# MIND GAMES

# MIND GAMES

Margaret Reyes Dempsey

KINGSBROOK PUBLISHING

MIND GAMES. Copyright © 2020 by Margaret Reyes Dempsey

Cover design © 2020 by Richard Lamb of Inspired Lamb Design

All rights reserved. No part of this book may be used, reproduced in any manner whatsoever, stored in a retrieval system, or transmitted, in any form or by any means, electronic, mechanical, photocopying, recording, or otherwise, without prior written permission from the author.

This is a work of fiction. The characters and events portrayed in this book are fictitious or are used fictitiously. Any similarity to real persons, living or dead, or actual events is purely coincidental and not intended by the author.

Published by Kingsbrook Publishing.

ISBN-13: 978-0-9903552-2-9

**For my husband, Richard.**
*You rock my world!*
UKT

# **One**

The first time it happens, I'm peeling carrots over the kitchen sink, distracted by a squirrel outside the window. He bites the rind from a black walnut and spits it over his shoulder. It reminds me of my childhood, eating watermelon and sending the seeds flying through the air because if I swallowed them, a watermelon tree would grow in my stomach. I can't remember which adult told me that, but the memory makes me smile. And yet, I'm perplexed. In my daydream, instead of my childhood backyard, I see concrete sidewalks and trees. No grass.

As I try to make sense of the image, the vegetable peeler slips from my wet hands, slicing a chunk of skin from the side of my index finger. I gasp, grab a hand towel, and wrap it around the wound. In the sink, watery red blood swirls around the carrot scrapings; and it happens. A loud whoosh. A rushing sensation in my head. I still stand at the sink, but in my mind, I've been transported to a room. Counters. Sink. A kitchen, but sterile and uninviting. Rage wracks my body, but fear rests at the root of my anger. Before I process the scene, a crash sucks me out of the vision.

The kitchen floor is a sea of rolling Cheerios. I try to block one with my foot, but I'm a second too late. It takes refuge under the refrigerator, where it will remain until an ant finds it next spring. I drop to my knees and sweep the Cheerios into a pile with my hands. The broom. I should get the broom. I stand and my body jolts at the sight of a baby in the high chair. I forgot she was there. Amanda. Her name is Amanda. She stares at me with a look that says, "Hey, Emily, you gonna pay me some attention or what?"

I grab the broom and sweep up the cereal. As I bend over to lift the dust pan, I feel I've forgotten something urgent. I pause for a moment, willing it to come back, but there's nothing. I toss the Cheerios into the garbage pail and lift a now fidgeting Amanda from her chair. In my arms, she frets even more, letting out a yell and arching backward when I sing a nursery rhyme and bounce her up and down. I pace back and forth but cannot console her. That a six-month-old baby can express such fury shocks me.

A ray of sunlight shines through the window, hits a crystal sun catcher, and disperses like a million diamonds over the granite countertops and beef stew ingredients waiting to be thrown into the Crock-Pot. Maple cabinets and newly painted sage walls should seem warm and inviting but feel alien. Did I decorate this room? It doesn't seem possible. Certainly I would have selected sleek black and stainless steel surfaces, a bit cool and aloof. A room where white, Chinese take-out containers with their silver-colored handles look like art on display. A kitchen that doesn't take itself too seriously or apply too much pressure to come up with a home-cooked meal.

Amanda continues to scream. I have a sudden urge to open the back door and run. Instead, I fill a glass with water and wash down a Tylenol for my raging headache.

I am not a natural mother. There it is. I've admitted it. I do not feel a bond with my daughter. We are like two strangers left alone in a room together. If it's possible for a baby to have opinions about such matters, I'd say she doesn't like me much at all. Maybe it's that postpartum depression people talk about messing with my mind, but it seems like a long time to be going through that. The oddest thing is, I don't feel guilty about my lack of affection. On the contrary, there is a rightness to it.

I place the glass in the sink and stare out the window. I'm struck again by the sensation, something floating just beyond the grasp of consciousness. What am I forgetting? My mind scampers this way and that in a futile attempt to uncover the lost memory. Outside, the squirrel digs hole after hole, searching for a hidden nut.

*\*\*\**

I sit up on the sofa, gasping for breath, my body in full-blown, fight-or-flight response. My gaze darts around the room, looking for some hidden menace. Someone walks toward me. It takes me a few seconds to realize it's my husband.

"I'm sorry. I didn't realize you were sleeping."

Brad bends down and kisses my forehead.

"What time is it?"

"Four-thirty. I decided to leave—"

I jump off the sofa and run into the kitchen, leaving him in mid-sentence. The high chair is empty. I twirl around and bump into him.

"Mmmm, it smells great in here."

He lifts the lid of the Crock-Pot and inhales the fragrant steam of beef stew. A beef stew I don't remember cooking. The kitchen sink is empty. No carrot peels, no glass. But there's a Band-Aid on my finger. I peel the edge of it, for some reason needing to see the cut. And then Brad's words come back to me. It's four-thirty.

I race up the stairs two at a time. I've been napping for five hours. Why hasn't Amanda awakened for lunch? I dash into her room. She lies in her crib, playing with her toy mobile. She glances at me, a bit of baby contempt in her eyes, and then goes back to her toy. Aside from a puffy diaper and her silent accusation, she is fine. Just as I reach down to pick her up, Brad sidles up beside me and beats me to it.

"There's my girl."

He carries her to the changing table, chattering baby nonsense as he puts a fresh diaper on her. She giggles, puffy diaper and bad Mommy forgotten.

Back in the kitchen, I start to take dishes out of the cabinet. Brad chuckles.

"The table's already set, Em. You must have had one heck of a day." He opens the pantry door. "What do you think about strained meat and carrots?" he asks Amanda. "Beef stew just like Mommy and Daddy."

I uncover the pot. The meat has fallen apart and looks succulent; the carrots are perfectly glazed. Brad puts Amanda in her high chair and then wraps his arms around my waist and nuzzles my neck.

Though I love my husband and have happy memories to prove it, lately I am startled by his touch. He reads my reaction as a titillated shiver, which makes him more amorous. In fact, just a few nights ago, we resumed our sex life at the cliffhanger we left it nearly eight months ago when I was committed to bed rest before giving birth. Between that and the twenty four-hour feeding schedule, it's not been an environment conducive to romance.

I feel his warm breath at my ear. "I see you've forgiven my aunt."

"What?"

"The Crock-Pot."

"What about it?"

"You vowed never to use it after we paid for her dinner at our wedding and she never showed up."

"I don't remember that."

"Really?"

"Really. Let's eat."

Brad guides a spoon of baby food into Amanda's mouth, offering words of encouragement. She smiles and bangs a plastic spoon on her tray, making him laugh. I marvel at the easy interaction. What am I doing wrong? Why can't I summon the smiles and laughter he has for her every night?

"Remember Karen? She came back from maternity leave

today." Brad takes a spoonful of beef stew and then opens his mouth, blowing out in childbirth-like pants. "She called the sitter a dozen times at least, poor thing."

"The sitter or Karen?" I ask.

"Huh, funny. She thinks you're lucky, getting to stay at home."

"It's only lucky if that's what you want to do. She gets to wake up and go into an office filled with adults who can talk back to her and take care of their own feeding and bathroom needs."

Brad stares at me, the next spoonful halfway to his mouth. "Do you want to go back to work?"

I think for a second and then shake my head. "Not to my public relations job."

"You love that job."

"I'm just not fit for public display these days."

Brad laughs. "I have no idea what that means."

"Neither do I." I blow on a carrot and pop it in my mouth.

"When you figure out what you want to do, let me know. We'll make it work."

I nod and he reaches across the table and takes my hand.

\*\*\*

The beef stew was such a success, it might be time to forgive Brad's aunt, whichever one it was. I'm in the bedroom rubbing moisturizer on my legs when he walks in. He stares at me for a moment and I know we are not headed for sleep.

I flinch when he runs his hand over my stomach.

"I can't believe how tight you are. Your stretch marks are completely gone."

I glance down. He's right. There's not a pregnancy trophy to be seen. "I guess the gym has helped."

He hooks his thumbs under the sides of my thong, bought to replace the granny bloomers I wore during and, I regret to admit, after my pregnancy. One day I awoke from my spell and recognized them for what they were—alien pods that had taken over my wardrobe. He slides them down as he kisses me. My skin tingles. There's that feeling of newness again, but it's uncomfortable rather than exciting.

No, we are not headed for sleep. And the thought fills me with dread.

# Two

The thumping of basketball on blacktop competes with the chick-uh-chick of the last cicada of the season, doomed to die a virgin. Jeremy Steele swipes the ball from his twelve-year-old son, pivots, and shoots.

"Swish," he says with a grin, glancing at his cell phone on the grass.

"You don't have to rub it in, Dad. That's poor sportsmanship." Robbie emphasizes the last words with quotation marks in the air.

Jeremy tousles the boy's sweaty hair. "You're right. But have some mercy. Another year and you'll squash me on the court." He takes a gulp of water, his gaze once again returning to his cell phone.

"Whaddaya say, sport? One more round?" he asks.

Robbie throws the ball at his chest. "Okay."

This time, Jeremy holds back, allowing Robbie to score some extra shots. Truth be told, he's tired. At nearly forty years old, he doesn't have the stamina he used to, despite eating right and exercising to counteract his sedentary career.

Accounting, he tells people when they ask. That stops any further questions. Especially when he adds the terms "pencil-pushing" and "civil servant" to the mix and punctuates his lie with a self-deprecating chuckle. Their eyes shift to look over his shoulder, seeking someone more interesting. And that's just the result he wants.

A loud wail interrupts his thoughts. His six-year-old daughter Kaylee lies sprawled on the pavement. As he strides toward her, he stoops to pick up his phone, checks the battery power, and drops it into the pocket of his cargo shorts.

"Awww, Kaylee." He looks down at her skinned knees. "It's okay, honey. We'll patch you up."

He carries her into the house and sets her on the vanity in the upstairs bathroom.

"Can I have ouch spray?"

"Sure you can, but we have to clean it first." He dabs at the wound, careful not to apply too much pressure.

"Ow, Daddy, it hurts."

"I know, honey, but only for a moment." He retrieves the antibacterial spray from the medicine chest and spritzes the wound with a cooling mist. While it dries, he grabs a box of Band-Aids.

"No, those are Elmo Band-Aids. Elmo's for babies."

"You're right! Why do we still have baby Band-Aids? We'll have to talk to Mommy about this." He opens the medicine chest again and considers the assortment of bandages. His kids are addicts, plastering them all over their bodies even when they're not injured.

"I want Dora," Kaylee says.

Jeremy pulls off the back of the largest one and applies it to her knee, gently pressing the edges.

"There you go. Better?"

She nods, her expression serious. He grins and kisses her forehead.

Back outside, Robbie studies an ant hill along the edge of the driveway. "Hey, Kaylee, look at this ant. It's carrying an injured one."

She runs over and peers down. "Maybe he fell down and hurt his knee."

Robbie rolls his eyes. "Ants don't have knees." He throws

the ball to his dad and their game is back on.

Seconds later, Jeremy's phone rings. He tosses the ball back to Robbie and pulls the phone from his pocket.

"I'm all ears."

"It's settled," the voice at the other end says. "They agreed this is the only way to go. But they're not happy."

Jeremy gnaws the inside of his cheek. Behind him, Kaylee says something about the ants. He stares in her direction.

"So, what are we telling the families?" he asks.

"MIA. That way, if we figure out a solution..."

"Yeah. That's best. So I guess they approved the budget to monitor them for the time being?"

"Of course. They were the cream of the crop, Jeremy. The big boys obviously feel a sense of obligation."

"And I'm sure they'll be watching our every move from now on."

"I don't think so. They're satisfied the military portion of the project has come to an end. Those guys have tunnel vision. They wouldn't see any problem with this if the subjects were non-military. Collateral damage."

Just then, Kaylee grabs his hand. "Daddy, come look. There's another ant carrying a hurt one."

"Just one second, honey," he says to her. To the caller, "Speaking of the non-military subjects—"

"Nothing to report. They seem to have assimilated. I'll keep you up to date."

As Jeremy ends the call, Robbie sighs. "Are we gonna finish now?"

"Take some practice shots with Kaylee, sport. I'm beat." He takes another sip of water.

"Are they taking him to the ant hospital?" Kaylee asks, her gaze fixed on the pavement.

"There's no such thing as an ant hospital," Robbie says.

"But he's all squished up. He won't be able to help the other ants build tunnels anymore."

Jeremy hears the tremble in her voice just as Robbie leans closer.

"I think he's dead!"

"No he's not!"

"Enough, Robbie," Jeremy says.

"Daddy, do you think they only save the ants that can help them build the tunnels?"

"I don't know, honey," he says without considering the question.

Robbie leans closer to the ant hill. "Nah. They're not like people. They take care of all the ants whether they're helpful or not."

"People should take care of each other, too," Jeremy says. "No matter what."

As he walks toward the house, his words, so easily spoken, replay in his mind like a news ticker. Any good father would have said the same thing. But today, in light of his phone conversation, his conscience adds one more word to the stream. Hypocrite.

# Three

I park the car and stumble over cobblestones, ten minutes late for lunch with my friend Susan. After settling the baby with the sitter and issuing the litany of do's, don'ts, and emergency numbers, I took a wrong turn on the way to a restaurant I've visited dozens of times.

Though not my oldest friend, Susan is my best friend. We met as college freshmen in St. Louis and pledged the same sorority, something of a shocker to me at present. I've come a long way from hanging out with gangs of girls. These days I prefer the one-on-one lunch date or just being by myself. Actually, the latter is truer. Susan coerced me into this lunch, laying on the guilt for being out of touch for the last month when it's been our ritual for years to have lunch once a week.

I trip again and my mood darkens. The cobblestones, old-fashioned lamp posts, and quaint façades do not hide the truth. This is just another strip mall on the South Shore of Long Island.

I stop at the corner for a speeding SUV and someone grabs my shoulder and twirls me around.

"Emily! I've been calling out to you for half a block," Susan says and engulfs me in a hug.

"I didn't hear you."

"People two blocks in front of you heard me. You were in another world." Susan breaks into a smile. "For a second, I almost thought it wasn't you."

"I'm sorry. I was fixated on the lack of creativity in neighborhood design."

"Huh?" Susan links her arm in mine as we cross the street.

"Never mind."

We enter the restaurant and a short, wiry waiter in a half-a-tuxedo uniform greets us with a thick, Italian accent.

"Buon giorno, signore. A pleasure to see you again." He leads us to a table for two against an exposed brick wall. "Your favorite, no?"

I glance around the room, not sure why this one would be a favorite over any other.

"You always remember, Giorgio. Thank you," Susan says.

Just another item to add to my growing list of forgotten memories. Giorgio hands me a menu and I skip right to the entrees. My taste buds crave something. Puttanesca. That's it.

Susan peers over the top of my open menu. "I gather from the way you're studying the menu you're not in the mood for our usual chicken parmigiana with a side of spaghetti."

I wince. "No. Is that okay?"

"Sure. I'll eat half and take the rest home to Ed."

The waiter brings two glasses of Chianti on the house. I take that first sip and feel the instantaneous effects in my blood. My shoulders drop an inch as I sigh.

"Signore, we have a special today of fresh buffalo mozzarella on sliced red tomatoes with a drizzle of extra virgin olive oil and basil. Very fresh."

The rolling of the r's in "very fresh" almost convinces me, but considering I have no knowledge of buffalo farms anywhere near Long Island, I guess fresh is a relative term. We decline and place our order. Giorgio bows and heads to the kitchen.

"I can't believe how thin you are," Susan says. "You actually have hollows under your cheekbones. You're a walking advertisement for the gym."

"It's the only thing keeping me sane after being in the house all day."

Susan leans in closer. "Is everything all right?"

I'm about to vent my motherhood issues when I consider my audience. Susan married a year before I did and started trying for a baby immediately. That she has not succeeded is an awkward point in our friendship now that Amanda has come along. I back step from my near blunder in sensitivity.

"I haven't been sleeping well. And when I do finally fall asleep, I have these horrible anxiety dreams."

"What about?"

"There's something urgent I've forgotten and I try desperately to remember what it is. I almost do, but just before it registers, I wake up, still grasping for it. And then it's gone." I snap my fingers in the air.

Susan sips her wine. "I think it probably all comes with the territory of being a new mother."

"Maybe that's it," I say in that way people have of agreeing with things they don't believe are true but don't have a better idea to present. "My brain feels fuzzy all the time. As if I'm between two stations on the radio, getting bits of both, but mostly static. Something will make perfect sense and at the same time not. Like the chicken parmigiana. I couldn't imagine wanting to eat that and yet it's our usual." I shake my head and wave my hand in the air. "Never mind. It's weird. I can't explain it."

"It's okay, Emily. It'll get easier. My sisters both went through this after they had their babies."

A spark of annoyance flares. I don't appreciate being lumped in with every other woman who has ever had a child. My feelings are never accepted as true, but attributed to a hormonal phase that will pass in time.

The appearance of the waiter with massive platters of pasta puttanesca and chicken parmigiana tamps down the emotion.

We go through the infuriating ritual of "Would you like fresh ground pepper on that?" followed by the equally annoying "Would you like fresh parmesan cheese on that?"

Yes, I'd like both, please. In huge, freakish quantities. So, leave the pepper mill and the bowl of parmesan right here, thank you very much. Of course, I don't say that. I watch closely, my eyes widening just a bit in what I hope looks like encouragement, as Giorgio sprinkles a dusting of cheese on my pasta. He then twists the four-foot-long mill with some muscle as I squint to see the microscopic particles of pepper in this Emperor's New Clothes-like charade.

With my first bite, I forget the circus act, focused on perfect al dente pasta with the tang of capers and the saltiness of anchovies. A low moan escapes my lips.

Susan laughs. "It sounds like you haven't eaten in days."

"Please, I've been eating constantly. There's nothing else to do."

Susan clears her throat. "Well, maybe by next year we'll be doing mommy things together."

I stop chewing and stare at her, eyes wide. She waves her hands in the air.

"No, no, not yet. But Ed and I decided to try IVF."

"What made you change your mind?"

Susan shrugs. "Mother Nature wasn't cooperating and artificial insemination didn't work. It's our last shot. We'll give it a chance, maybe two, depending on how bad it is."

I reach across the table and touch her hand. "It'll be all right. If I got through it, so will you."

She gives my hand a squeeze. We resume eating just as a large group of people enters the restaurant. They are loud and disruptive as Giorgio shows them to their table. The leader of the pack is a rotund man of about sixty who carries himself like he's somebody. In fact, he looks familiar, but I can't place him. He takes a seat, daring the chair to break beneath him.

"Where's Mario?" he asks Giorgio.

"He's not working today, signore," Giorgio says.

"Mario always takes good care of me. And I take care of him. You know what I'm saying?"

"Si, signore. Perfettamente."

I roll my eyes on poor Giorgio's behalf and Susan giggles.

"He sounds like a wannabe Mafia type."

And then it hits me. "Not a wannabe. That's Vincent Gargiulo. He's a mob boss from Brooklyn."

"How do you know that?" she asks.

I cock my head to the side. "I don't know." I shrug. "I must have seen him on the news."

We finish our lunch, conversation now impossible with Vincent the Gargantuan booming across the restaurant. He boasts to his lunch guests about his Italian tailor who makes all his custom suits. "Vincenzo, this-uh suit wuzza made-uh for you." We are privileged to hear how the Vegas casinos clear the tables for him. And we learn about all the people who respect him.

Other patrons have arrived at the restaurant for a pleasant lunch and have recognized this is not to be. Gluttons for punishment, Susan and I order cannoli and cappuccino for dessert. As I sip my coffee, Vincent stuffs his mouth with spaghetti and then continues talking.

"I'd like to walk over there and shove the heel of the Italian bread down his throat," I say.

Susan almost spits her coffee across the table. When she finally manages to swallow, she lets out a hearty laugh. "Who are you and what have you done with my sweet friend, Emily?"

Just then, Vincent erupts in a fit of coughing. I look over, expecting food to spray every which way. But that's not the case. The cough becomes muffled with a high-pitched wheezing sound. Vincent clamps his hand to his throat and two men at his table jump up. One of them encircles Vincent's significant girth from behind, his fists barely reaching around to perform the Heimlich maneuver.

The first attempt does not work. Vincent becomes more agitated. He struggles, tries to extract himself from his friend's arms, and the second guy jumps in to help. Meanwhile, the waiter has run into the kitchen, screaming in Italian, and returns with the owner. People jump up from their tables, toppling chairs, and shriek and shout advice. Across from me, Susan dials 911 and yells into her phone, her hand pressed to her opposite ear to block out the racket.

Everything seems to happen in slow motion, but a part of me knows Vincent has less than two minutes left to dislodge whatever is in his air pipe before he keels over onto the floor. The third attempt at the Heimlich fails. Vincent falls to the ground, taking his friend with him. His skin takes on a bluish hue.

I jump up, tipping the chair behind me. "Bring me a straw," I scream at the waiter as I sprint across the room. I grab a knife from Vincent's table. As I drop to my knees next to him, one of his Heimliching buddies—okay, let's be real, he's a henchman—lets out a yell and reaches for the knife in my hand. I swing away from him. "I'm going to save him, asshole."

Vincent's neck is fat, but I press until I find his Adam's apple and the Cricoid cartilage. With the knife, I cut a half-inch, horizontal incision. As I separate the slit in Vincent's throat, the waiter returns with the straw and collapses next to me. I grab the straw and insert it into the hole. When he doesn't start breathing on his own, I give two quick blows into the straw, wait five seconds, and blow again.

Vincent's chest rises on the fourth blow. His eyes flutter open. An ambulance siren screams outside the restaurant.

"Are you okay, Vincent?" I ask. "Can you breathe on your own?"

He stares at me without responding, but his body does what it's meant to do. The paramedics race in and take over. I back away to give them room. Only when Susan appears at my side and offers a napkin do I realize I am covered in blood. I take the napkin from her and see the shock in her eyes.

"Emily, how..."

I shake my head. "I don't know."

# Four

As soon as I get into the car, my body begins to shake. I fumble with the keys, jabbing blindly several times before I find the ignition. What the hell just happened? Emergency surgery! I performed emergency surgery. How? When did I learn that? And where? I try so hard to remember, it hurts. Images from the restaurant flash across my mind. The fearful cries of the other patrons. Chairs lying on their sides. Gargiulo and his men falling to the floor as he began to turn blue. And through it all, my cool detachment. I got to the end of it without thinking, much like you find yourself pulling into your driveway without remembering the drive home, as I've just done.

I race into the house, startling the babysitter who jumps up from the couch. She opens her mouth to say something, but then recoils at the sight of blood. I rush by and motion to indicate Susan is close behind.

In the bedroom, I pull off my blouse and buttons scatter on the wood floor as I strip off the rest of my clothes. I turn the shower on hot and climb in. The water running down the drain turns pink as I wash the bloody residue from my hands. I gag at the caked blood of Vincent Gargiulo under my nails and reach out of the shower to grab my toothbrush, the closest thing I have to a nail brush. As I scrub my nails, I shudder and remember a childhood memory.

I was playing with friends in an enclosed lot. We snuck in by digging a trench and sliding under the barbed-wire fence. On the other side of the lot, we played on huge mounds of dirt, oblivious to the approaching pick-up truck. A man stepped out and yelled at us. We couldn't escape the way we had entered since he was standing at our entry point. The only way out was over the fence. We climbed as far as we could to the top and then threw ourselves over to avoid the barbed wire. Other than being bruised from the landing, we were unscathed. All of us, that is, except Brian. He panicked, lost his footing, and was snared by the wire. I stared as he screamed in agony. The others ran even faster to get away, but I ran toward him as he fell to the ground, the wire ripping through his gut, hip, and the full length of his leg. I'd never seen that much blood before. I passed out instantly.

Ever since that day, the sight of blood makes me break out in a cold sweat, which makes what I did today very odd.

My body shivers and I realize the water has run cold. I reach for a towel with pruned fingers. By the time I pull on my robe and walk downstairs, the babysitter has gone and Susan sits holding Amanda on her lap.

"Are you okay?" she asks.

I nod and sit opposite her on the loveseat.

"Emily—"

"I don't have any answers for you. I truly do not understand what just happened."

"You can't even give blood…"

"I know."

"How did you—"

"I don't know."

She nods, accepting my answer, recognizing I'm just as at a loss as she is.

"Are you busy for the next two hours?" I ask.

"No, why?"

"I need to get out of here for a while. Would you watch

Amanda?"

"Of course. Where are you going?"

"The gym. If Brad gets home before I do, fill him in. I don't have the energy."

\*\*\*

Three in the afternoon is a good time to go to the gym. The nine-to-fivers haven't arrived yet, and the people who don't work have already gone. The only other person here is a woman in her mid-forties, shadowboxing in the corner. I head toward the treadmill in need of a good jog. As my legs pump, I relive the moments at the restaurant.

In hindsight, I realize how dangerous it could have been if Vincent's bodyguards had pulled out guns to stop me from getting close to him with the knife. And then, suddenly, I start to laugh. Not a quiet chuckle, but an out-of-control belly laugh with gasping breath. Had I cut just a bit deeper, I could have done serious damage to Vincent's vocal cords and what a blessing that would have been to hundreds, maybe thousands, of restaurant-goers in the future. I am laughing so hard by this point, I can't continue. I shut off the treadmill and fall to the floor, tears rolling down my cheeks. The suit that wuzza made-uh for him wasn't looking so good with all that blood covering it. I snort and laugh louder.

"What in God's name is so funny?"

My gym buddy, Trina, stares down at me, a curious expression on her face. When I've caught my breath, we settle down on mats in the corner of an empty aerobics room and I tell her in hushed tones about my day. Her intense brown eyes bore into mine as she listens. She is one of the more analytical people I know. When I get to the part about Vincent's vocal cords, a bit of hysteria bubbles to the surface again.

"You're in shock, you know," she says. "Maybe you should go see someone, Emily. I know a good therapist."

"Maybe. If things don't get better." I stand up. "I need to work out...get the adrenaline out."

Trina stretches out her arm, and I pull her to her feet. We return to the treadmills and jog in silence. My attention shifts between the middle-aged woman throwing punches at the heavy bag and the TV mounted from the ceiling. From the closed captioning, I gather the talk show host is discussing the first "test tube baby." Apparently, it has been over thirty-five years since that medical miracle. She relates the fuss made about it back then, the ethical objections, and how, today, in vitro fertilization is commonplace and not given a second thought except by the radically religious. It's hard to imagine what sinister plots people's minds invented back then.

Thirty minutes later, after a three-mile jog, we head over to the weight machines. On the way, I stop next to the woman struggling with the heavy bag. I raise my fists to eye level and punch straight from the shoulder in slow motion.

"You're letting your fists drop," I say to her. "You've got to keep them high."

When she mimics my position, I make minor adjustments to her form. "That's it. Remember, that's not a bag, that's your opponent and she's punching back."

The woman laughs. "Good tip." She throws a few more punches.

"A good way to remember to keep your fists up is to touch the side of your face with whichever hand is not hitting. You're right-handed, so if you're jabbing, your right glove should be in contact with your face." I demonstrate and she gives it a try.

"There you go."

She smiles and thanks me as Trina and I leave.

"I didn't know you boxed," Trina says.

I realize what just transpired and feel the anxiety return. "I don't."

Trina gives me an odd look. I feel compelled to explain myself, but for the life of me, I don't know what to say.

"I've watched a lot of boxing with my dad."

Trina accepts the lie with a nod.

At the weight machines, I do military presses and then bench presses. Trina works in between sets and we chat quietly about our routine. She reminds me to lift and lower slowly, using my muscles, not momentum, to bear the load. Her voice hypnotizes me. Knowing Trina, even for the short time I have, I'm aware this is her intention. We end our routine with bicep and tricep curls and then go to the mats for a few hundred crunches. Afterward, I'm tempted to do crunches hanging upside down from the bar, but she shakes her head.

"You've done enough. Time to call it a day."

I leave Trina at the entrance to the locker room. Once outside, I inhale the early fall air. It soothes my jangled nerves. As I stand on the curb, trying to remember where I parked my car, a black limousine pulls up in front of me. The door opens and a muscular guy in a suit steps out.

"Mrs. Cooke?"

I stare at him.

"Emily Cooke?"

"Yes."

"Mr. Gargiulo has requested to see you." The formality of the words contrasts with the strong, Brooklyn accent. I recognize him as one of the guys at the restaurant.

My breath catches as he grasps my arm and guides me toward the car. I'm not laughing about good old Vinny's vocal cords now.

I swallow hard. "Do you mind if I call my husband first to let him know I'm going to be late for dinner?"

"He knows. We stopped there first. He told us where you were."

"Oh." What the hell was Brad thinking? "Is Mr. Gargiulo all right?" I ask, still stalling.

"He's in the hospital." He motions for me to get into the car. My heart pounds in my chest. I look over my shoulder, but I'm alone in the parking lot. I consider making a run for it, but I'm sure this guy is armed.

"I have some things to do tonight. Can we just give him a call at the hospital?"

"He'd like to see you in person."

I think I've just been made an offer I can't refuse. I climb into the limousine and he follows me in and shuts the door. We're not alone.

"You did a good job slashing Mr. Gargiulo's throat," says the other guy from the restaurant, the one who almost attacked me when I picked up the knife.

Before I can respond to what sounds like an accusatory statement, his gaze shifts to the other goon and then lowers in a subservient way.

The twenty-minute ride to the hospital is silent and tense. I don't know what to expect, and neither of the well-dressed thugs in the limousine have bothered to provide any information. For all I know, I'm on my way to a processing plant where I'll be turned into human mulch and sprinkled on a landfill in Canarsie, Brooklyn.

When we pull up at the hospital, I breathe a sigh of relief. Upon walking through the automatic doors, the characteristic scent of hospital greets me like a long-lost friend. I don't know where to begin to analyze why that is, but it's no odder than a person with a blood phobia performing an emergency cricothyrotomy on a mob boss, right? How do I even know that word?

We finally arrive at the room and the henchman leading the way steps aside and gestures for me to enter. Vincent lies with his eyes closed, sheet pulled up to his chest, a hint of navy blue pajama top showing. Those pajamas are like a vortex that has sucked the power right out of him. The bandage over his throat and the IV drip in his arm don't help. If I had to guess, I'd say they're giving him broad spectrum antibiotics to counteract the effect of any cooties that were on the knife I used to save his life, along with some pain killers.

"Boss, she's here."

Vincent opens his eyes and stares at me, dark brown iris indistinguishable from pupil. With his sallow skin and obvious weakness, he in no way resembles the man reputed to have ordered hits on several dozen people, including his own blood brother when he wanted out of "the family."

He motions with his hand as if he's writing in the air and

his guy hands him a notebook and pen.

He takes his time writing my name. "Emily?"

"Yes."

He writes the word "repay." Then, looking at me with widened eyes, shrugs and shakes his head with his palms up.

"You don't need to repay me."

He attempts to speak. "Try." Then he points the pen and his guy steps up.

"To repay you for saving his life, Mr. Gargiulo is sending you and your guests to his private estate in the Cayman Islands."

"That's not necessary."

"To him it is—"

"No. I couldn't possibly accept a gift like that." I say no, I shake my head, but Vincent doesn't accept any of it.

He puts pen to paper and resumes his scribbling. "Yes!" He motions to his guy like he's holding a phone to his ear.

"I'll contact you tomorrow to get the dates you select. I'm Paulie, by the way."

"This is much too generous."

Gargiulo holds up his index finger to get my attention. I nod at him to continue and watch as his sausage fingers engulf the pen. When he finishes, he points to a woman in the drawing and points to me and points to a male genie coming out of a bottle and touches his chest with his hand.

Paulie leans over to look and laughs. "Hey, not bad, Boss. I didn't know I worked for Leonardo Da Vinci." Gargiulo smacks him affectionately in the head then waves his hand in the air in a sweeping gesture.

"Anything," Paulie translates. "Anything you need, you call."

"Okay," I say quietly. "Thank you for your generosity." I force myself to be polite because, at the moment, I'm just not feeling it. His indebtedness to me makes me feel uneasy, like I'm getting myself deeper into indebtedness to him.

On the ride back to the gym, I decide I won't sit in silence for another twenty minutes.

"Will he be able to talk again?" I ask.

Paulie turns his gaze on me. "Yeah, they just don't want him to try yet." He stares at me a few seconds in silence. "You a doctor or something?"

"No. Just a wife and mother."

"Nothing wrong with that. That's what women are supposed to be."

I'm about to argue, but reason kicks in and I just sit back and shut up. A twenty-minute silence is preferable to twenty minutes of ignorant conversation.

When we arrive at the gym, Paulie opens the door.

"Don't forget to pick the dates for your trip. I'll call you tomorrow."

I step out of the limousine.

"You're gonna have a good time. It's a nice place."

"You've been there?"

"Yeah, a few times. Mr. Gargiulo is a very generous man."

"I'm starting to get that sense."

I say goodbye and watch the limousine pull away. A fine mist has started to fall and the temperature has dropped since I left the gym earlier. I walk with my head down to protect my face and neck from the wind.

Inside my minivan, I start the engine and fiddle with the heating dials. Cool air blows out of the vents and I shiver and wait for it to warm. An upbeat song plays on the radio, but I'm not really listening. As soon as the air turns warm, I put the car in reverse. As I pull out, I think I see Trina in my rear view mirror standing in the parking lot, but when I turn to look, there's no one there.

Back at home, the front door flies open as I reach for the doorknob.

"I must have called you a hundred times," Brad says. "Where have you been?"

"Where have I been? I've been with the gangsters you sent to find me." I walk past him into the living room. "Where's Amanda?"

"Sleeping."

I offer up a silent thank you. "Did you know who they were when you told them I was at the gym?"

"Yeah, Susan told me. What's the big deal—you saved the man's life."

"I'm sure his future victims will thank me for that." In the kitchen, leftovers from dinner are wrapped on the counter. "You cooked?"

"Susan did."

When I start fiddling with the dishes, he grasps my upper arm. "Emily! Come and sit down."

I follow him back to the living room but remain standing as he plops into an arm chair. He sits there in khakis and a polo shirt, one leg crossed over the other, looking relaxed but for his jiggling knee.

"Susan was completely wound up, rambling a mile a minute. She said you saved some Mafia guy from choking. She used some medical term. I thought she meant the Heimlich, but then I saw the pile of bloody clothes on the bathroom floor. What the hell, Em? It looks like you murdered someone. Where did all that blood come from?"

I shudder and my gaze drops from his face. His bare feet are still tan from the summer. They are nice feet, as feet go, and I stare at them as I tell him what happened.

"It wasn't the Heimlich. It was an emergency cricothyrotomy."

"A what?"

"I cut his neck open with a knife and jammed a straw into his airway to—"

"You did what?"

As the memory of this afternoon resurfaces, a wave of dizziness has me grasping the end of the sofa.

"Whoa." Brad jumps up and grabs my arm. "Sit."

I perch on the edge of a cushion and focus on a spot on the floor.

"How would you know how to do something like that?" His voice is softer now.

"I don't know."

All at once, he is back on his feet, sanding the wood floor with his nervous shuffling. "You could have killed him."

"I know. But I didn't."

There's a long pause while Brad stands there, his face drained of color, his eyes darting back and forth as if he's caught in a waking version of REM sleep. It's a lot to process, I know. I've been doing it all afternoon.

Finally, he returns from his reverie. "What happened with those guys?"

"They took me to see Gargiulo in the hospital. He wants to send us to his place in Grand Cayman."

Brad's eyebrows shoot up. "Huh. That's generous."

"I can't say I'm thrilled to be involved with him. A simple thank you would have sufficed." I stand slowly, making sure the dizzy spell has passed. "I'm going to change and check on Amanda."

Brad encircles my wrist with his fingers. "Are you okay, Em? I know how you are about blood." He shakes his head, the look of disbelief returning. "I don't understand this."

"Neither do I."

He leans down and plants a kiss on my temple.


Upstairs, I slip by Amanda's room. She is sleeping soundly and I dare not make a peep for fear she will wake up. I don't have the energy for that right now. The bloody clothes have been cleared from the bathroom floor, bless Brad. I put on my version of pajamas—drawstring pants and a tee shirt. Glancing at my reflection in the mirror, I decide I am much cuter in pajamas than Vincent Gargiulo.

Just as I climb into bed, Amanda starts to cry. God, I need a vacation. And I guess I'm going to have one.

# Five

On Wednesday mornings, after they feed the kids and drop them off at school, Jeremy and his wife Stephanie take the train into Grand Central Station. Half a block down a side street sits the coffee shop where they met nearly fifteen years ago. Back then, they were two young people at the beginning of their careers, full of ambition and ideals. A bit older, a bit wiser, ideals on life support after a near fatal crash with reality, they return each week for muffins, egg sandwiches, and free refills on the coffee.

The ritual began the day Robbie started kindergarten and Stephanie returned to work. She selected Wednesday as her first day back because she wanted to ease herself back into the work force. Every Wednesday thereafter, they sat across from each other, her head buried in The New York Times, his in The Wall Street Journal. They sipped coffee and commented on what was happening in the world. It was their mid-week treat—something to keep them connected as the years passed and the demands of family and career increased.

These days, however, there is more reading and less conversation. Jeremy knows his recent preoccupation with work plays a leading role in this change, but it's all he can think of. Stephanie breaks off a piece of a cranberry-orange muffin and pops it in her mouth, her gaze never straying from the article she reads.

"Huh, yet another debate about Guantanamo and whether it should be closed."

Jeremy groans inwardly. He thought this one hour of his week would be a respite from work talk.

She looks up at him. "No comment?"

He takes a deep breath and exhales, his shoulders slumping.

She chuckles. "Okay, okay, I read you loud and clear."

He forces a smile and brushes a crumb from her lips. "I love you, you know."

"I know."

And he does. Deeply. He has found a partner in life. And though she can't know everything he is, she accepts the pieces he can share. Though others think he is an accountant, she knows he has security clearance, supposedly because of the projects whose budgets he manages. But he never thinks for a second that she believes this story. On the day he told it to her, she looked deep into his eyes in silence for what seemed an eternity and then just said, "Okay." With that one word, she silently said so many others. *I know that's not true. I know you can't tell me the truth. I understand. I accept it. I won't ask. I trust you.* Yes, he has met his partner in life and he loves her very much indeed.

She looks at her wristwatch. "Are you ready? Your meeting is in twenty minutes."

"I'm ready," he says softly.

She narrows her eyes at him but doesn't say anything.

"I'm sorry I'm so quiet. I have a lot of fires to put out."

She swings her bag over her arm and kisses his cheek. When they get outside, they kiss again, this time on the lips. She frowns at him before heading crosstown. He enters a building on the next block, flashes an ID badge to the security guard in the lobby, and makes it into the elevator just as the doors close.

As he steps onto the 17$^{th}$ floor, his cell phone beeps. He glances down at the number and swears softly. A voice mail from Agent Turner can only mean trouble.

He nods at the receptionist, whose name he doesn't know and won't bother to learn. She'll soon be replaced. Standard operating procedure. She's just a body to sit at a desk in case someone shows up on this floor. In that unlikely event, she'll phone a number and lead the visitor to an office at the opposite end of the hallway. Jeremy hasn't spent much time imagining what happens after that.

He places his right index finger on a scanner plate. A beep sounds before the heavy, steel door slides open.

On the other side of the door, walled cubicles sit like an island in the center of the floor, with offices and conference rooms around the perimeter. He walks into his office, flicks on the lights, and relishes the quiet. Most of his staff are assigned to the project site. That operation has taken on new importance in light of recent snafus. He sighs and accesses his voicemail.

"Hey, Boss. Nothing catastrophic. Had an unusual incident here, but I have it under control. I'll let you know if there's any change."

Jeremy sighs again, wondering what the hell happened. But he trusts Turner, one of his best agents, to handle it while he gets on with more important matters. As he pulls up a file on his computer, there's a brisk knock on his opened door.

"Reynold. Come in."

Reynold Mortimer lowers his six-foot-five body into a chair and brushes a piece of lint from his knee. His reputation of being a high-maintenance kind of guy when it comes to personal grooming has earned him the nickname GQ, but Jeremy figures at that height, he probably has to put some effort into planning his wardrobe. Getting the job done without breaking a sweat is why Jeremy has chosen him for the next stage of the project that has become his biggest nightmare.

"Your email said I was being transferred from the TSA Task Force to Project Grey. Do you think that's wise considering how much time I've invested—"

"Yes," Jeremy says. "It's crucial. What I'm about to tell you doesn't leave this room."

Reynold nods, but still sits relaxed in his chair.

"Project Grey's primary focus was to develop methods to extract information from uncooperative terrorists."

"What kind of methods?"

"Psychological ones. A team of researchers developed a way to transfer memories from one person to another."

At this, Reynold leans forward in his chair.

"We transferred terrorist memories to non-terrorists and then interrogated them. The transfer worked, but we didn't get the results we expected."

"What happened?" Reynold asks.

"The subjects who received the terrorist memories wouldn't give up the information."

"Why not?"

"We're not sure."

"Wait a minute. If they won't give up the information, how do you know the transfer worked in the first place?"

Jeremy taps the eraser end of a pencil against his desk. He knows he has to provide full disclosure so Reynold can take over the project, but the urge to cover his ass is still strong. "There were some other indicators."

Reynold considers his vague statement. "So they know the information, but they refuse to divulge it. Is that what you're saying? Just like the terrorists."

"That's correct."

"Could your procedure have transferred more than just memories?"

"What do you mean?"

"It sounds as if you transferred their will as well as their memories. Those guys will die before revealing anything to us."

"It's possible, but the subjects we used to test this process were pretty willful guys themselves. Trained to resist torture techniques. So, the question is, whose will are we fighting?"

"Trained to resist torture techniques? We're torturing test subjects?" Reynold asks.

"They signed up for it knowing it might be a possibility."

"Who the fuck does that?"

Jeremy flinches at Reynold's uncharacteristic tone. "People who love their country and want to ensure the safety of its citizens." He glances down at his desk and exhales. "Navy SEALS."

Reynold rests his forearms on his upper thighs and stares straight ahead. Jeremy can practically hear the gears in his brain processing this information.

"So you tried to torture the information out of SEALS and it didn't work. Jesus."

Jeremy's gut clenches. "They signed up for it. They knew that might be part of it."

Reynold finally makes eye contact. Maybe it's just paranoia, but Jeremy can't help feeling there's some judgment in his gaze.

"If the experiment didn't work, why am I being brought in when it's over?"

"It's not over. When the memories were transferred, the SEALS lost their own memories."

Reynolds eyes widen. "Can't you just reverse the process?"

"It's not that simple. It's as if their memories were overwritten."

Reynold's expression of horror correlates with Jeremy's stabbing gut pain.

"We need to continue the research on a larger scale. And fast. Not just to extract information from the new subjects, but to figure out a way to give everyone their own memories back."

"Considering my background isn't psychology or mind control, what role do I play?" Reynold asks.

"The powers-that-be know about the fuck-up with the SEALS. They're not happy. I need someone I trust in there to fix this."

"Right. Tell me what you're thinking."

Reynold's return to stoic business mode soothes Jeremy. "The researchers need a new test population. Your role is to orchestrate that."

Reynold squints. "More military guys?"

"Absolutely not."

"Then who?"

"That's up to you."

"Are you kidding? This is crazy. Do we place an ad? *Volunteers needed to be tortured for the sake of your country.* Who's going to sign up for that?"

"Reynold. You're not thinking. We can't use average citizens for this. There's a good chance several trials will go wrong before they go right. How would we return people to their lives without raising suspicion?"

"Average citizens," Reynold repeats out loud to himself. "So who do we use?"

"I have confidence you'll figure something out." Jeremy stands, ready to be finished with this conversation.

Reynold unfolds himself from the chair and towers over Jeremy. "If I'm unsuccessful, I guess I'll be taking the fall?"

Jeremy gives him credit for speaking his mind. "If this fails, we'll all take the fall."

On his way out, Reynold pauses at the door. "What happened to the SEALS who, for all intents and purposes, are now radical Islamic extremists?"

"We told their families they're MIA. They're being housed at the barracks on Governors Island. That's where the research facility is and where you'll be stationed. I'm counting on you to make this operation a well-oiled machine so the psychologists can fix what they fucked up."

# Six

Susan and I sink into the luxurious seats of first class and sip complimentary cocktails. We switched places so the guys could sit together to watch an action thriller. Susan, who was already bubbling over with enthusiasm for this trip, is bubbling over a bit more after a glass of wine.

When we arrive in Grand Cayman, we step down the plane stairs and cross the tarmac toward the terminal. Palm trees sway in the breeze. I'm amazed at how laid back the airport is, much different than Kennedy Airport in New York. There's even an open-air observation deck for people to watch their loved ones take off. As we make our way through the airport, I focus on the chauffeurs' signs, looking for my name.

"I guess he's not here yet."

My three companions burst into laughter.

"What?"

I follow their gaze and find I am standing shoulder-to-shoulder with a dark-skinned man with a broad smile, holding a sign with the name Emily Cooke clearly printed on it. Weird thing is, I already read his sign and it didn't register.

"How many of those complimentary cocktails did you have?" Brad teases.

The man greets us and ushers us to a white van. After

putting our luggage into the back, he hops in and looks over his shoulder. "And we're off," he says in an accented voice.

We all chuckle, feeling light and ready for some fun. I open my window and breathe the fresh air, feeling more at peace than I have for a long while. Our tour guide, Raymond, points out the sights. A casuarina pine. A smooth-billed ani. The home of a celebrity. This is just what the doctor ordered, or at least what Vincent Gargiulo ordered. At that unwelcome thought, some uneasiness creeps in, but I refuse to let it ruin the trip.

As if reading my mind, Brad asks Raymond how long he has worked for Gargiulo.

"About fifteen years. I began driving for Mr. Vincent when I was seventeen years old."

"That's a long time," Brad says. "How did you meet him?"

"My mother cleaned for him many years ago. We had a house fire and he invited my family to move into his home."

"That was nice of him."

"Mr. Vincent is a very generous man. He sent me and my sister to college."

My ears perk up, and I try to reconcile what I know about Gargiulo against Raymond's stories.

"My degree is in accounting and my sister attended culinary school. You'll experience her magic in the kitchen later this evening."

"I'm looking forward to that," Susan says.

While the others enthusiastically agree, I ponder Gargiulo's generosity and Raymond's degree in accounting. Is Gargiulo a philanthropist at heart or did he consider the convenience of having someone from the island hide his ill-gotten wealth?

The van slows and turns into a gated estate. At first, all I see is a long road that winds around a hill. Palm trees and lush, tropical plants I can't name line the way. Then we round a bend and there it is. To call it a house would be an understatement. This is a palace. A woman appears at the front door, wearing a cap-sleeved blouse and a knee-length skirt overlaid by a pristine, white apron.

"That is my sister, Dora." Raymond says. "She will take care of all your needs at the house."

When Dora smiles, there's no mistaking the family resemblance. She bows her head, her hands clasped in front of her, and then leads the way through the double doors into a main hall of marble, pillars, and cathedral ceilings. I shiver at the cooler air inside.

As we move farther into the house, Dora points at a rounded staircase. "The bedroom suites are upstairs. I'll show you to your rooms in a moment. But first, this is where the real living happens, as Mr. Gargiulo says."

I suck in my breath at the sight of the kitchen. The cooking areas are gleaming stainless and granite. Several seating areas at counter height allow guests to interact with the cook. The dining table is so long, Jesus could have invited a lot more people to the Last Supper. Bottles of olive oil, crushed red pepper flakes, and salt and pepper mills rest in the center. If they leave the grated cheese on the table at meal time, I'll think Vincent and I are kindred spirits.

"Oh my God. Look at this view, Emily." Susan stands at the back of the kitchen, peering through a glass wall that offers a panoramic view of the expansive yard. The back patio features lush gardens, a pool, and hot tub. Beyond that, the turquoise ocean beckons. Brad opens the French doors to the patio. The landscaping around the free-form pool has transformed it into a lagoon, wild and serene. I imagine how beautiful it must be at night, with the lights on and the palms swaying in the breeze.

"When you're ready," Dora says, "I can show you to your rooms to rest, or perhaps change into bathing suits and explore the beach?"

Too excited to rest, we agree on the beach. Dora leads us through another set of French doors to a massive living room. The ceilings are high with several fans twirling lazily over cognac-colored leather couches. There's a wet bar and the biggest flat screen TV I've ever seen. Ed reaches for the remote control on one of the cocktail tables and Susan grabs it from his hand.

"Don't even think about it."

He shrugs and exchanges a look with Brad. I suspect Susan and I will spend time on the beach drinking frothy concoctions with little umbrellas while the guys flip channels.

We climb the staircase to a circular landing overlooking the entry hall below. Each door opens to a bedroom suite. When Dora shows me and Brad to our room, the king-sized bed with its white, crisp linens almost convinces me to nap. But then the breeze parts the long, sheer curtains and I spot the ocean again. The air carries a hint of salt and sweetness with a pungent tang. Heaven.

"Hey, come look at this bathroom," Brad says.

I walk into the recessed alcove. The shower area is the size of a small room with jets on each of the walls. A deep, wide Jacuzzi is placed against a glass wall, and I picture myself staring at the ocean as I bathe. A display of fluffy towels, scented soaps and oils, and other bath products makes me sigh with delight.

Raymond has carried our suitcases into a huge, walk-in closet. I'm itching to get back outside, but I want to unpack my things first and get settled. In the closet, Brad grabs me and twirls me around the space. "This closet is bigger than our bedroom at home," he says. We laugh and do another turn around the room.

After unpacking, I put on my new bikini, bought just for this trip, and slip into my flip flops.

"Wow," Brad says. "That's nice."

"It was time to put the skirted one-piece to rest."

He trails his fingertips from my waist to hip and I stiffen.

"You're so ticklish," he says and I'm relieved he's misinterpreted my reaction.

"For the record, you looked hot in the old suit, too."

"It didn't fit anymore anyway. I must have lost weight."

"I think so. I can feel it." He wraps his arms around me to demonstrate. "See."

I look up at him. His eyes reveal kindness and love. His lips curve in a mischievous smile that transmits his desire. He is not unattractive. And yet, I struggle to not recoil from his touch.

"Come on, I want to go to the beach." I grasp his hand and pull him behind me.

Susan and Ed wait for us down on the sand. The four of us follow a winding stone path and end up on a private beach with the whitest sand I've ever seen. The sea is just yards away and I can no longer contain myself. I flip off my shoes and run down to the edge, dipping my toes in the frothy surf, warm as bath water. The waves crash and rush up around my legs and my feet sink into the soft sand. The water is pristine and just a few perfect white shells lie on the beach as if placed for effect. It wouldn't surprise me if Vincent has an employee who improves on Mother Nature.

Susan grabs my arm. "Isn't this amazing?"

She beams, and I'm glad she and Ed have joined us on this trip. It seems to be exactly what we all need. With Susan and Ed's IVF trials about to start, I hope this vacation will put them in a relaxed state of mind and that their dreams of being parents will finally come true.

Raymond appears from around the bend with a small cooler. "Dora packed a picnic lunch. You can have it on the beach, or I can take you out on the boat." He points to a sail boat docked at the end of a long pier.

"Let's do the boat," I say, and Susan links her arm with mine.

Behind us, Brad and Ed discuss the technical aspects of the boat, even though neither of them are boaters. As we board, Brad turns to me with a mischievous grin. "Shall I find you a life vest?"

I'm not sure what he means, but before I can ask, Raymond interrupts to give him instructions on how to work the sails.

Susan and I find a spot to lounge and lift our noses to the sun. I feel alive, yet calm. I'm not scattered. There's no static on my mental radio. The only station I'm getting is sunshine.

"I can't believe what your body looks like after having a baby. It's amazing. I hope I have the same luck," Susan says.

I glance down at my taut stomach and curvy but firm thighs. "Thanks. I'm sure you'll be fine."

"Who am I kidding? I'd give up every ounce of vanity if it meant having a baby." Susan stares off in the distance.

A few minutes later, the boat is flying through the water. Pure exhilaration. Schools of brightly colored fish slip by like ribbons pulled through the water. Raymond points out houses on the shore that belong to famous people. Finally, we slow down and drop anchor. He starts unpacking the food, and Susan sidles up next to him to investigate what goodies we're about to eat. I lounge on the front of the boat, the sun beating down on me. I decide to get a cool drink, but when I stand, the clear water is a hypnotic suggestion I am powerless to refuse. I run and dive off the boat. A split second of a man's scream registers before the water envelops me in silence.

# Seven

When I surface, I hear frenzied splashing behind me. Something crashes into my hip. I scream and instinctively push away with my fists and legs.

"It's okay! I've got you," Brad yells.

We both tread water, staring at each other.

"What are you doing?" I scream.

"Rescuing you. What the hell were you thinking?"

His tone raises my defensive hackles. "I'm taking a dip before lunch."

"Are you insane? You can't swim. You're deathly afraid of water."

Suddenly, Brad's earlier teasing about the life vest makes sense. But then again, it doesn't. Pushing back from him, I swim on my back then flip over and switch to a breast stroke. I stop several yards away. "Of course I can swim." But even as I say it, the statement feels wrong and the uneasiness I've felt of late returns. Brad's look of amazement does not help.

At the boat, Ed and Susan reach down to offer a hand.

"Are you okay?" Susan asks as she wraps a towel around me. Her expression is filled with confusion and fear, much like the day she handed me the napkin to wipe Gargiulo's blood from my hands. Why is she so concerned? Ed just stares at me as Brad dries off. I'm embarrassed for making a spectacle of myself and ruining the carefree afternoon, even though I'm not sure what I've done wrong.

"I'm fine. What's the problem?"

"You could've drowned," Susan says. "You can't just jump off a boat when you don't know how to swim."

"But I do know how to swim."

"Since when?" Susan and Brad ask at the same time.

Goosebumps raise on my arms though the sun warms my skin. Since when? That question stumps me. I have no memory of learning to swim. It's as if my mind is a blank canvas. No memory of swimming, no memory of performing emergency surgeries. What is happening to me? Did I have a stroke or TIA? Susan and Brad still stare at me, waiting for a response.

I lie, which seems to be a new habit, but only because I have no other answer. "I've been taking lessons at the gym. Guess I should have mentioned it."

Ed and Susan look satisfied but Brad gives me a strange look. "When did—"

"Lunch is served," Raymond calls out.

Just like that, the swimming incident is forgotten. The spread looks more like art than a buffet. Everyone loads up their plates with spicy jerk tuna, conch fritters, rice and peas. There's an avocado and red onion salad and a succulent fruit salad of fresh pineapple, mango, and citrus fruits. I go through the motions of serving myself, but I can't imagine I'll be able to eat any of it. Behind me, the pop of a champagne bottle inspires a chorus of happy sounds. Raymond offers me a crystal flute. I stare at the bubbles rising to the surface and wonder, what the hell is going on here?

***

Dora welcomes us back and informs us dinner will be at seven p.m. Upstairs, I select the mango coconut soap and turn on the shower. I lather up and let the water pulse on my back. I love that the shower is completely open, no door, but that also means nothing shields me from Brad's stare when he walks into the bathroom. An odd reaction to have about my own husband, I know.

He leans against the wall and watches me a moment. "So when did you learn how to swim?"

Here we go. "When I started going to the gym after the baby."

"Amanda is six months old, Emily. When were you going to tell me?"

I feel exposed standing naked in front of him during this inquisition. "I guess I didn't think it was a big deal. I learned to swim across the pool and I kept doing it until my muscles got used to it and didn't get tired."

"And got so good you could take a running leap off the side of a boat?"

"What can I say, Brad? I practiced. Why are you so upset?"

"Why am I upset? It's a big thing to overcome a phobia. I'd think you'd want to share that. I feel like I'm on the outside looking in."

"I'm sorry. It's not like that. You know it's been a tough few months. The moment I walk in the door from "me time" at the gym, it's back to Mommy chores."

Brad's dejected expression morphs into a dreamy smile, and I wonder what he's thinking.

"I guess it just slipped my mind in the daily chaos," I add.

"I get it. Hard to believe that little sweetie of ours can cause so much confusion." He gets lost in his thoughts for a split second. "I miss her."

"Yeah," I manage to say.

The truth is, I haven't thought of her until just this moment.

\*\*\*

On the last night of our week in Grand Cayman, all I feel is dread about returning home to the responsibility that awaits me. I excuse myself early to take my last bath in the Jacuzzi and then crawl into bed. I'll have time in the morning to pack my things.

I drift off into a deep sleep and, before long, slip into a vivid dream. In it, I walk down a long corridor lined with open doors. Two people with clip charts whisper to each other. Their white coats identify them as medical professionals. If this is a hospital, it must be after visiting hours. The lights are dimmed.

I round a corner and the hall lights have been completely turned off in this wing. My footsteps echo on the tile floors. I wonder if anyone else can hear them. A quick look over my shoulder confirms I am alone. I walk a few more yards and then turn into a room on the left. The flickering of a television illuminates the room. The man in the bed turns toward the door and his eyeglasses flash glints of light. He gasps and his mouth falls open.

"Surprised to see me?" I ask. "Did you think I was going to accept this and just go on with my life?"

He doesn't reply but instead searches frantically for the call button. I grab the line and pull it out of his reach.

"It ends here."

The man's eyes go wide. Then there is blood, a lot of blood. It flows like a river from the room, out into the corridor. Someone screams and I hear running footsteps getting closer. I start to run but slip in the blood. A baby cries, loudly and incessantly. I look down and notice I am wearing my new bikini. But my body is fat and flaccid and feels stretched out. Bright red tracks run from just under my breasts to my hip bones.

The scene suddenly changes. Now my thinner body is in the bikini, but the red marks are still there and blink like neon lights. I am running through another building. I enter a room, this one an office, and sweep my arms across the surfaces, sending everything crashing to the floor. Broken glass flies in every direction, but I persist until the room is trashed. There is blood on my hands again. The baby still cries in the distance. Louder and louder.

Jolted from my dream, I sit up, gasping for breath. I listen for Amanda but hear only silence. The crying baby was in my dream. At my side, Brad sleeps peacefully. We are still in Grand Cayman; Amanda is not here.

I settle back down in bed, but my heart continues to pound. The dream has left me with information that does not recede with my wakefulness, a bit of mind residue I know is absolutely true. And this frightens me more than I can say. Because to believe something is true when you know it is impossible is a bad sign. At the same time, a wave of relief washes over me. I relax into it and let my mind tell me the truth—the truth I've been fighting to remember.

My name is not Emily Cooke. I am Madison Thorpe, and I think I killed a man.

# Eight

At our final breakfast in Grand Cayman, I eat without gusto and cast furtive glances at my companions. They laugh and rehash the trip, but I can't join in. The same thought loops over and over again in my mind: I am Madison Thorpe and I am a murderer.

Why do these people call me Emily? Do they know I am Madison? Why have I forgotten my identity? Did I suffer a head injury? Do I have amnesia? If so, why would everyone seem so comfortable with the name Emily?

And then there are my parents. We dropped Amanda off with them before leaving for our trip. Why do they call me Emily? Surely they know I am Madison. What kind of game is being played here? Who is in on it? I scan the faces around the table again. When I get to Susan, she stares back at me. She scrunches her eyebrows in a silent "are you okay," the easy way a person might with her best friend. I nod and go back to eating my fruit. Why doesn't my best friend know who I am? Or does she and is she pretending not to? Can I trust her?

Later, on the plane, we are again sitting side-by-side. I turn to her and, in the most casual voice I can muster, ask "Do you remember a girl from college named Madison?"

Susan thinks for a moment and then shakes her head.

"What did she look like?"

"About five foot seven, athletic figure, green eyes, and shoulder length straight hair, brown." *Will she realize I just described myself?*

Susan gives it some thought. "No. Why?"

I shrug, trying to seem nonchalant, but watch her every expression. "She just popped into my head for some reason. Don't know what made me think of her."

I shut my eyes then and pretend to sleep, but my mind races the rest of the trip home. I believe I am someone other than who everyone else believes I am. That means I've lost my grip on reality, but not enough to leave me unaware I've lost my grip on reality. That is the only reassuring thing to grasp onto right now.

***

I've been home from Grand Cayman only four hours, but I'm anxious to work out. It's the one part of my day when I feel like me—the me who is Madison Thorpe. Brad looked surprised when I told him I was going to the gym. He was ready for some snuggly family time on the couch.

Trina waves to me from a treadmill. I hop on the one next to hers.

"How was your trip?" she asks, huffing as if she's been at it for a while.

"Grand Cayman is beautiful. Have you ever been?"

"No. But I've seen The Firm."

"We saw where they filmed that."

"How was your benefactor's place?" she asks.

"A mansion. The kitchen was the size of the entire downstairs of my house. The walk-in closet in the bedroom was bigger than my bedroom. And the bathroom..." I sigh. "Don't even get me started. With a nice lock on the door, it would have made the perfect sanctuary."

"So I gather this wasn't a second honeymoon."

"Oh, I didn't mean it that way. But no, it wasn't quite that."

I'm quiet for a moment and so is Trina. I like this about her, along with the way she makes eye contact when we talk. She really listens.

"Something odd happened on the trip."

She waits as I consider my words.

"What would you say if I told you I can't swim, I'm deathly afraid of water, yet I took a running leap off a boat in the middle of the ocean and swam like a pro."

"Congratulations?"

I swat her arm. "Very funny. Don't you think it's odd?"

Trina shrugs. "Not really. My mother threw my brothers and me into a pool when we were just babies and we swam. Technically, I think anyone can swim. It's just the fear that keeps some people from doing it."

"Maybe, but I'm not talking dog paddle. I dove into the water and swam with complete ease and proficiency as if I had been doing it all my life. Think about the first time you went to a gym. You didn't get on the treadmill and run 10 miles your first time, right? You had to build up."

"True."

"Here's the really weird part. I don't have any memory of being deathly afraid of water or of not being able to swim."

"So how do you know then?"

"My husband and friend Susan told me. They were in a panic when I jumped off the boat. Thought I'd lost my mind."

"Hmmmm. Well, if you suddenly decided you wanted to swim, I don't see why you wouldn't be able to. God knows you're in great physical shape."

One of the things I like about Trina is that she's analytical and can usually see both sides of an issue. Already, she's made me feel better, but then I remember the other, bigger issue.

"There's more."

I tell her about my dream and how, upon waking, I was convinced I was someone else.

"Some dreams linger longer than others," she says. "I've had the same experience."

Trina's tone seems nonchalant, but is that alarm I see in her eyes? Or maybe that's just a projection of my own alarm.

"Do you still feel the same way?"

"Yes."

"But the dream was only last night, or even early this morning. Not so long ago. Haven't you ever had a disturbing dream that affected your mood for a day or two afterward?"

"Yeah, I suppose."

"You know, it's probably nothing, but you could go talk to that therapist I know. He's really good at drawing things out and making connections. I call him whenever I need to work something out. I have the utmost confidence in him."

"Maybe."

"Even if you don't end up signing up for regular sessions, one talk might make you feel better." Trina picks up her towel and wipes her brow. "Come on, let's take a break. I've been doing this at least twenty minutes longer than you."

Trina jumps off the treadmill and walks toward the weights. I'm about to step off when my gaze lands on Trina's final mileage and time. She was running exactly one minute and thirty seconds longer than I was. Either she meant she was at the gym twenty minutes longer than I was or I'm not the only one with a memory issue.

Trina holds down the military press bar and motions for me to sit. She places it in my hands and I begin my reps—one, two, three—

"The thing is, what if I really am someone else? I mean, besides my believing it, what if there is evidence that proves I am?"

"Focus. Six. Seven. Eight. Nine. Ten. Eleven. Twelve. What kind of evidence?"

I release the bar and lean forward to increase the weights. "I haven't got that far yet. But if there were, how would you explain that everyone around me, the people who are closest to me, call me Emily?"

"There is no evidence. This is all a bunch of what-ifs. You undoubtedly have a social security card that says who you are, a birth certificate even. You can't go back much further than that."

I can't argue with her logic. If I am certain my name is Madison Thorpe, then I had to have been old enough to be cognizant of that fact.

"The scary part is, I do have memories of being Emily—and very far back, too—but they seem hazy." A horrible thought creeps into my mind. "Do you think it's possible I have multiple personality disorder?"

The expression in Trina's eyes, usually intense and probing, softens. "That's extremely unlikely." She touches my arm. "Go see my friend, Emily. Please. He'll put your fears to rest."

"Okay, I will," I hear myself say.

"Good. Now come on, one more set."

\*\*\*

Though I took the name of Trina's therapist, I did not immediately set up an appointment. For some reason, I was more comfortable Googling ghastly physical possibilities for my identity confusion than calling a shrink. Several hours of internet research convinced me a brain tumor was a strong possibility and I made an appointment with a neurologist, thereby postponing my date with the therapist a while longer.

I've never had an MRI and I'm not claustrophobic, so I thought the worst part would be lying perfectly still for forty-five minutes, feeling as if I had to scratch my nose and knowing if I did, they'd have to start all over again.

I was wrong. As soon as the technician slides me into the tunnel, an unwelcome sense of déjà vu overcomes me. In my right hand, I clutch a bulb to squeeze if I need assistance. The first few rounds are uneventful. But then, in the middle, something changes. My insides suddenly feel as if they are going to explode inside out. My throat closes. Mini spasms attack my intestines and legs, which aren't even in the machine. When my heart begins to constrict, I almost cave and press the bulb, but there's no way I can repeat this experience. I call out to the technician, hoping the sound of her voice will soothe me, but as she warned, she doesn't hear me over the din of the machine.

Is it possible to feel electrons moving to other parts of your cells, removed from their orbiting lives? If they were sentient beings, would this qualify as a near death experience for them? Would it feel as if they were being called home to the "great magnet in the sky"?

I will myself to think pleasant thoughts, to pray. But I can't keep the words straight to prayers I've been saying all my life. Finally, it is finished. But I don't feel better. The technician slides me out.

"I felt it," I say. "I thought you're not supposed to feel it."

"What did you feel?" she asks.

I try to explain but my words don't make sense even to me. She looks at me with a disbelieving expression on her face.

"I think you just had an anxiety attack," she says. "You can't possibly have felt *anegdhb bladgh dlbkskw*..."

Her words are as jumbled as the Our Father and Hail Mary were moments ago. Something is not right. My body shakes with the tension of emotion held back as I wait for her to get me the films. On the way to the car, my eyes tear up. Once I am ensconced safely inside, I break down and sob uncontrollably.

\*\*\*

There's nothing wrong with my brain. That's what the neurologist said after viewing my MRI results. This news did not fill me with as much relief as you might think. At least if there were something wrong, we could take steps to fix it. There *is* something wrong, but I'm the only one who knows it. I finally admit defeat. I need help. And so I sit in Dr. Robert Snelling's office, hoping he is as good as Trina says. As I wait, I read the framed quotations hanging on the walls. They are all about the mind. Some are statistics, some are sayings. One that catches my eye is "Mind over matter is successful only when you engage the correct part of the mind to reign over the matter in question — R.L. Snelling." The quote, initially intriguing, is less appealing when I see Dr. Snelling's name tagged onto the end of it. In fact, many of the posters hanging in the room have sayings attributed to him. I prepare myself to meet the egomaniac.

Right on cue, Dr. Snelling walks out of his office. He appears to be in his mid-forties, a bit of silver sprinkled through his wavy, brown hair. I extend my hand as he introduces himself. His is dry and warm.

"Please, come in. Make yourself comfortable."

I consider the seating options and choose an arm chair over the couch. I plan to get through this session from a position of power. In a surprise move, Dr. Snelling sits on the couch across from me. Or maybe not so surprising if it's a tactic to make me feel in control. I glance around the room. Wood bookcases line the walls. Snelling's desk is long and deep, and made of the same rich wood. Soft, golden lighting complements the autumn earth tones of the décor. There will be no fluorescent inquisitions in this office.

"Can I get you a cup of tea or coffee?"

I decline, knowing I am too nervous to drink anything.

"Has Trina told you anything about my issue?"

"No. I would never discuss a patient with another person. Plus, I prefer to hear the story from the source. Preconceived notions are mental quicksand."

I imagine that saying hanging with the rest on the walls. "Can I ask you a question before we start?"

"Go right ahead." Dr. Snelling smiles at me.

"That quote on the wall outside about mind over matter, what does that mean exactly?"

Dr. Snelling leans into the back of the couch and crosses his leg over his knee. He gathers his thoughts, comfortable in the extended silence. "People use the phrase 'mind over matter' as if it's some cure-all. As if all one has to do is think positive thoughts and they can accomplish anything. But that's a dangerous oversimplification that sets people up for possible failure and feelings of worthlessness."

"The self-help industry has made a fortune selling that message," I say.

"Indeed. For some people it works, but they are the exception, not the rule. If it were that simple, there would be no need for gastric bypass surgery, more people would enter and finish the New York City marathon, procrastination wouldn't exist."

"So what do you mean by the correct part of the mind? What is it and how do you access it?"

"Do you ever try to get into a mind over matter state and find a part of you has risen above the part you call your mind? It feels as if that is the real you and the mind you're trying to harness is just a minion of it."

"Yes, yes, I know exactly what you mean. That's how I feel when I'm in the zone at the gym, completely in the flow."

"That's right. That's also your mind, but it is a higher mind. It watches the lower mind decide not to eat cake anymore and then fail to influence behavior. This higher mind is the part that must be engaged for success."

"Have you figured out how to do that?"

He pauses a moment. "I believe I have. The next step is testing it on all those people for whom positive thinking alone has not worked." He smiles and fiddles with his watch. "So, tell me Emily, what brings you here today?"

I tell him. Everything. In a non-stop list. The sense that I've forgotten something important. The disconnection with Amanda and my life in the suburbs. Performing an emergency cricothyrotomy when I'm terrified of blood and have no medical training. The running leap off the boat. And finally, the dream that led to the realization that I am someone else. I omit only one detail—the belief that I may have killed someone.

Snelling never interrupts even though I talk non-stop for at least twenty minutes. He weathers the tsunami of information and emotion with the barest of nods. I have to admit, I feel relieved after telling my story. I almost believe I've purged it and things will get back to normal.

"How long have you been married?" he asks.

"Just over four years."

"How long did you know your husband before marrying him?"

"Two years. We met at a business event. He worked for one of my clients."

"What do you do?"

"Public relations and marketing, but I'm currently at home with the baby."

Snelling nods, but continues his rapid-fire questioning. "Where did you attend college?"

"Washington University in St. Louis."

"Are you still in touch with classmates?"

"Yes, my best friend Susan lives nearby."

"And she knew you as Emily Cooke?"

"Well, back in college, my maiden name was Sangiacomo."

"What about your family? Are your parents alive?"

"Yes."

"Any siblings?"

"No."

"Do you have memories of your childhood?"

"Sure."

"Who was your favorite teacher in elementary school?"

What the heck? Why is that relevant? I think for a moment. "Mrs. Ronell. Second grade."

"Do you remember how they used to make you write a heading at the top of each page in your notebook? Usually the school and class number or teacher's name were on the left and your name and the date were on the right?"

"Yeah."

Snelling hands me a blank piece of paper and a pen. "Write your heading as you did in that class."

I write the school name in the upper-left corner and Mrs. Ronell's name beneath it. In the upper-right corner I write my name with the date beneath it and hand the paper back to Snelling.

He glances at it. "How old were you in second grade?"

"About eight, I guess."

"I notice you wrote your name as Emily Sangiacomo."

I tense, immediately understanding where he's heading with this non-hypnotic regression.

"At what point do you think you were not Emily Sangiacomo? Was it before second grade?"

The pulse in my neck flutters. Snelling waits for my response.

But I don't have one. From as early as I can remember, I was Emily Sangiacomo and then Emily Cooke. And yet, something inside of me is so sure I am Madison Thorpe.

Snelling discreetly touches a button on his wrist watch.

"I guess my time is up."

"Yes."

I'm grateful he doesn't push me for an answer.

"This was a productive first session. If you decide you wish to continue, there's more we can work on."

Funny thing is, I do want to come back. I like him more than I thought I would.

After saying our goodbyes, I make my way down the elevator. I feel lighter. The static in my mind seems to have lifted. My mood is a bit manic and I have the sudden urge to dance. This is what relief feels like.

As I walk into the sunny, fall day, a breeze blows my hair across my face and I smile and push it behind my ears. Everything is going to be all right.

"Madison!" a man calls out from behind me.

My response is instantaneous. Almost as soon as the "Mad" is out of his mouth, I spin around. My heart races as a man approaches a woman with wavy, red hair.

She smiles in surprise. "What are you doing here?"

I stare at them as they embrace until I realize how strange I must look, gaping at them.

Back in the minivan, I put my forehead to the steering wheel, and in a repeat performance like the one after my MRI, I sob.

# Nine

When I arrive home, Brad greets me at the door with Amanda in his arms.

"What are you doing home so early?" I ask.

"I just felt like coming home to see my girls." He kisses my cheek. "Where've you been?"

"I had an appointment."

Brad bounces Amanda in his arms. I reach out to take her, but she snuggles closer to his shoulder. The characteristic pang cuts my insides. Determined to get this right, I take her from Brad's arms despite her annoyed yelp. I bounce her a bit as he did to get her settled, singing a silly made-up song with her name in it. But she frets and struggles and eventually lets out a wail that ends in full-blown sobs.

"Just take her!" I push her back into Brad's arms and storm up the stairs. Within minutes, Brad's cooing and coddling has calmed her down. I hear him place her in the crib.

A moment later he stands in the doorway of our bedroom. "Mind telling me what the heck that was about?"

"That kid wants nothing to do with me. It's like I'm a stranger instead of her mother."

"*That kid* is a baby, Emily. They get cranky, just like we do. What are you getting so upset about?" His exasperated tone makes me want to throw something across the room.

"Easy for you to say. She likes you."

"She's six months old. You're being ridiculous." He caresses my shoulder, but it's no antidote for the word ridiculous. "What's going on with you? You seem...different."

"Different how?"

"I don't know. Distant. You were the perfect mother from the day Amanda came home from the hospital, but in the last month or so, I've watched you fall apart before my eyes."

The perfect mother when she came home from the hospital? I sit on the edge of the bed and stare at the floor trying to remember, but it's all a blur.

"I know I've been on edge. I know my patience hasn't been high—"

"It's more than that, Em. When you first came home, you'd sit in your glider with the baby and nurse her. You said it was your moment of bliss, that the chemicals that were released every time you fed her were the best high ever. Every day, every two hours, bliss. And then one day, she fussed a bit and you packed it in. Just gave up doing something you loved. Bought a case of formula and you've been miserable ever since."

Though I don't remember the bliss he claims I felt, I do remember the day I bought the formula. I felt unwell. Woke up late. Missed a feeding. Amanda was already fussing and when I tried to nurse her, she went into full-blown baby rage.

"Is it some kind of depression? Maybe you should see someone."

It's now or never. "That's where I was today."

"Really?" Brad asks. He sits down next to me. "Who?"

"Someone my friend Trina from the gym recommended. I liked him. He had a reassuring way about him."

Brad nods, but has a lost expression on his face. That makes me reconsider telling him the truth, but I'm already half way in.

"I've been having some odd sensations and dreams. I get a feeling, a very strong feeling, I'm forgetting something important and I just can't remember it, no matter what I do."

"That sounds like normal, new mother stuff. We've heard other people say that. Remember that couple in our birthing class? How her sister came home from shopping and went to check on the baby and panicked when he wasn't in his crib?"

"No, I don't remember. Where was the baby?"

"Still in the car. She'd forgotten the baby had been with her."

Though I understand Brad's attempt to downplay my feelings, he's making me feel worse by not acknowledging the realness of this to me, the terror of it. Perhaps I haven't conveyed it as seriously as I feel it.

"There's more to it than that, Brad. One of the dreams I had was a lot more detailed. I'm not sure I understand totally what happens in it, but when I woke up I felt like I was someone else."

"Someone else?"

"I'm not Emily."

"What do you mean? That you've changed? That—"

"No. I mean I'm not Emily Cooke. Really not her. My name is Madison Thorpe."

"So you're saying that's what you dreamed."

"No, when I woke up from the dream, I was convinced I *am* Madison Thorpe."

"For how long? You don't think that now, right?"

"I do."

Brad's head does this weird backward snap as if an invisible hand has slapped him. Silence reigns for a long moment as he tries to make sense of it all.

"What did the doctor say?"

"The neurologist said there's nothing wrong with my brain."

"Neurologist? I thought you went to a therapist?"

"I did, after the neurologist. He did an MRI."

Brad jumps up from the bed. "Jeez, Emily. Why haven't you told me any of this before now? Clearly you think it's serious enough to warrant visits to specialists."

"I'm sorry. I was afraid. Do you hear how crazy this sounds? I needed time to sort it out for myself."

"Okay." Brad holds up his palms and his voice gets softer. "So, what makes you so sure you're Madison whatever-her-name-is?"

"I just know it. Don't you have things you just know in your very core that you can't explain?"

That makes him stop and think a moment, which is better than his anger.

"Anyway, my brain was fine physically, so I went to the therapist. I've only gone this one time and we just handled background kind of stuff. If I decide to go back, I guess we'll pick up from there."

"What do you mean if you decide to go back?"

"When I left there, I felt purged somehow of all the weird feelings. But then, as I was walking to my car, someone called out the name Madison. I spun around so fast, even before he'd said the whole name."

"Someone called you Madison?"

"No, the guy was calling out to another woman, but my reaction scared me. I thought he was calling me. I'm not purged of it. There's something in me that knows I'm Madison."

"You could have been responding to the shouting rather than the name."

His refusal to accept what I say strikes me like an angry bolt of lightning. I stand and start counting off the evidence on my fingers.

"I didn't respond to the name Emily when Susan called out to me on the street the other day, despite the fact she called out louder and louder, multiple times. I performed a fucking emergency cricothyrotomy on Vincent Gargiulo, despite my supposed aversion to the sight of blood and lack of surgery skills. Hell, I don't even feel connected to Amanda. It's like she's not my child."

"What the hell is that supposed to mean? Are you thinking you're not her mother now? Who is, then, for Christ's sake?"

"Okay, maybe that's not the best example. What about that running dive I took off the boat and how I can swim like a pro despite your claims I'm deathly afraid of water and can't swim. And then there's a whole bunch of stuff I don't remember, like being mad at your aunt about my bridal shower and the Crock-Pot, the couple at our birthing class, how much more proof do you need?"

"I thought you learned to swim at the gym."

I wince. "I lied about that."

"What? Why would you lie about that?"

"Because you were clearly upset by the incident. I didn't understand what was happening and I just wanted to fix the moment. That seemed the easiest way."

"So, you're telling me you have never taken a swimming class, that you've never gone swimming at the gym?"

"Not even once."

Brad's hair stands up in every direction from his nervous raking. "This is unbelievable."

"I know. I know."

"I think you need to go back to that therapist and work this out."

Work. This. Out. Those three words slice through me. "So you want me to go off and fix myself and come back your perfect little Emily again?"

"That's not what I meant and you know it."

"I don't know much of anything right now."

Brad tries to put an arm around me, but I knock it away and take refuge in the bathroom, the click of the lock my final word on the subject.

# Ten

Jeremy watches through the window as Agent Turner strides toward the conference room, exactly on time. Head held high, shoulders back, laser gaze focused straight ahead. Her confidence bleeds over into toughness and Jeremy understands the roots of that. A native New Yorker with generations of her family from the Hell's Kitchen section of the City before it became the fashionable part of town, she learned early how to communicate a don't-mess-with-me message via body language.

The harshness evaporates when she spots him through the glass and flashes a smile. It was that same smile that convinced Jeremy during her interview several years before that she would be a team player. Her respect for authority, though unexpected, has won Jeremy's faith. Time and again she has carried out her orders without complaint or debate.

"Hey, Boss." She drops her bag on the table. "Is it just us? I thought it was a project meeting."

"I decided to break it up into several meetings. No one knows yet about your side of it, and I'd like to keep it that way a while longer." Jeremy notes to himself that she doesn't know one hundred percent of her side of it either.

Turner slips out of her suit jacket. Despite the cool, autumn weather, she wears a short-sleeved shirt that shows off defined biceps and triceps.

"Jealous?" she asks.

Jeremy feels the heat in his face. "I didn't mean to gawk. Looks like we're paying you to work out."

"Pretty much. She's a bull. Really intense."

"How's it going?"

"After that episode a few weeks ago with Gargiulo, she was pretty shaken up. I suggested she see someone and casually mentioned Snelling's name."

"Did she bite?"

"Not at first. She's not really the therapy type. But then she started with the odd thoughts."

Jeremy has a hard time maintaining his typical poker face now that a feeling of dread has become a constant companion.

"She went on vacation and realized she could swim. Except everyone around her is telling her she's always been afraid of water. No big deal, right? But then she starts feeling like she's someone else."

Jeremy feels his throat drying. "Who does she think she is?"

"Someone named Madison Thorpe."

He sits perfectly still, but his mind screams with the implications. Could there be hope for the military guys?

"What does she say about Madison Thorpe?"

"Not much. She doesn't seem to have any knowledge of her except that she woke up one morning with that name in her head and the sense she was that person."

"So, it's not specific memories of a life led as Madison Thorpe, but rather a generalized sense of being Madison Thorpe."

"That's right. I spoke to Snelling. She made an appointment. According to him, it went well. She seemed calmer by the end of it."

Mixed feelings have Jeremy's stomach roiling. If anyone finds out about this project, his career will be over. From that point of view, he's glad Snelling was able to calm her. On the other hand, if she continues down this path, it might lead to a solution, allowing him to restore his military subjects and send them home. Either scenario contains the danger of exposure. One tiny leak and his name becomes a headline, his family disgraced. Maybe some psycho decides to exact his own brand of punishment. Basically, he's fucked.

"Is Snelling seeing her again?"

"She hasn't set up another appointment. If she confides any more in me, I'll try to convince her to return."

"Make that the goal. It would be best if Snelling was monitoring her in light of her recent breakthroughs. It could be traumatic for her." And me, he thinks.

"Okay, Boss. I'll work on it. Hmmm. I wonder..."

"What?"

"Snelling said she was interested in one of the quotes he had hanging in his office. Something about mind over matter. Maybe we can orchestrate some discussion group to get her back."

"Whatever it takes."

Just then, the security door opens and Reynold and his team enter.

"Are we late?" he asks as he walks into the conference room, checking his watch. He sits across from Turner and puts his laptop case on the table.

"No, I was just finishing up with Agent Turner. Turner, you've met Reynold."

She flashes an uncharacteristic coquettish smile. "Yes. I have."

"This is his team." Jeremy's cell phone rings just as he finishes the introductions. He excuses himself and exits the conference room.

"Hi, hun? Is everything okay?" he asks his wife.

"The school just called. Kaylee has a fever. I'm on my way to pick her up."

"Why didn't you have Teresa get her?"

"I wasn't that busy at work. I hope she doesn't pass it on to Robbie. We'll end up spending our Thanksgiving in lockdown."

As she chats on, Jeremy glances through the conference room window. He can't hear the conversation, but this absence of sound makes his visual perception stronger. What he sees confuses him. Turner has never been one to use feminine charms on a man. In fact, she's more like one of the guys. But Jeremy notices her eyelashes lowered a tad longer than a typical blink before she looks up at Reynold again from her slightly lowered gaze. Flirtation for sure, though no one else notices.

"Jeremy, are you there?"

"I'm sorry. I stepped out of a meeting to take your call. I really have to get back in."

"Okay." Stephanie sighs.

"I'll be home early tonight to help you medicate and soothe our little invalid."

"You're the best." She blows him a kiss before hanging up.

Turner and Reynold tense slightly when Jeremy returns to the conference room. And that's when he understands. They aren't flirting. They're trying not to flirt. Turner and Reynold already have something going on. Shit.

"Sorry about the interruption. Agent Turner, I think we've covered everything. Please let me know immediately if the status changes."

"Sure thing," she says. There's an awkward silence, and Jeremy realizes she doesn't recognize she's been dismissed. And why would she? He led her to believe she was more in the know than the others.

"Ah, you don't need me for the rest of this, right?"

"No, catch an early train back. I'm going to try to get home early myself. Sick kid at home."

She smiles, but Jeremy can see it is forced. She's confused and off-balance. He needs to do damage control.

He walks her to the security door. "Turner, thanks again. From now on, consider your assignment classified even among the team. I'll tell them the same about their assignments to keep the curiosity and competition at bay. That's why I need to have you leave before we begin."

Her expression lightens at his weak explanation.

Considering her cunning radar when it comes to people and bullshit, he can't help feeling disappointed by her reaction. But she wouldn't be the first person to accept something that couldn't possibly be true.

When he returns to the conference room, Reynold brings him up-to-date on the project. New subjects have been found to continue the experiment. And an ingenious method has been proposed to transport them to Governors Island, drastically lowering the chances of such a large, distinctive group being seen. Encouraged by the progress report, Jeremy announces the classified status going forward even within the team and then asks to speak to Reynold alone.

He waits until the other men have left the room.

"Reynold, my wife doesn't know what I do for a living. I suspect she doesn't believe what she's been told, but she has no idea what the specifics are."

"Okay." Reynold looks startled by the turn in discussion. Jeremy hasn't shared much of his personal life with his staff.

"That's the way it has to be. There are things we have to do in the pursuit of national security the average citizen wouldn't understand."

"I agree. It has to be that way."

"It becomes more complicated when two people with clearance begin a relationship."

Reynold's eyebrows knit together at first, but then the confusion lifts. "Oh. Was it that obvious?"

"No, not at all. But I picked up on it. Does she know what you're working on?"

"Definitely not. We're not that far along...as a couple."

"Yet."

Reynold nods his agreement. "Yet."

"You can't disclose what you're working on. I know you wouldn't under normal circumstances, but the project classification has changed, so I just wanted to make it clear that even though we're a team, we're on different need-to-knows."

"Got it."

Jeremy pauses a moment, hating what he has to do next.

"I have to ask that you break it off for now. I know you're not working side-by-side as partners, but this project demands maximum security and confidentiality."

Reynold nods once, the muscle in his cheek tensing.

"Thank you, Reynold. Good luck with the plan. If you need any resources carrying it out, just let me know."

# Eleven

It is Thanksgiving and this year I am thankful for the distraction of the day. To say things have been tense around here would be the understatement of the year. Brad and I speak only when necessary and our personal-space boundaries have expanded. As we pass in the hallway, he bends his body in barely perceptible ways to avoid touching me. Is he angry at me or afraid of me? I'm not sure, but I look forward to getting out of the house, to a change of scenery, different faces, traditional food. They'll be plenty of hands to hold Amanda, so it will be a day off from mommyhood as well.

I pack up the diaper bag in no time, having created a list that leaves nothing to chance. On our way to my parents' house, Amanda babbles happily in her car seat. I turn around to watch her and find myself breaking into a rare smile.

Twenty minutes later, we arrive at my childhood home, a modest cape on the border of Floral Park and Franklin Square. A warm rush of food-scented air greets us in the foyer, but my nose twitches with the sense something is not right.

The regular cast of characters has already arrived. Uncle Sal reclines in an arm chair, watching the football game on television. He takes Amanda from Brad and bounces her on his knee, singing silly rhymes.

Uncle Joe sits at the dining room table, whittling away at a loaf of Italian bread. "How are you, Emily?"

Before I can respond, the door between the kitchen and dining room swings open. My grandmother rushes in with two bowls and places them on the table.

"Ooooooh," she says as she rushes to engulf me in a cushiony embrace.

For some reason, I freeze. I pat her on the back to cover my awkward reaction but she's already moved on.

"Joe, don't eat all that bread. You know you're not supposed to eat that," she says to my uncle as she grabs a piece for herself and rushes off.

I follow her into the hair-curling heat and humidity of the kitchen. My dad lifts the heavy pan with the turkey and carries it to the kitchen table for carving. My mother swaps various pans in and out of the oven to warm them. Aunt Marge assembles food on a platter. It's a bee hive of activity, everyone too busy to do much more than coo when I enter.

"Everybody sit down," my mother says. "It's time to eat."

My dad pours red wine as trays of steaming food pass from one person to the next. Thoughts of Pilgrims, Native Americans, vegetables from the harvest, and an authentic New World meal come to a screeching halt when the first platter passes under my nose and I get the whiff of strong cheese and vinegar. No wonder my olfactory senses were confused when I walked in the door. For a moment, I stare at the antipasto platter of salami, provolone cheese, soppressata, olives, marinated eggplant, roasted red peppers, and fresh mozzarella cheese, then take a bit of mozzarella and a roasted pepper.

The next platter holds dozens of stuffed mushrooms. I select one before passing it on. Stuffed artichokes follow, but I'm not in the mood to dirty my hands on those. When everyone has been served, cries of "Salud" ring out and everyone raises their glasses. Let the eating begin.

As silverware clangs against china, my grandmother's head weaves this way and that as she tries to see through the platters on the table to my plate.

"Is that all you're eating? Look at you, you're wasting away to nothing. For heaven's sake." Her gaze moves to Brad's plate, which is practically empty despite the mound of food he had on it moments ago. "Emily, make your husband another plate," she says.

"I've got it," Brad says and winks to no one in particular.

Amanda lets out a scream and I jolt in my seat. She's dropped the heel of the bread she's been nibbling on. My dad grabs a new piece and hands it to her. She rewards him with a wide smile. The former clatter builds up to its original level as my mind recedes.

I return for a brief moment when the next course is served—lasagna. I have nothing against lasagna, but today it annoys me. My mother serves up huge, gloppy squares and everyone oohs and aahs. I ask for a tiny piece and my grandmother pipes up again about my eating habits.

"Ma, would you leave her alone," my mother says. "She lost all her baby weight. She's doing good."

My grandmother sniffs, not convinced. A dull pain begins to pulse behind my eyes.

Finally, it's the turkey and all the trimmings. I feel myself perking up as I help myself to white meat, cranberry sauce, and stuffing. But what's this? Broccoli rabe? Escarole? Where's the corn pudding, the turnips, the candied yams? Where is tradition? I look around the table at all the happy people consuming huge quantities of food. This is tradition. And yet, it doesn't feel like mine.

By the time the parade of desserts begins, I'm thinking a slice of pie and a cup of coffee would hit the spot. I pass the Italian cheese cake, the tiramisu, and assorted Italian pastries and cookies.

"No pumpkin pie?" I ask.

My mother looks at me as if I have three heads. "Pumpkin pie? Who eats pumpkin pie?"

"I do."

"Since when?"

That question stumps me. I'm a stranger dining in a foreign

land.

After dessert, everyone finds a spot to slump into a tryptophan coma. I stare at them through squinted eyes as I rub my temples. If aliens were going to swoop down to conquer the human race, right after Thanksgiving dinner would be the time to do it. I laugh at the irony of being probed by gadgets that look like pop-up turkey thermometers.

"What's so funny?" Brad asks.

I didn't realize I laughed out loud. "Oh nothing. Just thinking about aliens and human turkeys."

He gives me a strange look and turns back to the football game.

My head is now pounding. I go to the upstairs bathroom and swallow some ibuprofen with a chaser of tap water from my cupped hand. A solitary tear rolls down my cheek. I follow its path as I stare into the mirror. What's wrong with me? Surely the absence of turnips is not the problem. My eyes fill with tears and suddenly I'm swimming in a sea of blurred blue bathroom tiles. I splash water on my face and compose myself before stepping into the hallway. My feet sink into the plush carpeting in the dark, narrow hallway. As I make my way to the stairway, it occurs to me that I've walked this path thousands of times in my youth. So why does it feel so new?

Back downstairs, I whisper to Brad that I'm ready to go and then start packing Amanda's things.

"You're leaving already?" Uncle Sal says.

"Yeah, I'm really tired. It's tough being a new mother," I joke with him, though I'm not quite joking.

"What new?" he says. "She's eight months old."

I stare at him, speechless, shaken by his words. It's not his lack of understanding of what it's like to be a mother that leaves me temporarily paralyzed. It's the sense I haven't been doing this for so long. That it feels like only a couple of months rather than eight. This is not the melancholic sadness at the passage of time and how quickly Amanda is growing. On the contrary, it's about me and the sense I've lost something I may never find again. The only problem is, I don't know what that "something" is.

# Twelve

The Thanksgiving holiday has soothed Brad. The past week, he seemed his old self again, as if he's forgotten he has a crazy wife who thinks she's someone else. I, on the other hand, have sunk deeper into the abyss of obsession. It's 2 a.m. In typical male fashion, Brad sleeps soundly, not a care in the world, as I pace in the dark with my mind racing, a modern day Lady Macbeth. I'm either Madison Thorpe or I'm not. If I'm not, I'm crazy. If I am, I have a whole host of other problems. I've decided to proceed as if I am Madison to find the proof that substantiates that belief. Where would a detective begin? Google, my dear Watson.

I curl up on the couch with my laptop, not bothering to turn on the lights. I enter Madison Thorpe into the search field and groan at the number of results. By page fifteen, nothing has captured my attention. I stretch my arms and decide a cup of tea would be nice.

As I wait for the kettle to boil, I realize I may be able to narrow the search by making some assumptions. For example, my accent places me somewhere in the metro New York area. A local phone search might be the way to go. I pour water over an Earl Grey teabag and return to the den. I take a sip and let the essence of bergamot soothe my senses before consulting the phone listings.

There are no Madison Thorpes listed in New York. However, there are dozens of other Thorpes, some of whom may know this person I think I am. I begin compiling lists of everyone in the area. Once morning arrives, I'll make calls until I either find someone who knows me or exhaust the list without any clues. The latter option causes my stomach to clench.

\*\*\*

Four hours later, I wake up on the couch. Sunlight bends around the sides of the closed shades, blinding me. It feels as if I have a hangover but without having had the pleasure of drinking. I stumble to the kitchen to put on coffee before jumping into the shower. I need to be clear-headed for today's mission, and last night's poor sleep has already put me at a disadvantage.

When I return to the bedroom to dress, Brad sits on the side of the bed, staring into space and scratching his head. Usually, he is a perky morning person with smiles and good-natured chatter. While I am a quick riser, I do not enjoy conversation in the morning. I chuckle at the irony—I'm about to spend my morning in conversation with the Thorpes of New York.

Brad turns toward me. "What's so funny?"

"Oh, nothing really. Just a passing thought that wouldn't be as funny if spoken aloud."

"What are you going to do today?" he asks. I swear I see a wary expression on his face and then it hits me. It's his first day back to work after the Thanksgiving holiday and he'll be leaving crazy lady alone.

"Oh, I thought I'd plant eggs in the yard and see if chickens grow. After that, I'm going to break all the china and make a mosaic top for the dining room table." I shoot him a radiant smile.

"Ha, ha," he says without enthusiasm. "You know, I don't

think you're crazy."

I can't suppress my snort. "Of course you do." But then again, who wouldn't? A sobering thought. I can't talk to my parents about this. They won't understand and definitely couldn't make the leap to the possibility I am someone else, whatever the hell that means. I'm not even sure Susan would understand.

"Emily, did you hear me?"

"Huh?"

Brad stares at me. "I asked if you were going to be all right with Amanda."

Ah, Amanda. That's the reason for Brad's uncharacteristic pensiveness. I'd forgotten about Amanda. She will definitely impede my work today. Brad clearly thinks I am unfit to be with her. Best to kill two birds with one stone. "I'll call the babysitter. That way I'll be able to get some stuff done in the house."

"Good idea." As he passes me on his way to the bathroom, he leans in and kisses my forehead. I stiffen for a split second, but then it's over.

***

I sit on my bed, phone in hand. I've printed a list of all the area Thorpes, found a notebook and pen—one of those four-color ones that write in black, blue, red, or green at the click of a button. A cup of piping hot coffee sits on my bedside table. I take a tentative sip, followed by a deep breath. What's the best way to handle this? I think a moment and decide to identify myself as Emily Cooke and say I'm looking for an old friend for a reunion. That's a common enough occurrence these days. I glance at the phone. It's now or never. I take one more sip of coffee and am about to dial the first number when paranoia strikes.

Brad already thinks I'm nuts. What's to stop him from checking up on what I've been doing on the computer and the phone? That's all I need. I'll be in a padded cell in no time. I start up the laptop and delete my internet history. Then I gather up my stuff, call down to the baby sitter that I'm going out for a while, and head to the store to buy a prepaid cell phone.

I grab another cup of coffee from the Starbuck's drive-thru and end up parked back on my block with the new cell phone in hand. I dial the first number. My stomach knots as the phone rings. An elderly woman with a trembling voice answers.

In response to my introduction, she says, "No, I don't cook. I get the Meals on Wheels."

That one stumps me for a second.

"No, ma'am. I said, my name is Emily Cooke."

"You cook?"

"My. Name. Is. Em-i-ly. Cooke," I shout into the phone, glad I'm not making these calls from home or the babysitter would be dialing Psych Services. I take a deep breath. Life is short; I need to switch to the CliffsNotes version of my spiel. "Do. You. Know. Mad-i-son. Thorpe?"

"Madison? No, I don't know anyone named Madison? Who is she?"

A sigh escapes my lips. "Thank you. Have a nice day."

I hang up and erupt in laughter. Not a very good start. If I don't laugh, I'll cry.

Another sip of coffee, composure regained, I try again. The next two are "no answers." The fourth has an answering machine, but I decide not to leave a message and make a notation to try again later.

The next guy sounds as if I've woken him up. I apologize before beginning my speech. He's breathing heavy and sounds congested. I have a vision of a big-bellied guy, who spent the night eating Cheetos and watching TV before transporting his at-risk heart to bed. In response to my question, he grunts a no and hangs up. He's got to rest up for tonight's TV marathon, after all.

I dial the next number, belonging to R & R Thorpe, and this time a woman answers.

"Good morning, my name is Emily Cooke and I'm trying to locate a Madison Thorpe for a school reunion we're planning."

The woman chuckles, "Ha, ha, very funny. What are you up to, Maddie?"

Her comfortable, joking tone stops me in my tracks. Before I realize what she has just said, I suck in my breath hard. My heart feels as though it has come to a crashing halt, but in a microsecond it makes up for any missed beats with a pounding so fierce I can practically taste adrenaline. It's not just the name Maddie that has caused this reaction. No, there's something else. Something my mind cannot quite grasp.

"You know who this is?" My voice wavers.

"Uh, yes. Was that supposed to be a disguised voice because it sounds just like you."

A sob rumbles out. "You know who I am."

"Madison, what's wrong?"

And then my mind catches up. "Mom!"

"You're scaring the heck out of me. What's going on?" she asks.

I try to pull myself together, try to calm the hiccup-like sobs and sniffling. I wipe my eyes with my sleeve.

"I need to see you. Can I come there?"

"Of course."

I look at the Brooklyn address on my list. "333 Garden Place, right?"

There's a moment of silence. "Maybe I should come to you."

"No, I'm not where I should be," I say. "It's going to take me a while to get there. At least an hour once I catch the train."

"Where are you coming from?"

"Long Island."

"Okay, calm down, take your time, be safe. I'll be here waiting."

I can barely get the "okay" out of my mouth before hanging up. Stunned, I reach for my bag and open my wallet to make sure I have money. My wedding photo stares back at me. I'm wearing a Cinderella ball kind of bridal gown with a puffed skirt and glittery train. Something I would never choose. What is happening here? What kind of lie am I living? Who am I?

I leave the car and run the three blocks to the railroad station, afraid I won't find a parking space if I drive there. I pass the Victorian condo complex, a pretty compromise in a neighborhood obsessed with strip malls. I run past the strip mall next, the butcher with its advertisement-covered windows, the barber who does a thriving business, the florist who always sends a card on anniversaries and birthdays, the shoemaker who doesn't speak much English but can turn shoes one step away from the garbage into something wearable again. Across the street is the Five and Dime where you can find anything from a spool of thread to a Golden Book children's story to a length of replacement garden hose.

As I pass it all, I realize there's nothing wrong with this town. It's a fine place to live and raise a family. No, there's nothing wrong with it at all. I'm the one who doesn't fit.

A train pulls in to the station. I take the flight of steps two at a time, but it's the eastbound. I bend over at the waist, gasping for breath, my treadmill jogging no preparation for a long sprint. The early winter wind whips at my face, and I pull my jacket tighter. Five minutes later, the westbound pulls in. I slump down in a seat and pull off my jacket, now overheated from the forced hot air pumped into the car.

I know I should plan a strategy for how to handle this situation, but my mind won't go there. It chooses to observe the bare branches on the trees, the stores along Sunrise Highway that mark the various neighborhoods we pass—the King Kullen of Bellmore, the tile store in Merrick, the Home Depot in Freeport. Before I know it, we've arrived at Jamaica station and I switch to the train going to Atlantic Terminal in Brooklyn.

Now that I'm close, my mind switches to the issue at hand. Logic warns me I need to be cautious, but instinctively I know danger does not await me where I'm headed. When the train pulls in at Atlantic Terminal, I hop off and automatically make my way to the 4 train, walking briskly without thought or map.

After exiting the subway car, I climb the stairs to the street. Walk with purpose four blocks straight. Make a left. Halfway down the block is 333. It's as if I've been here a million times before. I climb the high, wide steps leading to the brownstone as my right hand instinctively goes into my pocket. Empty. I ring the doorbell and wait for what feels like a lifetime. A tall, thin woman with a chin-length bob answers the door.

"Why didn't you use your key?" She grasps my shoulders in a quick hug before stepping back and looking me in the eyes.

"I...I forgot it."

I follow her into the living room, the middle floor of three. The floors are gleaming hardwood, the ceilings high and adorned with crown moldings. The center, narrow staircase that leads to the bedrooms on the third floor is in front of me. Suddenly, I race up those stairs, turn right, and run to the end of the hallway. The door on what should be a bedroom is closed and I barge in.

It isn't a bedroom but a study with a computer set up in a fancy, wood armoire. That doesn't matter because I can see what used to be in this room—the single bed with the Hello Kitty comforter, the band posters of Pulp, Radiohead, and The Verve, a model of the DNA double helix. There is a door in the corner of the room. I already know it's a closet. I open it and find that the clothes bar has been replaced by shelving. I drop to my knees and stick my head under the lowest shelf, about a foot and a half off the floor. Tears blur my vision, but I don't need to see to know what is written on the wall.

*Madison Thorpe wuz here 6/10/95.*

That day was my thirteenth birthday and I was experiencing those first adolescent urges to record my existence.

"Madison, what on earth are you doing?"

I sit up with tears on my face.

Her eyes flash fear and she leads me to the loveseat on the other side of the room. We sit side-by-side, tilted toward one another. I pull a tissue from the box she offers and dab at my cheeks. This woman looks nothing like me. She's got light brown hair and medium brown eyes. Her nose is thin and slightly tilted up. The fact that I can't summon a single memory of her challenges the overwhelming sense that she is my mother. I've been fooled before.

"Your phone listing just had your initials. I don't remember your name," I say in a soft voice.

Her posture straightens even more as she inhales deeply. When she responds, her voice is softer than mine. "Regina."

"Who is the other R in the listing?"

"Richard."

"I feel like you're my parents—"

"Of course we are."

"But I don't remember you."

She sits in silence for a moment, staring at the rug. Then, with a voice as clear as a bell, she sings:

*Hydrogen has one proton, Helium has two,*
*One, two, THREE! has Lithium, peek-a-boo.*

My eyes pool with tears again as she holds up fingers to count and then covers and uncovers her eyes before saying boo. I throw my arms around her and sob. She stiffens for a split second before surrounding me in a firm embrace. The memory of my discomfort with the hugging on Thanksgiving comes to mind. This is my mother. My mother! I can't imagine how to tell my story so that Regina Thorpe—my mother—doesn't respond the way Brad did. This time it really matters to me.

I pull back from our embrace. "I have to tell you something. It's the craziest thing you've ever heard. You'll think I'm insane, but there are people who can confirm my story."

"Go on."

I take a deep breath. "I've been living on Long Island with my husband Brad and my daughter Amanda."

"What are you talking about?"

"It's true. I have a husband and a baby girl."

Her eyes narrow. "Madison, you're not married and you

don't have a daughter."

"Apparently I do. But there they call me Emily. Emily Cooke. And that's who I thought I was until I started having weird dreams and finally remembered my name was Madison. It's as if I've been living a double life, but I don't understand why or how it came to be."

Her intent gaze reminds me of Trina's. No surprise why we became fast friends.

"Maddie, even if you are living a double life, I think I would have noticed if you'd been pregnant."

She makes a good point.

"Okay, but if Amanda isn't mine, whose child is she?"

Just then, the phone rings. She glances at it but then returns her attention to me.

"It's okay," I say. "You can answer it."

"It can wait."

And it could have waited if the answering machine hadn't been invented. Regina's recorded voice tells the caller she's not available, leave a message.

Nothing has prepared us for what follows the beep.

"Hi, Mom, it's Madison. Give me a call when you get a chance. Bye."

# Thirteen

Regina lunges for the phone, but I grab her and pull her back.

"No," I say. "Not yet."

She twists out of my hold. "What the hell is going on here, Madison? This isn't funny."

Relief washes over me. Despite her confusion and anger, she still believes I am Madison.

"I don't know," I say, my heart pounding.

"Are you telling me you don't know anything about that phone call?"

"I swear."

She smooths the front of her blouse with trembling fingers and sits back down, her spine erect.

"This is some kind of hoax or scam. We need to think this through," I say. "We can't act rashly. I'm just getting my memory back, but I'm so relieved I'm not crazy."

"This is more than a hoax. Your memory loss...what caused that? You're convinced you've been living another life. Have you had head trauma—"

"No, I just had an MRI."

"How long do you think you've been living as this Emily person?"

"I'm not sure. I have a lifetime of Emily Cooke memories.

In fact, even now, I know only bits about who I really am. It's as if Emily's life has stifled Madison's."

"This makes no sense."

"No, it doesn't. I started to think I had been in an accident and lost my memory, but that didn't explain why I have an entire family and friends back in Long Island who know me as Emily."

"More than just the husband and baby?"

"Yes. Parents, a grandmother, uncles, aunts—"

"Why would Emily's family pretend you're their daughter?"

"Why, indeed? I even have a friend who says she attended Wash U with me."

"Wash U? You went to Columbia for both undergraduate and grad school."

"Columbia?" I ponder that for a moment but don't have any recollection of it. "What do I do for a living?"

"You're a scientist."

"You are, too, aren't you?" I ask.

"Yes, and your father."

I try to complete the puzzle with the pieces she's giving me.

"So, who just phoned?" she asks.

"I don't know. I didn't see that coming. But any way you look at it, there's no explaining this away. Someone is impersonating me in this family, and on the other side of town, an entire family is engaged in some kind of conspiracy, pretending I'm Emily Cooke."

"Hmmmm."

"What?"

"Well, I was just wondering. Does Emily Cooke really exist? Is there a paper trail we can follow?"

"I have a social security number—I mean, she does."

"Does she have a date of birth?"

"Yes, August 13, 1981."

"So, she's older than you, but not by much."

Her earlier question about how long I've been living as Emily Cooke pops into my mind.

"When was the last time you saw me?"

"Last week. At Thanksgiving dinner."

"That's not possible. I was on Long Island with the other family on Thanksgiving."

"I have pictures to prove it," my mother says.

"So do I."

She accesses the photo app and hands me her phone. I gasp. There I am smiling into the camera. My tears well up when I see a man I know is my dad. All of the photos display the date of Thanksgiving. How can this be? I walk over to the computer and sign into my online photo account. She stares in shock at my face on the screen.

"Do any of those people look familiar to you?" I ask.

"Not at all. Complete strangers."

I point to the screen. "This is Brad, and that's Amanda."

She leans in close to see. "Oh my Lord. This just can't be."

"What?"

"That baby looks exactly like you did."

"Are you sure?"

"Positive."

She bends to retrieve a photo album from a cabinet in the wall unit. When she starts flipping through it, I grab her arm to slow her down. She points to a picture.

"That's you at just under a year old."

"Oh my God. The resemblance is uncanny."

"It's more than a resemblance," she says.

I have to agree. As I flip through the album, I realize I know which photos are coming next. I turn to her. "On the last page of this photo album is a picture of Dad and me. I'm sitting on the hood of a car eating an ice cream cone that's smeared all over my face."

I turn to the back page and sure enough, there it is. A surge of relief flows through me.

"I think we should call your father. Have him come home. We need to figure out what's going on here."

"Okay, but don't tell him anything on the phone. We need to do it in person."

After she makes the phone call, we go downstairs to the

kitchen. She unpacks food cartons from a shopping bag.

"I ordered from the Greek place just before you arrived. We might have to warm it a bit."

"I can't believe it, but I'm actually hungry. It feels good to be home, even if I don't remember everything about my life yet."

My mother's worried frown reveals her fear, and mine—I may never completely remember my past or what has happened to me.

As we eat souvlaki and baba ghanoush, she asks me questions about my life as Emily. I tell her about Brad and Amanda, how the marriage seemed easy enough until I told him I thought I was someone else. I admit my lack of connection to Amanda. I tell her all the facts I know about Emily that don't resonate in me.

As we're cleaning up after lunch, Richard walks in. My dad. I study him as he kisses my mom on the cheek. He wraps his arm around my shoulder and kisses my forehead. "How you doing, Watson? What smells so good in here?"

"We just had take-out from the Greek restaurant," my mother says. "I made you a plate—"

My sob interrupts her response. They turn to me, shock in their eyes.

"What's wrong?" he asks.

"You called me Watson."

He watches, confused, as my mom pats my arm. He'd given me the nickname as a kid, after he brought home the DNA double helix model I remembered being in my bedroom. He'd explained the importance of the discovery by Watson and Crick. How the secret to our genetic code was in DNA, but until they figured out the double helix shape, it couldn't be unlocked. I'd asked so many questions that afternoon, he told me he was going to start calling me Crick. I protested and said I preferred Watson, having been a huge fan of Watson in the Sherlock Holmes stories, a man of exceptional talent himself who was perfectly content being in the shadow of Holmes. From that day on, the name Watson stuck.

"Sit down, Rich," Mom says. "There's a lot happening."

His plate of food sits untouched as we fill him in. He glances between my mother and me, his features frozen in an expression of disbelief, no doubt wondering if we have both gone mad. But when we get to the part about the phone call, he rushes to the answering machine to play the message.

"That's not you?" he asks.

"No. I was sitting next to Mom when that message came in."

"Well, there's only one thing to do," he says. "We call back this person claiming to be Madison and have her come over here right away."

"She can't possibly come here," Mom says. "This is all some kind of hoax. The game's over once she reveals herself."

"No, I think Dad is right. Let's flush her out. Call her bluff. And then we play it as it comes."

"Okay, then." She picks up the phone and stares into space a moment before dialing.

Dad and I watch intently and see it in her face the moment "Madison" answers.

"Hi, honey," Mom says in a stiff voice. "Listen, don't be alarmed, everything's okay, but Dad was having some chest pains." Mom pauses. "No, he's really okay, Madison, but I need to go out for his medications and pick up some groceries. Could you come sit with him for a couple of hours so he's not alone?"

"Did you have to put me at death's door?" Dad says when she finishes the call.

"She sounded truly upset. She's some actress, whoever she is."

I swipe through the photos again. "Tell me about Thanksgiving. Maybe I'll remember."

"It was just us, Uncle Ben and Catherine, and Fred and Lois."

"What did we eat?"

"What we always eat—turkey, candied yams, sausage and apple dressing, turnips, and Lois brought a corn pudding."

"Was there pumpkin pie?"

"Of course."

"Mmmm. Just what a Thanksgiving dinner should be. Not weird things like lasagna, stuffed artichokes, and Italian cheesecake."

"That's not what you said on Thanksgiving."

"What do you mean?"

"You asked why we don't ever have different things for Thanksgiving, like lasagna, or green vegetables like broccoli rabe."

"That's odd. I don't understand how I could have been in two places at once. What time did you eat dinner?"

"Six o'clock."

"We ate much earlier, but I remember all of that day and none of the one with you."

Dad takes the phone from me. "You look heavier in these photos." He holds the screen toward me.

"Yeah, it looks that way. My face is not that full."

He shows me another one.

Mom moves in closer to look at the photos. "Hmmm, we see you regularly, so we're not going to notice five pounds one way or the other. But I can see the difference from the pictures."

I study the photos.

"Smile," he says.

When I look up, he snaps a picture of me with his phone. We compare the photos.

"I've lost weight recently. I've been working out quite a bit."

"It's not even a week since Thanksgiving, Maddie," he says.

"What's your point?" I ask, exasperated by this sudden weight-loss tangent.

Before he can respond, a voice from the doorway makes us jump. "What's going on?"

# Fourteen

"Oh my God," Mom whispers. "Who are you?"

If the story about Dad's heart was fiction an hour ago, life might just imitate art. We are thunderstruck, staring at a heavier version of me in the doorway, swinging the house key casually from her index finger.

"What do you mean, who am I?" she asks, laughing.

But then her gaze meets mine. It's almost slow motion the way her jaw drops, pulling her smile into something akin to Edvard Munch's *The Scream*.

"What the heck is going on here?" Her voice trembles. "Who is that?" She points at me, and the house key falls to the floor.

"You have the key," Regina says.

I know what's coming next and Regina and Richard don't disappoint. They turn accusing eyes on me, the hollow-cheeked woman without the house key. Clearly not the person with whom they shared pumpkin pie at Thanksgiving dinner.

"Wait!" I put up my hands. "Mom, I just proved to you I knew things no one else would know."

"Mom? Why is she calling you that?" the other Madison says. "Is she...my twin? Why wouldn't you tell me I have a twin?"

"Because there are no twins," Regina says. "I gave birth to one child, a daughter, named Madison. That's it."

My mind churns. "That's impossible! We're obviously twins."

"I was awake for the birth."

"And I second it. I was there," Dad says.

Something teases the edges of my memory. "Did you conceive naturally?"

"If you were really Madison, you'd know we used in vitro fertilization."

*If you were really Madison.* Those few words are an acid that eats away at the security and well-being I felt just moments ago, despite the bizarre circumstances.

"Why are you calling her Madison?" my twin asks.

"Because that's my name."

She sinks to the floor. Dad jumps forward to assist her.

"I just need to sit a moment."

I turn back to Mom, determined to regain her trust. "What if the eggs harvested from you were implanted in someone else, who gave birth to her. It's a stretch, I know, that two different fertilized eggs would look exactly alike, but what's the alternative?"

"It's a long stretch," Dad says, "but the more interesting question right now concerns the odds of both of those offspring being named Madison."

The appearance of my doppelganger has thrown me for a loop, but when he says that, something clicks. The brain is a mysterious organ. It manages the entire operations of a body, it filters thoughts and stores them for later use. It dreams, and we mostly pay no attention. But one of my dreams now flashes in my mind like a neon sign. The dream of me in that silver bikini with the stretch marks.

"We're not both named Madison." I walk toward her. "Her name is Emily. Emily Cooke."

She looks up at me. "What are you talking about?"

"Stand up," I say. When she just stares at me, I say it again in a more forceful voice.

"Pull up your shirt."

"What? No."

"Do it. Come on, I'll do it too. It'll prove the point."

I lift my shirt and she does the same. My skin is smooth, toned, and unmarred. Hers is less elastic, her tummy is a bit loose, and she's got bright pink stretch marks on her abdomen. Even knowing what I was going to see, I am still in awe.

"Wow. She's not mine," I say.

I touch one of the pink tracks. When I look up at her, there are tears in my eyes.

"Your name is Emily Cooke—"

She shakes her head vigorously.

"You're married to a man, a very nice man, named Brad. You have a beautiful little girl named Amanda."

With that, a glimmer of recognition flashes in her eyes. "Amanda?" she whispers.

"Yes." I take her arm and lead her to the computer. A sob escapes her lips as I click through the Thanksgiving photos.

"This is going to sound weird...I don't remember from looking at her, but something inside feels right now that I know I have a daughter. I've been having a sensation of loss for months." She bursts out crying. I join her because I know exactly how she feels. There's not a dry eye in the room. And that's a bit rare in a family of analytical scientists.

As soon as the thought enters my mind, I know I've just had another breakthrough. "Have you been living my life?" I ask her.

"I...I don't know."

"A scientist?"

"Yes."

"What kind of scientist am I?" I ask.

"Genetics research."

I let out a mirthless laugh. "The irony of it all. You don't have a background in genetics. Are you physically doing my job?"

"Yes."

"How is that possible?"

"I don't know. But it's been stressful. I feel...blocked, like I've lost my mojo."

"That would be the Ph.D. in Genetics from Columbia. A minor detail."

This makes Emily giggle. I stiffen at the sound and then realize why. It is my giggle. The one I have tried to suppress all my life because it doesn't suit a serious scientist. It sounds much better on her.

"It's not the subject matter that's tripping me up," she says. "I understand what I'm working on, but my hands won't cooperate. I've been a complete klutz in the lab."

"No muscle memory," I say, almost to myself. "You're not alone. I've been trying to be a mother to your daughter and I don't have a clue. I think she knows I'm not you."

"Really?"

"Yes. In fact, I'm sure of it. Smart kid." Brad's words come back to me. How I just gave up breastfeeding one day. It all makes sense now. I was trying to feed a hungry baby with an empty breast and she wasn't having it. The best mother couldn't win that showdown.

My dad interrupts. "I don't want to rush the 'getting to know you' stage, but we still have a big problem here. Identical people who didn't know of the other's existence have been switched to live each other's life, complete with the memories of the other. Sounds like something out of a sci-fi movie."

He's not joking, and the truth rings through. Someone has switched Emily and me in every way possible. I am dizzy with the thought of it. I feel violated. Someone has invaded my mind. They've sucked out my memories and given them to someone else. And I've received a stranger's memories. It's insane. Who would do such a thing? And why? What purpose would it serve? Who would benefit? From the silence in the room, I suspect we're all pondering these questions.

We need to brainstorm, so I clear my throat and start asking the questions aloud. Emily Cooke, PR specialist, accustomed to being a human megaphone, doesn't disappoint. As we warm up, I tape printer paper to the wall and jot down terms and draw bubbles around them with a marker.

"Madison, that's going to bleed through on the wall," Mom says, stepping out of scientist mode for a moment to be a mother. My mother. Again.

I lift the paper to reassure her.

"Okay, who would do something like this?" I ask.

"Scientists, for sure," Dad says. "Even if they weren't driving it, they or someone in the medical profession would most likely be needed to orchestrate it."

"Why would they do it? What's the purpose?"

"To prove a hypothesis, for starters," he says.

"A hypothesis about what?"

"A theory about siblings, perhaps," Emily says.

My writing hand freezes in the air. I have to consider Emily a sibling. Although Mom and Dad claim they had only one child, other fertilized eggs from their in vitro trials could have been stolen.

"What theory about siblings?" I ask. "Why would you take siblings raised separately and suddenly switch them?"

"Maybe to see how similar or dissimilar they had turned out," Emily says.

"But that doesn't make sense. That would apply only if they hadn't switched our memories as well. What possible benefit could that have had in any research project on nature versus nurture?"

"What if it isn't a nature versus nurture project?" Emily says. "What if it's just a mind experiment to see if one person can be replaced seamlessly by an identical looking sibling?"

She raises a disturbing thought. Why would people need to know that? But I'm stuck in the past. I want to know how Emily and I were chosen for this project, and when? Why us and not another set of siblings? Or maybe there are others.

It's likely a scientific or medical community plays a role in our situation. I need to get back to my job to see if I can uncover anything. But then I look over at Emily and remember she recalls nothing of her real life. There's no way to return her to Brad and Amanda without causing a huge mess. Emily's expression is stuck in a frown. I imagine I look much the same. It's odd staring at myself.

"Is there any way we are all related?" Mom asks. "Not in a biological sense, but in a—"

"Six degrees of separation kind of way?" Emily says.

"Yes, exactly," Mom says.

"Unfortunately, I don't remember anything about my real life," Emily says, "so how do we figure out what the intersections are?"

"Perhaps Madison can fill in the missing pieces."

Emily says to me, "Why is it you know about my life but also remember your own? Why can't I do that?" Her voice trembles.

"I don't know. I don't remember a lot about my real life, but being here seems to help."

"Do you think I'll start to remember, too?"

I can't be sure, of course, but something in her eyes stops me from admitting that. "I don't see why not."

She lets out her breath. "Okay, so what do we know?"

"We can probably back into the date we were switched," I say. "I had my first anxiety moment in late September." I recall the day I made the beef stew in the Crock-Pot. The weird sensations. The lost time.

"What do you mean by anxiety moment?"

"A panicked feeling that I had forgotten something very important. I remember thinking that day I hadn't been feeling right for about a month. So perhaps we should look at that time period as the possible switch date. What else happened around then that will prove or disprove that hypothesis?"

"At the end of August, we were in Europe," Dad says.

"That's right," Mom says. "Switzerland, for three weeks."

"That was over three months ago, which puts Emily closer to when she gave birth, which means she may have been heavier than she is today. Do you remember a time we were together when you thought I was heavier than usual?"

"Now that you mention it, I did notice some weight gain when we returned," he says. "So, perhaps the switch happened while we were away. Sometime around August 25th."

I write it down on my brainstorm wall. "Emily, is there anything you remember from my life that's unusual. Any periods of stress that might help us with the dates and motives?"

"At work, I've had the sense there was some kind of turmoil. That I was being watched for screwing up in the past. Like maybe I was next to be fired." Emily struggles for the words to describe the sensations.

"That doesn't sound right," Dad says. "Madison is a respected scientist. She's been at HC Labs since her summers in high school. It's like a family."

"Do you have any memory of what I might have done?" I ask.

"No. It's all hazy."

I have a hint of what could have happened, but I ignore it.

"In August, we were moved to a different lab," Emily says.

"A different lab?"

"Still on the sixth floor, but they moved us to the lab at the end of the hall. The other lab was being renovated. There had been an accident or something. I don't really remember."

But I do. My dream comes back to me now in bits and pieces. In it, I am destroying the lab. There is blood on my hands. Could that have happened in reality? If it did, is it possible the dream of the man in the hospital is true as well? My menacing tone? All that blood? I shiver. That would make me a murderer, something I'm not ready to share yet.

"We're back in the original lab now," Emily says. "Things have been a bit easier, but I still feel like people are wary around me."

"I need to get back to my real life. Maybe being there again will trigger something and help me figure out what is going on."

"We can switch places," Emily says.

"Not yet. We need to take some time to debrief and exchange what we remember about our real lives and the lives we've been switched into." I think about how to word my next suggestion. "We also need to look as much the same as possible."

"Yeah, you really need to start eating more," Emily responds, taking me totally by surprise.

A second later, she erupts in laughter. "I'm sorry. That was a bad joke. I think I'm a bit hysterical from the shock of this. I actually just joined a gym, though I can't imagine why. It's not really my thing."

"That's you playing the role of me. The gym's my thing," I say. "If I lighten up on the working out and you go a bit stronger, we'll match in no time."

"I think we have to consider the strong possibility that you're being monitored," Dad says. "Otherwise, what was the point of all of this?"

He's right. Goosebumps raise up on my flesh. "We probably shouldn't use our regular phones to get back in touch. We'll get you a disposable cell phone." I glance at the window and notice it has grown dark outside. "Oh God, what time is it?"

"Five o'clock," he says.

"I need to get back. Remember, not a word of this to anyone. We keep playing the roles we've been playing. But keep an eye out for trouble."

"Do you think we might be in danger?" Emily asks.

I glance at my mother and father and remember my murderous dream.

"Anything's possible," I say.

# Fifteen

Blinking Christmas lights from the stores lend a festive atmosphere to the brisk, clear night, but Emily and I barely notice. We stand awkwardly outside the Duane Reade drugstore where we just purchased her a disposable cell phone and exchanged numbers. It's time to say goodbye for now, but neither of us knows how. Finally, Emily attacks me with a hug and it reminds me of my, um her, grandmother's embrace at Thanksgiving. This time, I'm more comfortable. I hug her back.

"Be careful," I say. "And remember, business as usual."

She nods, blinking back tears. "Give my baby a big hug and kiss for me, okay?"

"I will."

As I walk down the subway steps, I realize she didn't mention Brad. It occurs to me that no matter how much you love a man, it's nothing compared to the feelings you have for your child. Since I have no experience with such matters, I can only assume this is one of Emily's thoughts flitting through my mind.

I just make the train back to Long Island and settle in for an angst-filled ride. Now that I know the truth, or rather a fraction of the truth, I am more self-conscious about the role I must play. Can I pull it off? Is Emily's family complicit in this scam? My gut says no, but whose gut is telling me this—Emily's or mine? If it's Emily's, can it be trusted? If it is mine, well, who am I anyway? Returning to Long Island seems a brave act. Once again I wonder whose bravery, or stupidity—hers or mine? For now, it doesn't matter.

The sun set hours ago. I stare into my reflected face in the black train window. There's another me in the world. Another me who is nothing like me. She's warm and emotional. I'm cool and aloof. Her instinctive reaction to hearing she has a daughter, even though she doesn't remember her, showed more love than I've been able to summon in the months I've been in Amanda's life. It's not that I dislike the child. In fact, I'm more inclined to like her now that I know I'm not expected to feel a mother's undying devotion. My inability to summon that magnitude of feeling and the resulting guilt have caused the distance between us. It suddenly occurs to me that if Emily and I are biological siblings, then Amanda is my niece. My reflection smiles at me. Yes, I can be an aunt. When it comes to relationships, I'm more the "baby steps" kind of person than the "sudden immersion" kind.

As the train picks up speed, the dark scenery morphs into an ominous blur. Fear tightens my gut. Am I afraid of physical harm? Psychological damage? Learning the truth? They say the truth will set you free. Right now, I'm not so sure.

If this were a movie, I'd be screaming at the screen, "Go to the authorities!" Clearly, we need help. Something sinister has happened. At the very least, someone has tampered with two minds. My mind—the thing that guarantees I'm different and unique from anyone else in the world. That scares me so much, I can't allow myself to dwell on it or I will surely break.

What exactly could I do? Walk into the local precinct? Sit down in front of the heard-it-all-before desk cop? And say what? "I've been switched with another person?"

No, the local police precinct is not the place to take this. The FBI maybe. Though the low agent in the hierarchy wouldn't be much more help. Moreover, would their disbelief cause them to be careless and maybe tip off the enemy? They would have the advantage then. What if they went into hiding, leaving us to wonder what happened to us and why?

The station arrives too soon. As I step off the train, the darkness finally registers. I've been gone all day. It is well past dinner time. Brad will surely ask where I've been and why I haven't been in touch all day. As I walk up the same avenue I ran down hours earlier, the mood is completely different. The wind has whipped up and the remaining leaves, crunchy and dry, scrape against the otherwise quiet street. The street lights cast eerie shadows. I look over my shoulder every few feet, wondering if someone is watching me. My muscles relax as I turn into our block. Justified or not, I will feel safe once inside the house.

As I turn my key in the lock, the door swings open. Brad stands there with a dozing Amanda on his shoulder. Some survival instinct kicks in. I force a wide smile and wrap my arms around him and Amanda.

"I'm okay, Brad. It's going to be all right."

"Where have you been? I've been calling you all day."

"Really?" I pull out my phone. "The volume is off. I'm sorry."

"What if there had been an emergency?" he asks.

"I'm sorry. Really."

I take advantage of his struck-speechless-by-exasperation moment and fill the silence with my impromptu story.

"Something happened to me today," I pull off my coat and hang it in the hall closet, then reach for Amanda, carefully transferring her to my shoulder. Sitting on the sofa, Brad across from me, I close my eyes for a moment and pat Amanda's back. When I open my eyes, Brad stares at me, a concerned look on his face.

"It's okay," I reassure him, "It was something good." I take a deep breath and exhale in preparation for my Academy Award–winning performance. "I woke this morning and had the sense something had to give. I needed to be alone to figure out what's going on with me."

"Okay," Brad says.

"I took the railroad into Penn Station. I walked to Macy's to see the decorated store windows. Then I grabbed a coffee and sat in Bryant Park to think.

"I realized how much I love you and Amanda. I'm fortunate to have you as my family. I've been feeling isolated. A bit depressed. I think it's time for me to change things up a bit, maybe get back to work a few days per week. The isolation is driving me a bit batty."

My mouth is dry, my lips parched. I lick them, hoping my nervousness doesn't show and that Brad is buying this great big pile of crap.

"That's fine. I've always told you whatever you want to do is all right by me."

A sigh of relief threatens to give me away. I let my breath out in a barely perceptible stream, my shoulders dropping slightly now that the weight has been lifted.

"I love you, Em. I just want us to be happy."

"I am happy. I just needed to think it all through. It's like a giant weight has been lifted from my chest."

"Good. I'm glad. I was worried when I didn't hear from you."

"I know. I'm sorry about that. I lost track of time. I should've called."

"It's okay. I'm glad you're home, safe and sound." Brad extends his arms. "Let me put her down," he says quietly.

I pass Amanda to him. When our hands touch, Brad looks at me with that certain look. A jolt of electricity ricochets through me. I've been sleeping with Emily's husband. The thought makes me queasy.

"I think I'll go take a shower," I say. "I'm feeling kind of crampy. I got my period this afternoon."

Brad shuffles off to put Amanda in her crib. Womanhood's oldest trick in the book has worked again.

# Sixteen

Stephanie Steele watches her husband through the family room windows. Jeremy paces on the dormant lawn while talking on his cell phone. The temperature has dropped, making his breath appear in tense, staccato bursts. From inside the house, she can't hear what he says but she can tell none of it is good.

Over the past few weeks, she sensed he was in some kind of trouble at work, that something didn't go as expected, and that he was taking the heat. If she's honest, she resents that he doesn't share his troubles with her. In fact, he doesn't share much of anything with her these days.

Though they keep up their Wednesday morning ritual at the café, they're just going through the motions. He drinks his coffee in silence and stares at the table top, while she sneaks glances at him over the paper.

She doesn't bother to ask if she can help. The lie they live has permeated her existence. She knows she's not supposed to ask and so she doesn't.

As much as it bothers her, she signed up for this. She knew what she was getting herself into when she married him. Well, as much as she could know. Which was that she wasn't allowed to know anything. However, her kids haven't been given a choice, and she's not pleased with how remote Jeremy has become with them.

She glances at Robbie, his eyes glazed while pressing buttons on his video game controller. He's been at it all morning. At least Kaylee bustles around, talking to herself, using her imagination. Well, they'd get some time together when they went into town. He promised they'd take the kids to the local children's museum. Afterwards, they'll go to their favorite burger place.

When Jeremy comes inside, he stamps his feet on the mat as if he's shaking snow from boots even though there hasn't been any snowfall.

"Everything all right?" Stephanie asks.

"Yeah." He tucks his cell phone into his back pocket.

"Are you ready to head into town?"

"Uh, you know, I think we need to postpone that. I have some work to catch up on."

The anger builds inside Stephanie's chest, crowding out her heart, crushing her lungs.

"Robbie and Kaylee! Upstairs right now and get ready to go out."

Both kids look up, startled by her stern tone. They run up the stairs to their bedrooms without argument.

"We," she says, stalking toward him, "are taking those kids," she points in the direction they just ran, "into town for a fun afternoon."

Jeremy stares at her, his expression blank. "What's wrong? Why the tone?"

"Why the tone?" She laughs, but it's a mirthless sound. "The fact you asked the question answers it. You don't hear anymore. You don't see. You walk amongst us, but you're not quite here."

"Jeez." Jeremy rakes his fingers through his hair. "Where is this coming from?"

"It's coming from fifteen years of being on the outside looking in, except the windows are painted black." As her anger escalates, her voice goes low. "I'm finished with that life."

"What is that supposed to mean?"

"Finished. If you don't remember really fast that you're a father and a husband..."

"What?" he asks, his tone daring her to finish the sentence.

"Don't make me answer that, Jeremy." She hears the kids on the stairs. "Just plaster a smile on your face and let's have a good time with our children."

# Seventeen

It's been a few weeks since I saw Emily, though we've talked regularly over our disposable cell phones. Slowly but surely, she has lost some weight. I have stopped going to the gym so much and snacked a bit more. We've shared glimpses of memories from our real lives and have tried to fill in the missing pieces.

Today is an important day. My twin and I will waltz into a hair salon and request identical styles. After our makeovers, we'll grab lunch and discuss last minute strategies for the switch. I think she's more nervous than I am, especially since she remembers much less about her former life than I do. I'm hoping seeing Brad and Amanda will jog her memory.

I chose a salon far from any stomping grounds I may have frequented in my New York City existence. Emily has called in sick at work and will meet me.

When I enter the salon, a thin guy, dressed in all black, glides across the floor in my direction. He introduces himself as Jacques. I explain what we have planned for our hair.

He smirks. "That is a terrible idea. People will talk," he says with just the right amount of French-accented horror.

Before I can respond, Emily enters with her signature bubbly energy. She's wearing an oversized pair of dark sunglasses. When she embraces me and kisses my cheek, I smile at my increasing comfort level with public displays of affection.

"How are you?" she asks.

"I'm fine, but I fear I've upset Jacques with our hair plans."

"It's ridiculous," he says. "Grown women. You are not little girls anymore with matching outfits."

Emily lightly touches his arm. "Jacques, you and I both know this is a vulgar idea, but we're playing a practical joke on a friend. Once it's over, I promise we'll be back to have you give us individual looks. And I swear, if anyone asks, we will never admit you were involved."

Jacques' body visibly relaxes as he places a hand on his heart. "You've calmed me, ma chérie. You understand."

With that, he sneers at me before sashaying toward the back of the salon. "Come along, ladies."

Emily grins at me and follows him. From behind her, I murmur, "You may not remember all the details of your former life, but I'd say your background in Public Relations hasn't been totally wiped out."

Emily half turns her head. "Then the rest can't be too far away."

For both our sakes, I hope she is right.

When we arrive at Jacques' station, Emily pulls off her sunglasses, revealing a dark bruise on her upper cheek.

"What happened to you?" I ask.

"A passion for boxing with none of the skill, apparently."

"Huh." I think back to that moment in the gym with Trina. I raise my fists in front of my face and take a jab at Emily, who looks startled and backs away.

"Do you box?" she asks.

I consider the question for a moment. "Yes. I do."

"Ladies, please." Jacques motions for us to sit, no doubt thinking some sibling/twin rivalry has led to fisticuffs in his hair salon.

Emily and I exchange a glance and nearly burst into laughter. We decide on simple shoulder-length cuts with chunky, piecey layers—Jacques' words—in the front to frame the face.

As Jacques cuts, Emily and I engage in light conversation about the "sci-fi book" we are collaborating on in which two identical people are brainwashed and switched so they can live each other's lives. Every once in a while, I glance at Jacques' reflection in the mirror and he looks bored, not catching on that this is a true story and not the plot of some co-written novel.

An hour and a half later, Emily and I sit in a small, dark Persian restaurant eating succulent *jujeh kabob* over basmati rice. We are the only customers here, no reflection on the food, which is delicious.

"Let's focus on our relationships for a minute," I say. "I can't bring myself to believe my parents or yours have anything to do with this situation in a sinister sense. But maybe there is something that connects all of us, other than the obvious genetic link."

"The genetic link that doesn't make sense," Emily adds. "We're obviously identical but born of two different sets of parents. How can that be?"

"I don't know. That question has been troubling me more than I care to admit. Without a scientific answer, I think we should move on. We can't afford to get stuck."

"Fair enough," Emily says. "Okay, so connections between us...You're a genetics research scientist at a lab. I'm a public relations specialist for a corporation. Has your company ever needed someone to manage the public, maybe to announce an important discovery or sugarcoat a scandal?"

"Not that I'm aware." Once again the bloody dream comes to mind and I push it aside.

"I can't think of anything either from my 'planted memories.'" Her fingers make quotation marks in the air.

"What about our parents?" I ask. "Would their paths have crossed in any way? Career conversations haven't come up with your parents. Do you remember what they did for a living?"

Emily stares into space for a second, her eyebrows scrunched. "I don't even remember them, never mind what they did for a living."

"I have an image of your dad in a uniform of some kind," I say.

"Like a cop or firefighter?"

"No, something green."

"Green?"

"Yeah." I think for a moment. "The army green of fatigues comes to mind, but that doesn't seem right."

"Something maintenance oriented?" she asks.

"Maybe. I'm not sure."

I fight the frown trying to take over my face. I don't want to bring Emily down.

"So when do we switch places?" she asks.

"Right after Christmas. Just before the long New Year's weekend."

"Why then?"

"You'll call in sick on Thursday of that week. I'll report to your job, I mean my job, on Friday, and if I seem a bit off, I can blame it on having been sick. I have to go in only one day and then I'm off for the weekend. I want to ease in, give people a chance to accept any differences. Plus, since Brad will be working, too, it will give you a chance to come and spend some time with Amanda and get acclimated to your old life."

Emily's eyes are glassy. I reach across the table to touch her hand. "It's going to be okay," I say. "You're going to remember."

"Even though my mind doesn't quite remember yet, I'm getting the sense my soul has never forgotten."

"Oooooo, very new age, Emily," I say, wiggling my fingers in the air to lighten the atmosphere. I'm rewarded with her infectious giggle.

This time, when Emily and I say our goodbyes, the hug is tighter. I wonder if this new sensitive side will stick when the old me returns. I hope so.

Back on the train to Long Island, Emily's words about her

soul never forgetting come back to me. I've heard people say the soul comes into this world with a purpose, and though our conscious minds don't remember what that purpose is, we continually move toward it. I hope they're right, because without my memories, I'm going to need my soul's GPS capabilities to get me where I'm going.

Several stops before my own, I have an idea. I exit the train and walk to the library. At the only available computer, I search for HC Labs, where I've supposedly worked since getting my degree. I click from page to page and eventually land on the Company Profile page. Halfway down the page, I nearly rocket off the chair. The man from my dreams stares back at me. His name is Henry Chadwick and he's the founder of the company. Chadwick has a long list of impressive credentials. I wonder if he's dead by my hand. If he is, would they have kept his profile up? I notice the site was last updated in July. Before the switch. So, he could be dead.

I enter Henry Chadwick's name into Google. Dozens of pages display hits. The first page mostly links back to the website I just left. Some link to papers he has published in various journals, all dealing with genetics research. No obituaries, no news articles about his demise. I click on Chadwick's Linked-in page and read more of the same. Except for one piece of information: Chadwick has two doctoral degrees. One is in genetics.

The other is in psychology.

# Eighteen

My eyelids flutter open. The house is quiet. I must have slept through Brad dressing for work. Burrowing deeper into the covers, I feel at peace. That's odd, I know. How can I be at peace with all the turmoil and unknown? But now that I know I'm not crazy, everything else seems manageable. I will find out what happened to Emily and me. And I will find out who is responsible.

When Amanda stirs in her crib, I spring out of bed.

"Good morning, Amanda," I coo. I pick her up and kiss her smooth, pale cheek, then put her to my shoulder and make my way down to the kitchen. She snuggles in to my body, then reaches out and touches my face. My heart lurches and I am overcome, for the first time, with natural love for her. I think Amanda and I have come to a psychic understanding. She's always known I'm not her mother and she's decided to go easy on me now that I've caught up. I plan on being the best aunt she's ever known. And in the meantime, I'll be the best mother I can be to her. I owe that much to Emily.

As I prepare Amanda's breakfast, I sip coffee and eat my fruit and Greek yogurt while standing at the counter. When the babysitter arrives, I head out to visit Emily's parents. Well, to visit their home. They won't be there. I made sure of that.

I pull up in front of the house. It's that quiet mid-morning time. Neighbors have already left for work. Kids are already at school. I slip the key out of my pocket and let myself in.

For a moment, I stand in the stillness and listen. Then, I move slowly around the living room, letting my eyes fall on each object in the room, seeing if anything causes a reaction in me. I look at photos of Emily and other family members on the shelves. I pick up figurines and stare at artwork. Nothing stands out as an important piece of our puzzle, so I move directly to their bedroom. I open every drawer. Emily's mom's drawers are organized with dividers, her clothes color-coded by drawer. There's nothing unusual. Her only jewelry is costume jewelry. The good stuff is probably in a safe deposit box at the bank.

I peer into the one, small closet in the room. It holds mostly her clothes and a suit or two of her husband. Shoe boxes are stacked on a shelf, their contents clearly marked on the boxes. Just in case, I peer inside a few to make sure they contain shoes. Nothing out of the ordinary here.

I search the dresser across the room, which is filled with his boxers and socks. When I open a larger drawer at the bottom of the dresser, I hit pay dirt. Several army-green shirts and pants are neatly folded. A uniform. I unfold one set to see if there is anything embroidered on the shirt. Nothing. But the style of the uniform seems to indicate maintenance or custodial work. Somewhere in this house there has to be documentation indicating what his job is. In their tax records maybe. But before I leave the room, I open the drawer of a night table.

Inside are tissues, a spare eyeglass chain, a book light, and a suspense novel. I move on to the other night table, where I find a fistful of loose change, some pocket fuzz, and a crumpled drawing of a stick figure with the kid-written message "I love my daddy." That Emily was a sweetie even back then. I lift the drawing and my breath catches. Emily's dad stares back at me from an expired ID badge in the bottom of the drawer.

He works for HC Labs.

I freeze at the sound of a key in the front door. I close the drawer and hurry out to the living room just as Emily's mom enters the house. She jumps when she sees me.

"Oh my God, Emily, you almost gave me a heart attack."

"I'm sorry. I stopped by for a visit, but you weren't here."

"I told you when you called last night I was having breakfast with the girls."

In fact, she did tell me that, which is why I've been snooping around her home.

"I guess I forgot," I say.

"How about a cup of coffee?" she asks.

"Sure."

I settle into a kitchen chair and watch her go through the motions of making coffee. Within minutes, the coffee bubbles up into the glass percolator top, getting darker and darker as the fragrant steam perfumes the kitchen.

"Would you like something to eat?" she asks. "I can make you a frittata or pancakes, or I have those nice Portuguese rolls."

"I've already had breakfast."

She places a cup, teaspoon, and napkin in front of me and then decants a cup of steaming coffee. She pours cream into a small pitcher—no cartons on this table—and places the sugar bowl in front of me. But I'm suddenly having the urge for black coffee, which I imagine is how I drank it back in the day when I was truly me.

"So where's my gorgeous granddaughter?" She pours herself a cup of coffee and takes a seat opposite me.

"With the babysitter. I had to run some errands and decided to do them alone."

She smiles. "Yes, errands alone were like a vacation at times."

Donna and I don't have much in common, but on this we agree. My mind focuses on the new piece of the puzzle I've uncovered. I need more information to figure out how the heck we are all related.

"Mom, I'm thinking of writing a sort of memoir of my life

for Amanda, but there's lots I just don't remember."

"That's a wonderful idea. I had started something like that when you were little, but I didn't get very far. I'm not the writing type."

"Do you still have it?"

She frowns and her eyebrows do that scrunchy thing that Emily and I both do. It's then that I realize how strongly we resemble her. For all these years, I'm sure I looked for and found the features that were similar between me and my parents. Bad scientific practice. When you look for something, you usually find it. My parents claim they used IVF, with their own eggs and sperm, to conceive. And yet, here I sit, the spitting image of Emily's mother. That agitates me and my body feels tight.

"Emily?"

I am jolted out of my thoughts. Donna stands in the living room, holding a stack of photo albums in her arms.

"Come in here. We'll be more comfortable."

We settle down on the sofa. She opens the first album and mumbles to herself. "What would I have done with that journal?"

I scan the photos on the first page and start turning pages. They are all pictures of me as a baby and toddler. Except they are not me—they are Emily. One thing is for sure. Amanda is the spitting image of us as babies. It truly is uncanny, as my mother said when she first saw the pictures of her.

Nothing stands out in the photos until I get to the photo of Emily's dad Anthony holding Emily in his arms. He's got a big smile on his face and he's wearing a uniform similar to the ones I found in his drawer.

"Did Dad work for HC Labs that far back?" I ask.

"He got that job right before you were born. What a blessing that was. He had just been laid off from his previous job and we had no idea how we were going to survive."

"How did he find the job? Did he know someone at the company?"

"No. He got a letter in the mail inviting him to apply for

the job. It was right up his alley, and the pay was significantly better than his previous job."

My antenna go up at that statement. My heart starts to race. "Who was the letter from?"

"Someone from the company. Human resources I guess."

"But how did they know he needed a job?"

Donna shrugs. "Who knows? Maybe an angel intervened."

The lack of curiosity astounds me, but these are not scientists. These are straightforward, accepting people. And considering the circumstances, new baby, no job, I can't blame them for just being thrilled and moving on. But it makes my life a bit more difficult right now.

"Did Dad work in the same building all these years, or did he work at some of the other locations."

"No, same building, which was great. He got to stay on Long Island and his commute was easy. Remember how we'd always eat dinner just after 4:30 because he was home so early?"

"Yeah." I do have a vague recollection of that, but I know it's not my memory. It's Emily's.

I move through the rest of the albums, but nothing else catches my eye. I have more questions but Donna won't know the answers. I need to get Anthony alone and pick his brain about his job. I help Donna carry the albums back to the cabinet beneath the china closet and then top off my cup of coffee.

"So, did you and Dad have trouble conceiving?"

"Trouble? No. In fact, I got pregnant the first time we intended to." She looks at me with a pained expression. "I only wish you had it as easy." She sighs. "But that's all over now. You have your little miracle."

I'm stunned. If they conceived naturally, there's no chance of an IVF mix-up between Emily's parents and my parents. How the heck can Emily and I, identical as we are, have been born from different parents? That's impossible.

I say my goodbyes to Donna and exchange a hug and kiss. Out in the car, I call Emily.

"Hey," she says. "What's happening?"

For some reason, that makes me smile. "I just had a lovely visit with your mom after sort of letting myself into their home when no one was there."

"Do tell," she says.

"We looked through albums. I realized how much I, we, look like her. But she says she and your dad conceived naturally."

"I'm having a hard time wrapping my brain around all of this. How can that be?"

"I don't know. If both our parents had used IVF to conceive, I'd say the lab screwed up and inadvertently implanted your parents' fertilized eggs into my mother. That would explain why I resemble your mother, though it doesn't explain how we're identical. But if your parents conceived naturally, there were no fertilized eggs to get mixed up."

"Jeez. What a confusing mess," Emily says.

"No kidding. Every time I try to work through this mystery, my head hurts. It makes no sense. But forget about that for a moment. I have big news. Your dad works for the company I work for."

"What? Am I passing him in the hallway and not even realizing it?"

"No, he works at the Long Island building. Do you remember eating dinner very early when you were a kid because he worked so close to home?"

There's silence on the other end, then, "I think I do."

"And here's another bit of information that may or may not be relevant. Your dad lost his job while your mom was pregnant, which was a great source of worry. But sometime just before you were born, he received a letter in the mail from HC Labs inviting him to apply for his position."

"So what does that mean?"

"I'm not sure. But how many times do you receive letters in the mail from people you don't know offering you a job?"

"I see your point."

"It may turn out to be nothing. But it seemed strange, and

your mom couldn't tell me who sent the letter. She assumes it was human resources and she doesn't know how they would have known he was out of a job."

"They were probably just relieved."

"Exactly. So my next step is to try to interview your dad about his job. See what he can tell me."

"Sounds like a plan. How's my baby doing?"

"She was sweeter than sweet this morning. I think she's forgiven my lack of maternal instincts."

Emily giggles. "She takes after her momma."

"That, she does."

\*\*\*

After my Nancy Drew detective work and debriefing with Emily, I decide to stop at the gym for a workout. But I have one more errand to run. I head to the sporting goods store near my home and find the aisle with the boxing equipment. After a few moments' perusal, I settle for the best gloves I'm going to find at a sporting chain store in a shade of grimace-inducing, Pepto-Bismol pink. I add 180-inch hand wraps and make my way to the check-out counter. The heavy bag has beckoned ever since I saw that woman giving it a go. It's almost like a magnetic pull, and it feels good. Perhaps I'm returning to the old me.

When I enter the gym, it is once again quiet, just the odd person on a stationary bike or using the bench press machine. I head to the boxing corner, sit on a bench against the wall, and start wrapping my hands. Thumb through the loop. Three times around the wrist. Once around the thumb, then back around the wrist before looping through each of my fingers. The act is meditative, yet mindless. It's as if the wraps know what to do.

A quiet, focused energy rises up in me. But then something pokes at my memory, and my heart begins to pound. I can't access the visual, but the feeling is raw and angry. I shake it off and put on my new gloves.

Out on the floor, in front of the mirrors, I throw a double jab and cross at my reflection and can't help smiling at myself. It feels right. I turn away from the mirror and focus on the corner of the room, shadowboxing to warm up. I jab, jab, slip, come back with a hook and chuckle, somehow knowing I've been reprimanded for too many of those in the past. I throw a straight right and continue with my jabs, bouncing on the balls of my feet. My body starts to feel warm and flexible.

I'm practically in a trance, as if a portion of my mind has separated, a helium balloon floating, tethered only by the thinnest of strings. My body, on the other hand, is grounded and heavy, ready to engage something more substantial, so I move on to the heavy bag. I throw a punch and feel it reverberate up my arm and into my body. I throw a quick left-right.

Though my mind still floats, devoid of thoughts, my body remembers. Muscle memory ensures I can box without any cerebral knowledge that I've done it before. My muscles also remember another physical experience. Something violent and impulsive. As my punches intensify, the helium balloon that is my mind pops, releasing a gale of rage. I pound the bag, pummeling it with punch after punch. Sweat flies from my forehead and drips into my eyes, but I don't stop. I can't stop. The anger is palpable. My mind's eye sees flasks and petri dishes flying through the air. Test tubes shatter on counter tops. Inside I scream, outraged at a betrayal I cannot remember. In the vision, someone grabs me from behind and I push them away.

"Emily!"

Only then do I realize someone actually has grabbed me from behind. Trina is sprawled on her butt looking up at me like I've gone insane. And maybe I have. With my teeth, I rip open the Velcro closure of my glove and extract my hand to offer it to Trina.

"I'm so sorry. I was totally focused."

She gets to her feet. "I can see that," she says, somehow keeping good humor in her voice. "Those were some moves. I thought you said you didn't box."

I feel compelled to make light of this. "I don't. My dad and I used to goof around. He was always trying to teach me to defend myself."

Trina just nods as if trying to process it all.

"Well, I'm done for the day. I have to get back to Amanda. Have a good workout."

"Thanks," Trina says, and I can swear I feel her staring at my back as I walk to the locker room.

Inside, I sit on a narrow bench, remove my other glove, and start to unwrap my hands. Once again, I enter into a meditative rhythm and this time a vision of a bloody hand being wrapped in bandages flies across my mind. If this daydream contains any truth, it's no surprise Emily is experiencing surreptitious, wary stares back at the lab. I had a major meltdown for some reason, and people think I'm unstable, but I don't feel like eruptions are a normal part of my constitution.

So what the hell happened that drove me over the edge?

# Nineteen

The bracing wind, frosty and damp on Jeremy's face, forces the fog of worry from his mind. It's a bit of medicine he doesn't mind. At the end of the pier, he boards a motorboat.

"Good to see you, Owen. How are the fish biting?"

The burly, bearded man extends his hand and gives Jeremy's a hardy shake. "Not bad, not bad at all. I was thinking I'd head up to Canada and try my hand at a bit of ice fishing."

Jeremy chuckles. "Sounds cold."

Owen pats his solid, but protruded belly. "I got plenty of blubber to keep me warm. You ready to head out, boss?"

Jeremy nods and takes a seat as the boat pulls out and makes its way around the tip of Manhattan. Though a problem solver and analytical by nature, Jeremy has always preferred the arena of broad conceptual overviews. He appreciates that his agents provide their statuses without minute detail and doesn't worry he might be missing something because he trusts them implicitly. So, when Reynold called last night to request his presence at the project site, Jeremy knew it was serious.

As they approach the pier, Jeremy spots Reynold waiting and his stomach does a small lurch.

"I'll give you a call when I'm ready to head back," Jeremy says to Owen as he disembarks.

Reynold waves to Owen and then extends his hand to Jeremy. Despite the cold wind, Reynold's skin is pale and there are dark circles under his eyes. The two men climb into an old military jeep and drive a short distance to the complex.

Jeremy hasn't spent much time on Governors Island. The desolation gets his notice. The spirits of military families past seem to cling to the old barracks. It has a ghost town feel, despite the latest flurry of activity. One side of the island serves as a tourist destination, but with limited hours during the summer. The rest of the island is off limits and under construction. The project site is located at the border of the two sections.

They enter a row of barracks. Reynold leads him to an office that makes Jeremy's look posh by comparison. He sits in a rickety chair at a metal desk.

"In light of the snafu with the military guys," Reynold says, "I thought you should know what's happening here."

Jeremy wonders why Reynold couldn't just tell him over the phone. That worries him.

"We've been putting the new subjects through the experiment. The results so far seem to suggest the will of the terrorist is being transmitted."

"To what degree?" Jeremy asks.

"The subjects are putting up resistance." Reynold pauses. "Resistance we can't seem to tamp down, despite our...best efforts."

"Are there other things you can try?" Jeremy asks the question in a generic way, not meaning anything specific by it. He hasn't let his mind consider what they might have tried so far.

"We've had to move up to coercion."

Jeremy winces. The military guys signed up for the torture, but these new subjects hadn't. "How far have you gone?"

"Pretty far. Two guys died last night."

"Shit."

Reynold looks down for a moment. "What should we do with the bodies?"

Jeremy's mind races. He's already in knee-deep shit after the military failure. If this gets out, he's not sure he'll recover.

"It's not like anyone is going to be looking for them," Reynold says.

"We don't know that. There could be someone who checks up now and then. Or even the others in their make-shift communities."

"It's not static. They come and go, move on. It's only two people."

"So far," Jeremy says. "Can we leave the bodies to be found or is there evidence that will compromise the security of the project?"

"Maybe you should take a look for yourself," Reynold says as he clicks a few times on his laptop. He turns it around to face Jeremy.

A bedraggled man sits, secured to a chair. Another man interrogates him about a potential terrorist plot that has been on the radar for some time. The subject doesn't respond. He sits, mute but with a defiant posture. The interrogation continues. He watches as the subject remains silent despite escalating physical abuse. The video cuts out for a split second and returns, showing a scene some time later, as evidenced by the amount of damage done to the subject and the blood that covers him. Jeremy forces himself to calmly watch, forces himself not to shift in his seat as he watches a man, an innocent man, murdered in front of his eyes. The video fades out with the body on the floor, with the interrogator kicking it, not getting a response, taking vitals, and declaring the man dead.

The craziest image pops into his mind at that moment—former President George W. Bush sitting in that little chair in the kindergarten classroom when news of 9/11 was whispered into his ear. The President's eyes stared blank and lifeless for a microsecond before his brain recovered from the shock and undoubtedly began processing at lightning speed. There had been opinions, conspiracy theories, even jokes about that moment captured on tape. But Jeremy Steele—fierce patriot, lover of his country, card-carrying Republican—perceived it differently. He saw the leader of the country temporarily paralyzed between the whispered threats of terrorism and the happy squeals of children awaiting his next words.

He watched a man forced to make the most crucial decision of his life in a split second while maintaining his composure in front of school kids, teachers, and the still running cameras. Jeremy had never admitted this to another soul, not even Stephanie, but one night, as he watched the news, they ran that classroom clip for the umpteenth time and he started to cry. This may have frightened him more than the threat of future terrorist attacks. He wasn't accustomed to losing control. It had never happened again and he'd forgotten about it. But today, it was as if he had channeled George Bush's emotion on that day.

"So, what do you think?"

Jeremy looks up from his trance. "He's pretty beat up. If someone finds him, questions will be asked."

Reynold's expression is tight. And in that second, Jeremy knows exactly why this meeting had to happen in person—why Reynold didn't just call to ask what he should do. As the supervisor of this project site, Reynold doesn't have a soul he can tell about this. The weight is all on his shoulders. Jeremy is the only other one he can turn to. This insight strengthens Jeremy. He feels himself rising to the occasion, even though he really wants to crawl behind some bushes and vomit to purge the horror.

"We'll have to get rid of the bodies." A part of him wants to grab a couple of shovels and dig two graves for the lost souls who gave their lives in unofficial service to their country, even if their involvement will never be known. But with future development planned on Governors Island, the bodies would eventually be discovered. He couldn't take that risk.

"Call in the lab guys. They'll know how to handle it." He doesn't even want to ponder what they'll do to fix the problem. He imagines a mix of caustic chemicals, then pushes the thought from his mind.

Reynold's nod is robotic and lifeless.

"Where did you get the video footage?" Jeremy asks.

"I had a surveillance system installed."

"Why? Might be incriminating, don't you think?"

"I want to know what's happening on my watch."

Reynold knows he's on the line. He's grasping at whatever shred of control he can.

"Who knows about it?"

"Just me and the guy who installed it. I'm the only one who can access the videos."

"Let's keep it that way," Jeremy says. "So, what's next?"

"Some of the subjects show less resistance though they still haven't been helpful. The psych guys think they might be able to use drugs to lower their resistance."

"If they could do that, we'd never have had to torture anyone in the name of national security."

"In this case, they're thinking their will to resist might have been transmitted versus natural and, therefore, not as strong. It's worth a try."

Jeremy nods. What option does he have at this point? "Okay, keep in touch, Reynold."

"Will do." Their eyes meet for a moment. Jeremy feels a cord tightening between them. An umbilical cord, he thinks. And instead of nourishing Reynold as any mentoring boss would, Jeremy is poisoning him, encouraging him to continue down a path from which there is no return. And Reynold knows it, but he will follow Jeremy's orders to the letter.

# Twenty

Brad talks baby talk and whistles under his breath as we get Amanda into her car seat. The day is sunny and clear, mild for December. Emily's mom has invited us for Saturday dinner at 3 p.m. Brad is looking forward to the meal. Amanda will be pleased to see her grandma. As for me, well, there's that conversation I need to have with Emily's dad.

As we pull up to the house, Emily's mom gives a little hop of excitement in the doorway. She takes the baby into her arms, cooing and snuggling her. Amanda laughs and slaps her hands against her grandmother's cheeks, which makes Donna giggle.

"Where's Dad?" I ask.

"He's in the garage, fiddling with something," she says, so entranced with Amanda she doesn't look my way.

Brad carries the diaper bag into the living room as I cut through the side door to the garage. Anthony is engrossed in a lawnmower motor.

"Hi, Dad."

"Hiya, Emily." He kisses my cheek. "I figured I'd get this motor in shape before spring."

I unfold a chair and sit.

"So what's new with you?" he asks.

"Oh, nothing much," I say. If he only knew the truth. "Same old thing. Taking care of Amanda, going to the gym, then doing it all over again the next day."

He chuckles. The sound is gentle and endearing. "Yeah, I remember those days."

"How's work going?" I ask, leading in to the desired topic of conversation.

"Can't complain. Same routine every day for me, too, but I don't mind."

My need to know exactly how Anthony is connected to HC Labs almost has me asking my supposed father what he does for a living. Patience.

"All these years, I've known what you do, but I never really thought about the details. What's your typical day look like?"

"Clean the common areas, make sure the lights keep shining, repair doors that stick and locks that don't lock and toilets that don't flush." He drops a wrench and picks up a rag. "I putter around doing this or that."

His gaze meets mine as he wipes his hands.

"If you had it to do all over again, would you take the same job?" I ask.

He sits back on his heels, silent for a moment. I wonder at the thoughts I will never hear spoken.

"Yeah. It provided for you and Mom in a better way than I could have otherwise. That's the most important thing."

"If money hadn't been an issue, what do you think you would have done?"

A hint of a smile lifts the corner of his mouth. "I was a good ball player. I'm not saying I would have made the pros, but a man can dream, right?" He stares into space. "Maybe a phys ed teacher."

"Really?"

"Yeah."

"I can see that. You're a very patient person." A question pops into my head. I word it carefully in case I'm supposed to know the answer. "Didn't you box?"

"I dabbled in the day." He glances around the garage and

spots a plastic bin on a nearby shelf. He pulls out a pair of brown, leather boxing gloves that look like they could tell a tale or two.

I press the garage door opener and jog out to my car. I pop the trunk and pull out my boxing gloves, waving them in the air.

His face breaks into a grin. He puts on his gloves and strikes a pose in the driveway. I move opposite him and say "ding, ding, ding."

We spar for a bit, jabbing here and there. I throw a hook and he tells me to stick with the straight shots, like I haven't heard that before.

"Why? Why do people keep telling me that?"

"A straight shot is faster," he says.

"But if my straight shots are constantly blocked, why not throw a hook?"

"You've got to be in close to land a hook. Too far away, you're wasting your energy."

Just then I see my opening and take it. It's not very hard, because we're playing after all, but it's enough to make him step back.

"Good one, Emily."

When he says Emily, reality sets in. What the hell is Emily going to do when she returns home and her dad wants to spar with her?

With that thought, I wave the white flag and we pull off our gloves. "I'm impressed," he says. "You know what you're doing."

"I've been boxing at the gym," I say. "Great for losing baby weight."

He swats at the air. "Ah, you women are all the same. No one cares about that except you."

As we walk back to the garage, I glance at the front door and see Brad in the doorway watching us. Emily's mom stands behind him with Amanda in her arms. When Brad sees I've noticed him, he turns and walks back into the house.

I sigh. What story will I invent to explain why I haven't told "my husband" that I've learned how to box?

I follow Anthony back into the garage and close the door to banish the chill. "You know, Dad, maybe you should coach kids' teams or something to tap into that passion you had."

"I'm getting old, Emily. I don't have it in me anymore. Sometimes when you neglect things, they just get away from you."

We're quiet for a moment as he packs away his gloves and replaces the bin on the shelf. He stares at it longer than he needs to before turning back to the lawnmower motor.

"I was talking to Mom the other day about how you got the job with HC Labs. She said you'd been laid off and then got some mysterious letter in the mail inviting you to apply for a job."

"Nah, it wasn't so mysterious." The furrow in his forehead deepens. "You know this story, don't you?"

I shake my head. Oops.

"It was a month or so before you were born. We just found out you had some problems and doctors were parading in and out. One guy took an interest in our situation. I got talking to him and he'd come in every day while your mom was out having tests and keep me company. Hand me that wrench."

I place it into his palm, handle first, and wait for him to continue.

"We ended up talking about a lot of things besides you. I told him I'd been laid off. I tried to downplay it, acting like I was confident everything would turn out all right, but he saw through that. I'm pretty sure he put in a good word for me with the company."

"Do you remember his name?"

My throat feels dry and tight. I cough to clear it.

He twists in my direction, a perplexed expression on his face.

"I'll never forget it. And neither should you."

I have no idea what he means. I stare back at him, a bit deer-in-the-headlights. When I don't respond, he chuckles.

"That's a serious case of sleep deprivation you got there,

Emily. I'm old and senile and even I remember having this conversation when you mentioned your doctor's name."

"My doctor?"

"The one who helped you with your troubles and helped bring that beautiful granddaughter of mine into the world." He reaches out and knocks on my forehead with his knuckles. "Emily, you're scaring me. Dr. Henry Chadwick."

# Twenty-one

The Christmas tree comes to life as I insert plug into socket. Colored lights flicker and bounce off of Swarovski crystal snowflake ornaments. The effect is pretty even in daylight. Emily has just called to inform me her train arrived on time. She'll be here in minutes for the big switch.

I peek through the drawn, living room curtains for the tenth time, just as Emily rounds the corner. The blonde wig renders her unrecognizable. I open the door and we stare at each other in silence for just a second, both of us still startled by the presence of our twin. Her infectious grin soothes and we embrace. She smells like peaches. It suits her.

Emily follows me into the living room and gazes at the Christmas tree. I wonder if she remembers any of the ornaments.

"What a pretty tree."

Her head turns this way and that, taking in all the objects in the room, probably searching for something familiar. I lean close to her ear and remind her to be careful about what she says in case someone has bugged the house. She gives me a thumbs-up and then peeks into the kitchen.

"It's very homey, isn't it?"

"Uh, yeah, I guess you could say it is."

Emily grins. "You hate it."

I grin back at her. "I do."

She leans forward and whispers, "You'll be glad to get back to your place. Sleek black, white, and stainless steel."

"Music to my ears. I can't wait. But first things first." I motion for her to follow me up the stairs.

As I enter Amanda's room, Emily gasps when she realizes where we are. Amanda looks up, her eyes shining and alert. I lift her from the crib and turn toward Emily, whose own eyes are filled with tears.

"Do you remember?" I mouth the words as I carefully hand Amanda over to her.

"No," she says, but then her arms envelop Amanda and pull her close. They both adjust a bit until they are two pieces of a puzzle that perfectly fit together. It's that muscle memory again—our bodies remembering what our minds won't. My body knows how to box; Emily's knows how to nurture a baby. Just then, Amanda looks right at me, tucks her head into Emily's shoulder, sticks her thumb in her mouth, and closes her eyes.

"*She* does," I say to Emily. Her tears spill over onto her cheeks.

We head back to the living room, where I observe the two of them a moment longer. "Will you be all right?"

Emily nods, almost too quickly.

I lean in within murmuring distance. "Amanda doesn't seem to have any doubts about who you are. And Brad will be so happy you're not ranting about being someone else, he won't notice the switch back."

"That's one thing that will be uncomfortable." Emily directs her gaze my way.

I wince, but I knew the topic would come up eventually. Emily grasps my arm, concern on her face.

"No, it's okay," she says. "You didn't know."

I'm thinking how accepting she is that I've been sleeping with her husband when I realize it will be just as odd for her as it was for me. Though I had knowledge of Brad through

Emily's memories, my body recoiled from him as if he were a stranger, which he is. But Emily has no recollection of him.

Amanda stirs, lifting her head from Emily's shoulder. Her eyes are half-closed. Emily caresses her back and makes gentle shushing sounds until Amanda snuggles into her again.

"I should walk you around the house. Show you where everything is. Do you cook?"

"I have been. More than you do anyway."

"What do you mean? I cook here every night."

Emily chuckles. "Those must be my recipes you're remembering," she whispers. "You don't even have a salt and pepper shaker at your place. I suspect there's been a lot of take-out in your past."

I consider that a moment. A busy scientist living alone in the City. A sleek black, white, and stainless kitchen. It's probably true. And yet, I don't want it to be true anymore. There's something meditative about cooking—the chopping of vegetables, the measuring of ingredients. The sizzle as raw onions and garlic touch heated olive oil, their flavors melding in the pot, the rising aroma a gift to the chef.

I take Emily on a tour around the kitchen, opening cabinets, pointing out dishware, cutlery, the pantry. I speak freely, as if showing a friend my home, just in case someone is listening. Next is the tour of the bedrooms, bathrooms, and closets. I show her where Amanda's clothing and diapering supplies are. With Amanda still in her arms, she reaches out and strokes a soft, onesie in between her fingers.

When we enter the master bedroom, the awkwardness returns. "You sleep on the right side of the bed," I whisper, pointing my finger. "That's your closet." I open the door to a small, walk-in closet filled with Emily's clothes. For the first time, I realize how festive her wardrobe is with its colors and prints. I suspect my closets are filled with lots of black.

"The laundry is in the basement."

On the way, we put a sleeping Amanda down in her crib. Emily smiles down at her and strokes her hair. In the basement, I point out the supplies and then lean behind the washer.

"Brad is very helpful at home but he never does laundry." I pull a taped envelope from the back of the washer and hold it out to Emily.

Emily takes it from me, a quizzical look on her face. I watch as she skims notes of everything I know about her life to help her assimilate. Details about her parents, their jobs, their habits. Brad's little quirks. Her history with her best friend Susan and some recent conversations we've had. And some information about Trina and our workout routine at the gym.

"Ugh, the gym. Do I have to continue that madness?" she asks at normal volume.

I put my finger to my lips to remind her to be careful what she says.

She leans in. "I got the baby weight off. Please, please, say I don't have to."

I can't help laughing. Our differences are most pronounced, it seems, in the physical exertion area.

"Whatever you want. But in case you get the urge, you have a gym membership at House of Pain on Parkside."

"A fitting name."

I chuckle and grab my handbag as we enter the living room, pulling out the wallet with Emily's credit cards and driver's license.

Something about the driver's license makes me pause before handing it over.

"What's wrong?"

"Do I own a car?" I whisper.

"No."

"Do I know how to drive?"

"No."

"Wow. That explains a lot."

"What?"

"You drive." I wave the license at her. "I felt uncomfortable for a while about driving and I couldn't understand why. It was like I was doing it for the first time. Apparently, I was."

"Jeez Louise," Emily says. "Were you able to do it?"

"In the beginning, about as well as you box. Wide turns. A lead foot on the brake. It got easier over time. I'm just wondering if you'll be able to drive without the memories of having done so."

Emily gets a panicked look in her eye. "Oh God. I'm starting to feel sick."

"If you want, we can drive out to the parking field at the beach. No one is there at this time of year. I can practice with you."

"No, it's not just that. It's everything. I've been pulling off a charade without realizing it and now that I'm returning to my real life, it feels like this is the charade. It's overwhelming."

What can I say? She's right.

"I guess I'll have it easier. I'll be by myself at home so I won't have to play a role."

"Yeah, but you'll be doing the hard work at the lab, figuring out what's happened to us. What a mess this is, Madison."

Once again, I can't disagree.

Emily hands over her handbag and I look at my ID card for work, my credit cards, my gym membership card. Nothing is familiar and it's unsettling. Will I know how to do my job in the lab when I get there? Will people realize something is wrong?

The phone rings, interrupting my stream of thought. I motion for Emily to pick it up. No time like now to start being yourself, right?

Her "hello" is hesitant. I lean my head next to hers to listen.

"Hi, babe. It's me. I'm not feeling great. I'm coming home. Do you need anything from the store?"

We look at each other wide-eyed. Diapers, I mouth to her, and she repeats it and then adds wipes, tomatoes. And tampons. With that last one, I know she's biding her time.

When she hangs up, we go into fast-forward mode, exchanging the last bits of information we deem crucial for the switch. She hands over notes of her knowledge of my former life. I wish there was time to review them now. She helps me put on the wig, and I fuss with it a bit to get it looking natural. Then, I take her coat and put it on.

Emily grabs my arm. "I don't want you to leave."

"It'll be all right. We have the phones to call each other."

Emily nods. I don't know if she looks more sad or scared. I glance up at the clock on the kitchen wall. Time is running out. I dash up the stairs and peer down at Amanda. She is still sleeping. I brush a wispy curl off her forehead. She stirs but doesn't wake up. The lump in my throat comes as a surprise. I'm going to miss her.

At the front door, Emily and I embrace. Neither of us wants to let go. Minutes later, I'm walking to the train, sad for Emily but looking forward to returning to my life and remembering more about who I was, what has happened to me, and why.

# Twenty-two

After spending the weekend familiarizing myself with my apartment and life, I've decided my former existence was a bit cold. I'm not about to rush out and purchase a floral sofa or paint my walls dusty mauve, but I don't feel as comfortable as I thought I would. It isn't...cozy. That upsets me, but not for the expected reason. Rather, it terrifies me that someone has messed with my brain at such a deep level, it has affected even my decorating preferences.

I am no longer me, though I struggle to find my way back. It seems I am irreparably altered. I've become an Emily-Madison hybrid. Why does this horrify me? Emily has many fine qualities that would definitely round out a personality. But I can't help feeling a satisfaction with who I was, even though I don't really know what that means. The memory has died, but the pride has not. I want to be me. I want to be the accomplished scientist with degrees from Columbia and work that matters in the scientific community.

Adrenaline courses through my body as I enter the center. Without my memories, it's essentially my first day of work, but I have to squash any tourist tendencies and make it seem like I've been here all along. I flash my ID badge.

"Good morning, Dr. Thorpe."

I turn toward the voice. A man in a security uniform gives me a warm smile. He is not familiar. His name tag identifies him as Jake Dyson. Emily has not mentioned him in her debriefing notes.

I take a breath to steady my voice. "Good morning, Jake."

"Have a good holiday?" he asks.

"As a matter of fact, I did."

At this point in countless other conversations, I'd be on my way, the superficial exchange of pleasantries over. But Jake smiles again and I pause, not quite ready to go up to the lab. Though not classically good-looking, he's appealing...and something else. Comforting. Odd, but it's true. His gaze reassures me.

"It's been so quiet here this week with the holidays, I started reading this book." He holds it out to me. "Interesting, so far. The author is a neuroscientist who studies how memories are created."

Neither the title nor the author is familiar to me. Just as I hold out the book to Jake, he continues, "It really makes you wonder. What would we be without our memories?"

The book slips from my trembling hands and lands with a thump.

"Oh, I'm so sorry." I stoop to pick it up just as he does, and we bump heads. He chuckles and supports my elbow as I stand up and hand the book back to him.

"It sounds interesting." My voice is shaky and barely audible.

"I'll pass it on to you when I'm finished, if you like."

"I would, actually."

Once again his gaze meets mine. "Sure thing."

In the elevator ride to the sixth floor, I take deep, steadying breaths. But when I step into the corridor, my lack of memory cannot steal the comfortable feeling that seeps into my soul.

The lab feels like a ghost town with everyone out for the holiday week. One person nods and smiles at me as I walk past. I nod back. Inside the lab, counters are organized, supplies stacked neatly, cabinets labeled. A few people in lab coats and goggles sit on stools, focused on their work. I walk to the office and exchange my wool coat for a lab coat. It's time to find out if I still have what it takes to do my job.

On the way back to the lab, a sign on the door of the office next to mine catches my attention—Dr. Henry Chadwick. Through the open door, I see an office so perfectly in order it seems he hasn't worked there for a while. I'm staring into the office when an Asian man approaches. From Emily's description, I surmise this is Andrew Peng.

"Shame what happened to him. Such a talented man," he says.

A bead of sweat drips down my back. I need to know what the shame part means. Is Chadwick dead? Did I kill him? If so, how did I get away with it?

I turn to Andrew. "Yes. It's not the same without him."

"Damn tickers. You never know when they're going to give out."

And just like that, I have my answer. Henry Chadwick is dead from an apparent heart attack. But that still doesn't absolve me from guilt since I don't know the events that led up to his heart attack. If my dream in Grand Cayman is any indication, those events have something to do with me.

Overwhelming despair washes over me. If Chadwick is dead, what hope do I have of uncovering the mystery of what happened to Emily and me? He's my only link. Without that, I am doomed to live out the rest of my life as someone else.

Andrew pats my arm and walks away. I head to the lab and find my spot. Emily has provided extensive notes on my work. I've been studying how to prevent aging by examining accelerated aging disorders. I have no recollection of this, nor do I understand how aging works. Where I was at an advantage with implanted memories of driving a car, Emily was at an advantage with all of my knowledge. I'm sure her laboratory technique was no better than my driving at first, but the memory was 99% of it.

I reread her notes and examine my old logs and test results. Hours later, I still have no clue what I'm doing. I'm finished.

Life as I knew it is over. I have no skills that will allow me to continue in this existence. I know how to take care of a baby, though I don't have the inclination to. And I can drive a car. Emily's old work in Public Relations isn't much of a memory for me. Perhaps Emily was so consumed with motherhood those other memories didn't transfer in the same way my work memories transferred to her. So, we're back to driving a car.

My surroundings blur through a veil of tears. I can get my hack license and drive a cab. That's what I'll do with my multiple degrees from Columbia. A sob rises up in my throat and I hurry from the lab to the stairwell. I climb a flight before breaking out in ugly, choking sobs. Part of me wants to run and never look back. But even a small chance I can recover what I've lost means I must continue to show up here until I find the answers. I wipe my tears away, take a few deep breaths, and head back to the lab. At the landing, I hear footsteps below and self-consciously glance down the stairs to see who's approaching.

Jake stares at me with a concerned look on his face, confirming how terrible I must look.

"Are you okay, Dr. Thorpe?"

"Yes. Mini-meltdown. But I'm okay."

He pauses a moment. "Let me know if you need anything."

I thank him and, after holding the door open for me, he turns toward the elevator banks while I return to the lab.

I decide to put my efforts in another direction. I enter Chadwick's office and sit down at his desk, willing some trace of memory, no matter how small, to materialize. But there's nothing. Maybe I'm trying too hard. I think of the times I've glimpsed my past. They were when I'd been rested after sleep or on vacation. Maybe the stress is preventing me from accessing data. I flip through the files on Chadwick's desk, skimming each one. I open his drawers and go through files there. I touch pencils and pens and gadgets and desk toys he's accumulated over the years. Finally, I get up and peruse his bookshelves. They are mostly scientific volumes and some of them are so old, they're most likely out of date.

Exhausted, I sit back in his chair and glance at the clock. I've been at it for hours. Time to call it a day. When I leave his office, no one is left in the lab. Only one light is on and I shut it and make my way back to my office. My footsteps echo in the eerie silence. I wish Emily weren't so far away. I don't want to go home to an empty apartment. I could use some of her bubbly energy.

I put on my coat and grab my bag. Maybe I'll stop for Indian food at a little place I passed this morning. Surely it's a good sign to crave an ethnic food that wouldn't interest Emily in the least.

As I enter the lobby, I glance at the security desk. Jake has been replaced by someone new who doesn't bother to look up at the sound of my approaching footsteps. Disappointment wells up in me. It would have been comforting to see Jake again, especially now, with this mood taking over.

As I exit the building, a strong gust of wind whips my hair across my face. I pull up the collar of my coat to keep out the chill and slide my hands into my pockets. My fingers feel the clink of coins and the crunch of paper bills. I smile at the find and think of Emily, carelessly stuffing change from a purchase into her coat pocket.

Warm, spiced air envelops me upon entering the Indian restaurant. A man with a welcoming lilt to his voice greets me. Suddenly, I am starving for both food and company. This will be my sanctuary for the next hour. Rather than getting take-out, I sit and peruse the menu. When the waiter returns, I order samosas to start and then chicken korma and a side of naan. I decline the offer of wine and opt instead for hot tea.

After eating, I review the events of the day. Jake's comment about the book comes to mind. Who am I without my memories? I make a mental note to read that book and perhaps consult with the doctor who wrote it. Maybe there's hope, even if I can't find out what happened to me and who is behind it. This thought brings me a momentary lightness and the courage to return to that sterile apartment I once called home.

As I pay the check, I pull out the contents of my coat pocket and put the money Emily left behind into my wallet. Stuck in between the dollar bills is a slip of paper, the writing in neat, uppercase print.

*YOU'RE IN DANGER. C IS ALIVE AND WANTS TO MEET WITH YOU. I CAN TAKE YOU TO HIM. TRUST NO ONE ELSE. CALL ME AT 917-555-1389 FROM A DISPOSABLE PHONE. J*

# Twenty-three

I stare at the message. What is this? Why wouldn't Emily have told me about this note? Then I register the J, and the exchange with the security guy Jake comes back to mind. The talk about memory, my dropping the book, Jake grabbing my elbow to help me up. Clutching the elbow on the same side as the pocket with the note. Did he really find me in the stairwell by chance or did he see me on the security cameras? Could C be Chadwick?

My inclination is to call immediately and find out what this means. But that would be foolish. Who is Jake? And why should I trust him?

Outside the restaurant, the wind blows debris along the curb. The scuffling noises have me looking every which way in the moonless night.

I duck into a store to buy a new throwaway phone. I don't want to compromise the one I use to call Emily, just in case Jake has a way to trace it. But before calling him, I need to speak to Emily. To say a bit of paranoia has seeped into the mix would be a gross understatement. I huddle in the doorway of a store front, closed for the night. I've walked all the way to the west side of the city. It's a bit seedier but feels like a wiser option. The people I have to fear are not the ones wandering with bottles of liquor in brown paper bags.

Emily answers and says my name as a breathy exclamation. I am at once nervous that something bad has happened.

"No, no, nothing like that," she reassures me. "It's just good to hear your voice. I've been thinking about you, wondering how you did today." She pauses, but before I can respond, she adds, "Plus, it's nice to talk to someone who knows who I am."

I consider the irony of that statement. She is surrounded by people who have known her her entire life.

"I know what you mean," I say. "How is it going?"

She lets out a deep sigh. "It's stressful worrying I'm not going to respond properly when I don't remember something, but it's going well. We visited my parents last night. They didn't seem to notice any difference in me. Unfortunately, I don't remember them at all. But it doesn't matter. They're good people. I like them. I'll just move forward."

I'm shocked at Emily's quick acceptance of our plight.

"Madison, are you still there?"

"Yeah, I was just thinking."

"How did it go at work today?"

"Not too well. I discovered Chadwick died of a heart attack, or that's the story at least."

"Why would it be a story? Do you doubt it?"

I pause, not certain I want to answer that question. But there's no one else I can tell. "I think I killed him."

"What? Why would you think that?"

"A dream I had. I destroyed the lab. There was blood everywhere. Then I saw Chadwick."

"You remembered him?"

"Not exactly. I had the dream and then found a photo of Chadwick online."

"But if he had a heart attack, that doesn't match up with your dream."

"What if something I did caused the heart attack?"

"Madison, I don't think you have it in you to harm someone. I just don't. Don't make yourself crazy with this. It can't be true."

Emily's certainty brings tears to my eyes. I want to believe her but I'm not there yet. It will have to be enough that she's sure for now. This new teary episode reminds me of my breakdown in the stairwell. Suddenly, Jake pops into mind.

"Hey, do you know a security guard named Jake Dyson who works at the front desk?"

"Jake. Hmmm. I don't think so. What does he look like?"

"Late thirties, dark short hair, light brown eyes. Athletic build, nice smile, very friendly."

Emily snickers. "Anything else?"

I feel the warmth in my face despite the cold night. "No, that's it."

"Uh huh." She giggles again. "No, I don't know him. I think I would have remembered someone who looked like that. Who is he?"

"I don't know. We had the oddest exchange this morning about a book he was reading. He said something about memory that seemed so targeted to me."

"That sounds a wee bit paranoid."

"Yeah, I convinced myself the same thing, until I found a note from him shoved into my coat pocket tonight."

"What?"

"He claims Chadwick is alive and needs to talk to me, and..." I inadvertently swallow with a gulp-like sound and hope Emily hasn't registered my fear. "...and that I'm in danger."

"Oh my God. What are you going to do?"

"Call him. See what he has to say."

"I don't know. Maybe you should just go to the police. I mean, what do you really know about this guy? Maybe he's lying to you. How could Chadwick still be alive? You said he died of a heart attack. Was there a wake, a funeral? This is not some blockbuster thriller movie. How would someone orchestrate this in real life?"

She has a point, but hope that Chadwick is still alive burns in me like a fever. He is the key to all of this. I'm sure of it. "I'll be careful. I'll just call him. I won't go anywhere with him. I promise."

Emily provides reluctant acceptance, but I can sense her fretting over the phone line.

"How are things going with Brad?" I ask, interrupting the uneasy silence.

"Last night, after we got home from my parents' house, we put Amanda down to sleep. We were staring down at her sweet face and he pulled me into his arms for a hug. It was the strangest thing. I fit perfectly against his chest with my head under his chin. It was like that spot was made for me."

I am speechless once again and feel alone.

"It felt warm...and safe. I still don't remember our past, but I'm optimistic about our future."

A tear slides down my cheek and I wipe it away. "That's really great, Emily. I'm so happy it's working out."

"Don't cry, Madison."

"I'm not crying."

"Yes you are. Look, I don't think I'm ever going to get my memory back. If seeing Amanda didn't jolt something in my brain, nothing will. I have to live with what I have, and what I have here is not so bad."

"No, it's not. Brad is a good man. And Amanda is beautiful."

"You already have some of your memory back and I think you'll eventually get more of it. Look at how far you've come, figuring out your real name and finding Regina and Richard."

My shoulders begin to shake. When I speak, my words ride the wave of a sob. "I don't remember my work. I'm useless there."

"You will, Madison. I know you will. I'll help you any way I can. You know that."

I sniff. "Thank you."

"You don't have to thank me. We're sisters, after all."

Her comment catches me by surprise. In all the discussions we've had, we focused on the scientific facts of how there could be two of us. The term biological siblings may have even been uttered. Never once did the practical implications come to mind. I have a sister. A sister.

I can barely say goodbye. Seconds later, I'm bawling again. In some ways, I wish I could be like Emily, content to let go of my past, of who I was, and accept a future that is unknown and new and something that needs to be built one brick at a time.

But I'm not like Emily. I am Madison. Madison Thorpe. And I'm determined to find out exactly what that means.

Fortified with intention, I take out the new throwaway phone and dial the number on the scrap of paper. It starts to ring. In the distance, I hear a faint ringing sound. The phone rings again, and some other phone nearby rings with a split-second delay. On the third ring, it sinks in. I turn toward the sound and see Jake striding towards me, just half a block away.

That's all the confirmation I need that he's been following me. Boxing be damned. I turn and run as fast as I can.

# Twenty-four

Jeremy brings another handful of popcorn to his mouth. It's become a rhythm as he sits in the dark room, the glow of the television the only light. Stephanie has selected the movie, a foreign film with subtitles. Jeremy lost track of what was happening almost from the beginning. He just keeps shoveling in the popcorn and chasing thoughts around his mind. If Stephanie knew, she'd probably leave.

He glances over at her. She seems perfectly content, focused on the ribbon of words flashing on the screen. The kids are sleeping over at her parents' house. Tonight is a date of sorts, a chance to connect again after the recent tension. Stephanie has whipped up his favorite snacks for the occasion. He's all for it in theory and yet, his thoughts are far away. He'd never say it aloud, but there are matters more important than his marriage.

Right on schedule, his cell phone rings. Stephanie sighs and pauses the movie as he answers and walks into the kitchen.

"Hi, Boss. It's Turner. Sorry about intruding on your Friday night, but I've got some interesting developments here."

Jeremy's pulse quickens. Each new communication from his agents puts him into temporary panic.

"What's happening?"

"Maybe it's nothing but there seems to be a loss of physical strength. Some muscle weakness."

"I'm not sure I'm following you."

"Well, just what I said. She's not as strong as before. It's noticeable. I guess I just wondered if it's significant. If maybe the procedure could be responsible."

"I don't see why the procedure would have any impact on physical strength."

"Mmmmm. I figured so, but since I don't know exactly what was done, I wanted to make sure. It's odd. Maybe something else is wrong."

"Is it possible the recent holidays have something to do with it. I know my workouts aren't as good after all the feasting and napping."

"I suppose..."

"But you're not convinced."

"No, call it woman's intuition, whatever. My gut is telling me something is off."

Jeremy frowns. He knows the role instinct plays in their jobs. He can't discount it, especially with so much at stake.

"Okay, Turner. I believe you. Keep an eye on it and call me immediately if there's any change."

"You got it. Um, one more thing..."

Turner pauses for what seems an eternity.

"You still there, Turner?"

"Yeah. It's about Reynold."

"What about him?"

"I'm gonna go out on a limb here..."

"Okay."

"I wouldn't be having this conversation with you if I didn't think it was important."

"Spit it out, Turner."

"Right, well, Reynold and I, outside of work, have become...friendly."

Jeremy curses silently, angry that Reynold has ignored his order to break it off with Turner. "I'm well aware."

"Oh."

"What's the issue?"

"He's different."

"How so?"

"He seems...haunted."

"Haunted?"

"I think he might be depressed. He hasn't been sleeping. He's completely withdrawn. Claims there's nothing wrong, but there's clearly something wrong."

Jeremy knows exactly what's wrong. The fact Turner doesn't means Reynold has at least kept his side of the project classified. "I'll have a talk with him. Thanks, Turner."

"Don't say I told you."

"I won't. I appreciate the heads-up. We're all under a lot of pressure. Thanks."

Jeremy leans against the kitchen counter and lets out his breath. He considers Reynold and Turner's relationship, wondering how much conversation there could possibly be when neither party is at liberty to speak of their job.

Just then, Stephanie pads into the kitchen and stares at him. He knows how little conversation there is when just one person isn't at liberty to speak of his job.

# Twenty-five

The desolate avenue stretches ahead, no one in sight. I run a block and then cut up a side street, heading East to a more populated area. But it's cold and windy and already close to 9 p.m. The masses have settled in front of the television for the night, unaware of the danger behind me.

I hear Jake shout "Madison," ditching the formality of Dr. Thorpe.

Despite my physical conditioning, the fear factor takes its toll and I'm winded. Judging by the sound of his footsteps, he's gaining ground. Realizing there's no way I can outrun him, I blast through the doors of a gyro place. The guy slicing meat from the rotating spit turns and stares at me, as does the customer waiting for his sandwich.

"There's a man chasing me."

The customer, a guy about twenty who may be a college student, looks over my shoulder. I follow his gaze but no one's there.

I bend over at the waist and gasp for breath. What the hell do I do now? I can't go home. I obviously can't go to Emily's. I consider my parents, but if I'm followed I'd be putting them in danger as well.

The counter guy wraps up the gyro in aluminum foil, puts it

into a white paper bag and hands it to the customer. As the kid pays for it, I'm stunned neither of them seems concerned that someone is stalking me.

As the customer takes his change and turns to leave, I grab his arm. "Please, can you hail me a cab? When it comes, I'll jump in."

He nods and I watch from the door as he walks out into the street and raises his arm. My eyes scan the sidewalk on both sides of the street, but there is no sign of Jake. A cab pulls up. The guy opens the door, says something to the driver, and then turns toward me. I bolt out of the shop and practically dive head first into the cab.

"Just drive. I haven't decided where I'm going yet." I turn and stare out the back window. "Make lots of turns."

"Is someone following you?" the driver asks in his singsong Pakistani accent.

"It's a possibility."

"You should go to the police."

I keep careful watch out the back window as the driver speeds up, takes a corner on practically two wheels, races to the next corner, makes a right, speeds four blocks, takes a left. We go on like this for a few minutes. I don't see any sign of Jake.

"44th between 5th and 6th," I tell the cab driver.

As he circles back, I look at the meter and pull money out of my wallet. I don't want to linger outside once we get there. I include a nice tip for his trouble. He thanks me and wishes me luck.

I slide out of the cab and speed walk into the hotel, looking up and down the block one last time to be sure I haven't been followed.

When I've checked in, I ride up in the elevator. As I make my way to my room, I scan the hallway, looking for the emergency stairways. Once inside the room, I double lock the door and affix the chain. Then, I drag the desk chair across the floor. It's not the right height to wedge under the doorknob, but it's heavy enough that it'll make some noise if someone tries to get in. Precious seconds.

I collapse onto the foot of the bed and peel my coat off my shoulders. Despite the chilly evening, my body is damp with perspiration. A hot shower will do me good, even if I don't have fresh clothes to change into.

As the steaming water hits my body, I begin to relax. I need a plan and I do my best thinking in the shower. There's no point going back to work. I don't remember what I do. Chadwick's office has offered up no clues. Moreover, I don't know who I can trust there. If Chadwick really is alive, I need to find him. But I'm not ready to trust Jake to lead me to him. The message that I am in danger may be true, but it also might be a ruse to get me scared enough to follow Jake wherever he leads. I'm not desperate enough yet to do that.

I revisit the events of the day. I understand now why I picked up a vibe from Jake. His interaction with me, from the book to the quote to the note, was meant to transmit a message. Or, maybe it was to gauge my reaction. I think back to how that quote on memory jarred me. What did he make of that? What was the "right" response? What was he looking for and why? Does he know about Emily and me or is this some weird coincidence? Does Chadwick know what's happened to us? I have no memory of that, but the dream that makes me feel I have something violent in my past feels so out of character, I have to believe it is somehow related.

I'm rinsing the last of the soap from my skin when a chill spreads throughout my body. I found the note at the Indian restaurant and walked to a remote part of town. I was careful. I didn't see anyone following me. And yet, he found me. Maybe I'm paranoid, but I can't afford to take anything for granted. I jump out of the shower, not even bothering to dry myself, and pull on the hotel robe. I run to the bedroom and pick up my coat, turning the pockets inside out and scanning every inch of them. I run my fingers over the lining, paying special attention to the elbow where Jake grabbed my arm to assist me when I retrieved the book I had dropped. Nothing.

I fall back on the bed and let out a long breath. I stare at the ceiling while I think it through again. Am I making more of it than it is? I pull my bag towards me, retrieve the note and reread it. Then I remember the money and change in my pocket. The bills may be gone by now after paying for dinner and the cab, but the change is still scattered in the inside pocket of my purse. I take it out and look at each coin—a quarter, two nickels, a dime, three pennies, and a black disk the size of a quarter.

The rising panic paralyzes me. How long was I in the shower? Enough time for someone to track me here?

I throw off my robe and dress as fast as I can. I have to get out of here. I leave the disk on the bedside table, then toss my bag over my shoulder. I remove the chair from under the doorknob and peek through the peep hole. When I'm certain the hallway is empty, I unlock the door and rush toward the elevator. At the last moment, I decide the stairs are safer.

I open the stairwell door and pause a moment to listen. It's quiet. I close the door with a gentle click and descend the stairs, slowly and carefully, making as little noise as possible. On each landing, I look down to make sure no one's lurking. The whole time I'm hoping the tracking device I found was the only one.

When I get to the lobby level, the disciplined person I am almost wants to stop at the desk to officially check out, but I come to my senses. I walk out into the night and jump into a waiting cab.

The driver looks back at me for a destination. Without even thinking, I say Brooklyn. But it's not Regina and Richard I have in mind. I pull out my wallet and extract the card given to me the day I saved Vincent Gargiulo's life. By his own admission, a trip to the Cayman Islands couldn't repay my deed. I figure I have a favor coming to me.

Just as I reach for the Emily phone, the other throwaway starts ringing. Stupid, stupid, stupid. What is wrong with me? I totally forgot about that phone, and Jake now has my number from the call I made to his. I'm not sure if a throwaway can be traced, but if it can it's probably possible whether or not I answer it. In the safety of the cab, my curiosity gets the best of me.

Jake doesn't even wait for me to say hello. His voice no longer reflects the warm, reassuring friendliness of this morning's encounter.

"Madison. Listen to me. I'm not the enemy here, but you do have one."

"And who might that be?"

"Chadwick is the man to ask about that."

"He's really alive?"

"Yes, I've seen him with my own eyes."

"You're sure the man you've seen is Chadwick?"

"Yes."

"Has he told you what's going on?"

"No. All I know is you're in danger and I have to take you to him so he can fill you in."

"How can you be sure he doesn't mean to harm me?"

"I know people."

I snort.

Jake's breath rushes out in a frustrated sigh. "You know you want to believe me or you wouldn't be asking all these questions."

"What was that conversation really about this morning? And that book you're supposedly reading."

"Not supposedly. I did read it."

"Why?"

"Chadwick told me you might be suffering from amnesia."

"So why would someone hired as a body guard need to read up on memory?"

"I like to understand the people I work with."

"And what did that little conversation have you understanding about me?"

"That you're aware of the memory issue...and you're afraid of something."

I'm silent.

"Listen, I'm in the lobby of your hotel. Either let me come up to your room or you come down if you're more comfortable with that. We can talk face-to-face."

Just then, the cab driver swerves to avoid another cab. He presses down on the horn and screams at the other driver, gesticulating like a madman.

"What the hell? Wait! Where are you?" Jake says.

"Not where you think I am. But if you want your GPS disk back, it's on my bedside table."

"Shit. You have no idea what you're up against. You have to come back and let me get you to Chadwick."

"I don't think so. Bye."

"Wait—"

I hang up and throw the cell phone out the window.

"So where in Brooklyn am I heading?" the cab driver asks.

"The underworld," I say under my breath.

# Twenty-six

All eyes turn my way when I enter the men's club in Sheepshead Bay. It's like a scene out of The Godfather. At some tables, men play cards and argue. At others, they feast on heaping portions of Italian food brought from the kitchen by a rotund man in a soiled, white apron. The few seconds I stand in the doorway feel like a lifetime until Paulie, the guy who escorted me to visit Gargiulo in the hospital, approaches me.

"Good to see you again, Mrs. Cooke."

Now that I know I'm Madison Thorpe, it's odd to hear myself referred to as Mrs. Cooke. I don't bother correcting him. Instead, I greet him with a smile. Everything is relative and right now I'm happy to have these guys on my side.

"Follow me. Mr. Gargiulo is expecting you."

In the distance, Gargiulo stands to greet me.

"Emily, it's so good to see you again." He takes my hand in his and holds it rather than shaking it.

"The feeling is mutual," I say, and mean it.

He gestures in the air. "Paulie, get Ms. Cooke some food." To me, he says, "What do you like? Carbonara? Or something with red sauce?"

"No, thank you. I had dinner at an Indian restaurant a few hours ago."

Gargiulo winces. "You like that stuff?"

"I do."

"To each his own. I can't even get you some antipasto to pick on?"

"No, but if you have it, I would love a glass of wine."

"*If we have it*. That's like asking if a Chinese restaurant has rice. Paulie, get the lady some wine." He motions for me to follow him. "Let's go into my office where we can talk privately."

His corpulent body falls into the chair, suggesting his knees are shot from carrying around so much weight. Paulie arrives with a glass of red wine. Before I can thank him, Gargiulo instructs him to close the door on the way out. Ensconced in this cave-like office with a Mafia man who wants to make me comfortable and feed me, I have never felt safer.

Gargiulo leans back in his chair. "So, I have to tell ya. I'm a little surprised you called. Don't take that wrong. I'm happy you did, but I didn't get the sense our paths would cross again. I'm intrigued."

"I think I may be in danger."

"Danger? From who?"

"I'm not sure. But there's someone who claims to know. He wants to help me. I just don't know if I can trust him."

Gargiulo squints and two deep furrows appear above his nose. "I can't imagine someone would want to harm you. Is it a domestic thing...an ex-boyfriend or husband?"

"No, nothing like that. It's...complicated, mostly because I haven't put all the pieces together yet. But the ones I have—well, if I told you that part, I'd have to kill you."

Gargiulo stares at me, his expression serious, and then erupts in a bark of laughter that sets off a wheezy cough.

"Are you okay?" I ask. "I don't have to take another steak knife to you, do I?"

He pats his chest with his pudgy hand and finally calms down. "You're a funny lady."

"What I can tell you is something very strange has happened to me. If I told you what, you'd think I was crazy.

It's like a sci-fi movie. Or a bad dream. But I know it's true because I found someone else who is involved. She's the missing piece that proved I wasn't losing my mind."

Gargiulo listens intently, nodding every now and then.

"I respect you don't want to tell me more, but how can I help you then?"

I didn't have the answer to that question when I decided to come here, but now it's perfectly clear. "I need you to protect me while I figure out the rest and who's behind it."

"That I can do. So this guy, the one you said knows something but you're not sure you can trust him, where is he?"

"I don't know. I got away from him."

"Got away?"

"He was tracking me but I found the device. I left it behind to throw him off my trail before coming here. I have a contact number, though."

"You're clever. I like that." Gargiulo beams at me with admiration, and I feel confident there's a position waiting for me with the mob if the lab job doesn't work out.

He pushes the phone across the desk. "Call him. Tell him to come here. You'll be safe. He can tell you what he knows. Then you can decide if you trust him or not."

The idea of turning Jake into the one with something to fear brings me satisfaction.

I make the call, and Jake picks up with a brusque "Yeah." The competitive part of me wants to gloat that I got away from him, not once but twice.

"I'm ready to talk to you," I say instead without identifying myself.

"Nice to hear you've come to your senses. Where would you like to meet?"

I give him the address and he repeats it back with surprise.

"Do you know where that is?" I ask.

"Uh, yeah, I know it well. I'll be there in half an hour. You're a very unpredictable woman."

Twenty-eight minutes later, as indicated by the ticking grandfather clock I've been unable to ignore, Jake walks in the door accompanied by two of Gargiulo's men. One of them holds a gun.

"He's packing, Boss."

My body tenses at the sight of the gun and how narrowly I escaped harm.

"It's okay," Gargiulo says. "Give it back to him."

What? Before I can protest, the man hands Jake his gun and leaves the office. Gargiulo seems as relaxed as ever.

"Good to see you again, Detective Dyson."

When I hear the word Detective, I'm stunned.

"It's just Jake, now. I work for myself."

"Smart man. I never understood why anyone would stick around past the twenty-year mark when you could collect half your pay as pension and get another job on the side. But that's just me."

Gargiulo motions for Jake to sit in the chair next to me. To say I feel foolish about being afraid of a former New York City Police Detective would be an understatement. Why the hell didn't he just identify himself to me?

"So, it seems we have a confusing situation here," Gargiulo says. "This nice lady, who happened to save my life, fears for her safety. I know you're not a concern. Is there someone who is?"

"I believe so, yes. I was hired by...my client, who claims she's in danger. I don't know the specifics myself. My job is to get her safely to him so he can give her the information she needs."

"How do you know your client doesn't have ulterior motives?"

"He's not a stranger to me."

"Why couldn't he just meet with her in a public place?"

"He's in hiding."

"From who?"

"I don't know."

"Why not just write the information in a note and send it to her?"

"I suspect he can't write the information down because it

either wouldn't be safe to create a record of it or it's so complicated that a conversation is required to answer the questions. I'm convinced he's not the enemy, but it's obvious he's extremely worried for her safety."

Gargiulo nods. "If you say he's safe, that's good enough for me. I always felt you were someone a man could trust...if that man were playing on the side of the law."

Now that I know the gun wasn't intended for me, Jake's reassuring aura has returned. He sits back, his posture relaxed, arms open and resting on the sides of the chair. His easy gaze belies the shrewd calculations I suspect are running through his mind. I have no doubt he could be out of that chair in a second with Gargiulo's ample neck enclosed in his clenched fingers. Gargiulo is not a stupid man. He has to know it, too. The fact that he sits here unguarded with Jake inches away convinces me I'll be safe with him.

"What's the next step?" Gargiulo asks.

"I take her to my client."

"I want to send one of my guys with you, just in case."

"Not possible. I can't compromise my client's safety."

"And I can't compromise mine," Gargiulo says, nodding in my direction.

"It's okay," I say. "I'm sufficiently reassured Jake is not the enemy. And I don't doubt he can take care of himself...and me."

Jake gives a quick bow of his head. "We'll stay in a hotel tonight and meet up with my client tomorrow. Would you mind having someone drive us into downtown Brooklyn?"

"It would be my pleasure."

It hasn't escaped my notice that not once during this conversation has Jake mentioned Chadwick's name or even referred to him as my boss. He gets an extra point for discretion.

I say my goodbyes to Gargiulo and thank him for his help.

"This sounds like it's just beginning. If you need me again, you know where to find me."

Jake and I follow one of Gargiulo's men outside and climb

into the back of a black limousine. Jake looks out the window, the muscle in his cheek alternately tensing and relaxing. When I open my mouth to ask him about Chadwick, he gives me a barely perceptible shake of the head, a warning.

When we reach the hotel, I follow Jake inside.

"Do you have any information on the Circle Line Tours?" He smiles politely at the man behind the registration desk.

That catches me off guard. The front-desk clerk gathers up brochures and prattles on about the schedule.

"Thank you. Tomorrow's our last day in New York and we want to make the most of it."

He flashes another smile at the clerk, then takes my hand and leads me to the elevator. We take it in silence to the third floor, get off, and take the stairs back down to the lobby level. From there, we exit into a back service hallway, parade through the mostly empty kitchen and out onto a back street.

"What the heck are we doing?"

"Making sure only we know where we're staying."

"You think Gargiulo's guys are watching us?"

"Maybe not. I just want to make sure he's out of the loop."

My heartbeat quickens. Was that a veiled threat?

As if hearing my thoughts, he says, "You'll be safe with me. I don't need any complications or people in the know blackmailing you in the future."

Jake looks up and down the block and then knocks on the window of a parked, out-of-service cab.

"I'm off-duty," the driver says.

"I know. I'm only going a few miles. I'll give you four times the fare."

The driver nods. Minutes later, we pull up in front of a different hotel. Before I can protest, Jake registers for one room and guides me to the elevator.

"I'd like my own room," I say once we're inside.

"No."

My eyebrows raise. "No?"

"Uh uh. Just in case you get any more bright ideas about taking off on your own."

My anger erupts like hot lava. "I would have been more of an idiot to trust a guy who claims to want to help me, but never identifies himself as a cop."

"I'm not a cop anymore."

"Yes, I heard. You have impeccable financial sense, but you're not so good at convincing people you're not a threat."

"I figured Chadwick's name was enough."

"I thought Chadwick was dead," I say as we exit the elevator.

He turns to me in the hallway. "Why would you think that?"

"Because I have a vague memory of killing him."

"Why would you kill him?"

"I don't know. I don't remember that part. I don't remember much at all. You should try it sometime and see how trusting *you* are."

Jake opens the door, scans the room, and then steps back so I can enter. "I'm sorry," he says. "Understand that I know as little as you do. Usually my clients provide all the gory details. Not so in this case. I sensed Chadwick intentionally left out some details. It has me on guard. That's why I've been secretive about being a former cop and why I contacted you in the manner I did. I'm operating blind."

"That's reassuring."

He smiles and this time it seems genuine—not one he uses for front-desk clerks and unknowing women whom he wants to take on potentially dangerous journeys.

The sight of the two double beds makes me realize I'm exhausted. The stress of the day has taken its toll.

"I need to sleep."

I lock myself in the bathroom, splash cold water on my face, and rinse out my mouth. The desire for fresh clothes is fierce. I wash my bra, panties, and blouse in the sink. Jake will just have to deal with my feminine clutter. With everything washed and hanging, I pull on the hotel robe and walk back into the room. Jake sits on the bed closest to the door, playing with his cell phone. His shoes are off and his gun, a bleak reminder of what a mess my life has become, lies on the bedside table.

I murmur a quiet good night and slip under the covers. When I look up, Jake is staring at me.

"Good night," he says and quickly looks back down at his cell phone.

# Twenty-seven

When I awake, Jake is already up, pacing the room. I mumble a good morning, wriggle back into my robe, and head to the bathroom for a quick shower. A grateful sigh escapes my lips as I slip on my fresh undergarments and blouse. The things we take for granted.

When I come out, a tray with coffee, croissant, fruit cup, and scrambled eggs awaits me.

"I didn't know if you were one of those anti-bread people," Jake says, "so I ordered you fruit and eggs, too.

"I'm so hungry, I'll eat it all." But first things first. I take a sip of coffee and the calm takes hold.

"Aren't you hungry?" I ask.

"I ate hours ago."

"Hours? What time is it?"

Jake glances at the clock between the beds. "Almost ten."

I can't believe I slept so soundly with a stranger in the next bed. I'm letting down my guard and that's not a good thing.

After breakfast, we head out for the meeting with Chadwick. My stomach starts to grumble and I question the intelligence of eating such a large breakfast when nerves are a big part of the equation.

Outside the hotel, we hail a cab and go a short distance

before pulling over at a Beaux Arts-style building in downtown Brooklyn. We enter through the front door and, ignoring the calls of the doorman, walk down a hallway and exit through the side doors. Jake calmly looks both ways and then grabs my hand.

"Let's go," he says, breaking into a jog.

We run to the end of the block, round the corner, and race down the steps to a subway station. Except it's not. It's the New York Transit Museum.

I have no idea what he's up to, but there's no time to ask questions. After paying for two tickets, Jake leads me down to the subway car exhibit, a string of train cars through the ages. Judging by the tracks leading into the tunnel, this was once a functioning station.

Before I realize what's happening, he walks to the back of the last subway car and jumps down onto the tracks.

"What the hell are you doing?"

"We're being tailed."

"Who? I didn't see anyone."

Jake motions for me to jump down. "Gargiulo's guys, I think. But I'm not taking any chances."

"Who else would—"

"Jump, dammit!"

I do and he steadies me when I land.

"Let's go."

We take off through the tunnel. It's dark and smelly and every once in a while I hear a scuffling sound. I don't need much of an imagination to conjure up the cat-sized rat in the shadows.

"This part of the tracks isn't used any more. But we'll have to cross through an active tunnel to catch a train to Chadwick. Just keep to the walls. It's wide enough."

He speaks the words so calmly—it's wide enough. Active tunnel. Is he kidding? But I follow, glad I can't see what's in front of him. My skin is clammy and I'm short of breath. I force myself to ignore the signs of an impending anxiety attack. One foot in front of the other. Keep close behind Jake. Don't think. These words become my mantra.

At the end of the tunnel, there's an intersection. The familiar screeching noise up ahead means we've reached the active tunnel. My body freezes. Jake turns around.

"Are you ready?"

My mind screams no, but I nod. His gaze lingers. This guy doesn't miss a thing.

"It'll be okay. Stay to the side. If a train approaches, turn your face to the wall."

We cross the tracks, carefully stepping over the electrified third rail he points out. I hear a distant rumbling. My prayers have not been answered. A train is going to pass us. My chest tightens. I can't breathe. The rumble becomes a monstrous roar. The train rounds the bend, headlights glaring. It races toward us. Closer and closer.

It's too late to turn back, but my body hasn't gotten the memo. It moves in the direction of the inactive tunnel. As if reading my mind, Jake grabs me. He presses my head into his chest and pushes me against the tunnel wall.

The train hurtles by, the noise deafening. I panic at the force and wind and start to struggle, but I'm locked tight against Jake. Finally, he pulls back.

"Are you okay?"

I respond with what sounds like the last gasp of a dying man.

"Come on. We've got a small window before the next train."

"Can we take it at a jog?"

"Yeah, just be careful you don't fall. A skinned knee in this place and you'll be dead from some unknown disease."

Within a few moments, the lights of the station appear. I hear the rumble of another approaching train. We need to get out of the tunnel and up onto the platform.

"Run," I shout. He gets to the end of the platform and in one strong, graceful movement pulls himself up. I look to the right and see train lights approaching. That expression "deer in the headlights" exists for a reason.

"Madison! Give me your hands."

Like a child who wants to be picked up by a parent, I reach up and close my eyes. And then I'm on the platform and we're running for the stairs of the Hoyt-Schermerhorn station. In typical New York fashion, people waiting for the train look at us with disinterest.

At the A train, we hop on just as the doors are about to close. Gasping for breath, I huddle in a corner seat by the pass-through door with my head in my hands. Just when I think it can't get worse, I feel tears pooling as my body trembles. Jake stands in front of me, holding onto the overhead bar. It's obvious he's aware of my emotions when he gently touches the back of my head.

"It's okay, Madison," he says softly.

But it's not. None of this is okay. And I don't have much hope left it will turn out well. It's a nightmare I can't escape, like when you know you're dreaming and all you have to do is open your eyes, but you can't. That's what my life has become.

I'm numb. I follow Jake in a trance. I have no idea when we transferred from the A train to the 4, but eventually I find myself settled in a window seat on the Hudson Line of a Metro North train. The scenery flies by so quickly, I can barely take it in. It parallels my state of mind. Racing, jumbled thoughts. Multi-colored streaks without form. I close my eyes and rest my forehead against the hard plastic surrounding the window. Seconds later, Jake's arm is around me, and he pulls me into his muscular shoulder, reassuring and welcoming. Sleep beckons and I rush to meet it.

***

The big moment has arrived. My pulse races despite attempts to calm myself. In front of us, a tall building sits nestled among sprawling grounds dotted with trees and fallow garden beds. We approach the security booth and Jake identifies us as Mr. and Mrs. Smith and hands over a driver's license for inspection. The guard nods and tells us to proceed through.

"Smith?" I mutter once we're out of hearing range. "That's original."

"Exactly the point," he says as he casually takes in our surroundings.

As we pass through the front doors, he scans the lobby and then leads me to an elevator bank. He punches in eleven and turns my way as I tie a knot in my hair to keep it back from my face.

I bear his scrutiny in silence. Why the heck is he staring at me? What is he thinking?

I lean away when he reaches out and puts his index finger on my temple. "You have a chicken pox scar."

"What?" With a million tries, I never would have guessed his thoughts.

"I hadn't noticed it until you pulled your hair back."

"How lucky that I can hide my deformity by letting down my hair."

He stares at me, his face devoid of expression, and then lets out a hearty laugh. The serious, in-control mask he's worn shatters, revealing deep lines at the outer corners of his eyes and mouth. Too deep to be new. This is a man with a sense of humor.

I can't help smiling at the infectious sound. I welcome the break in tension, no matter how brief. The ping of the elevator brings reality rushing back. Jake's expression turns serious again. I imagine mine must be somewhere between grim and panicked.

A million thoughts race through my head in the seconds it takes us to walk to Chadwick's door. But one pushes its way to the front: Do you really want to know the truth?

Before Jake knocks, the door opens. My former boss stands before me, tall but frail, his blue eyes large in his thin face. He holds reading glasses in his hand and I wonder if he's reading a scientific article or something light. At the moment, I can't imagine being able to read either.

"Madison. You look well."

"You don't," I think.

Chadwick ushers us in and gestures to a sofa.

"Please, have a seat. Can I get you anything?"

Jake and I decline. Chadwick sits across from us in a leather, wing chair. He turns and stares out the floor-to-ceiling window that I assume overlooks the rear gardens. At eleven floors up, all I see is sky.

"It's a pretty day for confessions," he says so softly I barely hear him. "Thank you, Jake, for bringing her here safely."

"No problem," Jake says, all business, but I sense something more to their relationship than my delivery at Chadwick's door.

Chadwick takes a deep breath. "I'll start from the beginning. You need to know everything."

"Wait! How much does Jake know about this matter?"

Jake and Chadwick start to answer at the same time, but Jake defers to him.

"None of it," Chadwick says.

"All I know is you're in some kind of danger and you have some memory loss," Jake adds. "I already told you that."

"I don't want him here," I say to Chadwick.

Chadwick begins to protest. "I think it's best—"

"No, it's okay." Jake rises. "She deserves some privacy."

"You know, you can trust him," Chadwick says after the door shuts behind Jake. "I've known him a very long time."

"How?"

"My apartment in the City was on his beat back when he was a police officer. He worked nights and I often arrived home late from the lab. We became friendly."

"That doesn't seem like much of a history."

"When he made detective and moved to the day shift, we'd grab dinner or a beer and talk. He's smart. And honest. I'd trust him with my life."

"Not all of us have a choice."

Chadwick nods once, slowly, then clears his throat to speak. His expression is pained. I've never been so frightened in my life.

"Back when I was a young and enthusiastic doctor, I did

something incredibly foolish. Some good came out of it, and that would have been all if I hadn't told anyone. But besides being young and enthusiastic, I was proud. It was a lethal combination."

He stares out the window for so long, it seems he's forgotten I'm in the room.

"Go on," I say.

"I had opened an in vitro clinic, and my success rate was quite high. I brought people happiness with my work, and that in turn made me happy. And rich. But it wasn't enough. I became interested in the nature versus nurture argument. Would genes win out, or could a child's upbringing counteract their effects?"

I think of my twin Emily. Were we his subjects in this experiment? Twins brought up in different households? But how?

"I considered that embryos from Emily's mother had been implanted into my mother," I say, "but Emily's mom conceived naturally."

Chadwick pauses. "Even if she hadn't, Madison, that wouldn't have been a very good experiment. In vitro embryos are fraternal twins, not identical ones."

"Of course. So did you figure out a way to split the cells to turn them into identical twins?"

"You've just said she conceived naturally. There could have been no intervention on my part."

I'm not thinking straight. Silence ensues. His blue, watery gaze penetrates my confused one. It's as if he's willing me to guess some big secret. And then it clicks. My heart pounds. Perspiration seeps from my pores. My subconscious has picked up something my conscious mind has not yet registered.

Chadwick notices the physical change in me. "So you've figured it out."

"No. Tell me."

He's so still, he could be a statue. His unblinking eyes shine with a blinding intensity—as if he's vacated his body but left floodlights on to make it appear someone's home. He licks his parched lips and leans forward.

"You're a clone, Madison. I cloned Emily to create you."

# Twenty-eight

I let out a piercing scream, the sound of a mortally wounded animal, as I lunge from the sofa toward Chadwick. A flash of memory tells me I've been here before. I *did* trash the lab. Chadwick had already confessed to me. Before my memories were taken away.

"You son of a bitch," I scream, my fists in the air as I hurl myself at Chadwick. The front door crashes open. Jake grabs me from behind and pins my arms to my side.

"Let go of me!" I struggle to free myself.

"What the hell's going on?" Jake says.

Chadwick collapses back into his chair and stares into space. I break away from Jake and storm out the door. At the elevator, I pound on the buttons. When it doesn't come, I start running down eleven flights of stairs.

Chadwick's words replay in a continuous loop in my mind. *Cloned Emily to create you. Cloned Emily to create you. Cloned Emily to create you.* I falter at the bottom of a landing and fly over a few stairs, almost crashing to my knees. A door slams above me. My footsteps are so loud, I can't tell if anyone has entered the stairwell. I continue racing down flight after flight and finally exit to the back garden.

A large pond sits in the distance, surrounded by bare

weeping willows and benches scattered here and there. I take a few deep breaths and walk toward it. I stare down into the water and imagine the wriggling of tiny fish born of millions of eggs, each one genetically different from the next. Nature doing its thing, not being manipulated by an egomaniac for his own amusement and curiosity.

I am a clone of Emily. I am someone else. I am not me. The me I know is genetically someone else. In trying to create something, Chadwick has created nothing. I am nothing.

"Madison."

I jump at the sound of Jake's voice.

"Are you okay?"

"Did he tell you?" I ask.

"No, he wouldn't without your permission."

"I'm not okay. I'm not anything."

"You don't have to tell me what he said, but I need to know why you're in danger and who is after you. Without that, Madison, I'm seriously handicapped in the protection department."

Jake's practicality snaps me out of my self-pity. I shudder and rub the goose bumps on my upper arms.

"I don't know why I'm in danger or who's after me."

"Then you need to go back in there and find out everything he knows."

He's right, but I'm filled with dread. I recall the reality of my life for the past few months. Emily's memories instead of my own. Living in Emily's life instead of my own. How had I come to take over her existence and she take over mine? In light of the cloning experiment, it seems more ominous than ever. My imagination has a field day dreaming up all the possible reasons I might be in danger. I need to find out the truth.

We walk back to the building in silence. At Chadwick's apartment, Jake stops at the door.

"Come in with me," I say.

"Are you sure?"

"Yes."

Chadwick stands at the window, staring down at the garden, like God surveying his creation. Jake and I return to the same seats.

"Start again," I say to Chadwick. "Jake needs to hear everything you've told me so far."

As he recounts the story, he never lifts his gaze from coffee-table height. Earlier, his eyes bored into mine, begging for forgiveness. But now, with Jake, it's shame coming through.

I'm half listening to his retelling when the word "clone" penetrates my drifting thoughts.

"Shit," Jake mutters.

The rage builds up again, this time in the form of blinding tears. I try to force them back, but one escapes and rolls down my cheek. I swipe it away. Jake's expression of horror says it all. I am the result of a freakish laboratory experiment. My next thought puts me over the edge and I erupt into hysterical laughter. I double over, holding my stomach, tears pouring down my face. I try to tell him what's so funny, but I can't get the words out.

Jake says something to Chadwick and Chadwick leaves the room. Jake moves next to me on the sofa.

"What's so funny?" he asks.

"I was thinking...I was thinking I'm the freakish result of a laboratory experiment...and...and..." Another peal of laughter escapes. "And that I have a ch...chicken pox scar." I lean back on the couch. My side aches from laughing so hard and still I can't stop. But Jake does not laugh. He leans over and lifts me effortlessly onto his lap. With my face buried in the crook of his neck, my laughter turns to sobs. He rocks and shushes me as if I am a helpless child.

I sense Chadwick standing in front of us and open my eyes. Jake takes a cut-crystal tumbler from him.

"Take a sip," he says.

I wince at the whiskey fumes and erupt into a full grimace after the first gulp. Liquid fire flows down my throat, but it instantly warms and soothes. I take the glass in hand and extricate myself from Jake's embrace, embarrassed at the spectacle I've made of myself.

But then I ask myself what the hell I have to be ashamed about. Chadwick holds out a box of tissues. I dab at my face and take another sip of whiskey.

"I need to splash some water on my face."

Chadwick gestures to a hallway. "First door on the left."

Inside the cream-colored powder room, I stare at my reflected face. Puffy, red-rimmed eyes return my gaze. I splash cool water on my face and rinse my mouth. I wish I could hide out here forever, but Chadwick has information I need.

When I return to the living room, both men sip whiskey in silence. The muscle in Jake's cheek contracts in a rhythmic pattern and I wonder what he's thinking. His expression softens when he looks at me, but he doesn't speak.

"I'm okay now," I say. "Continue the story."

Chadwick finishes his whiskey and places his glass on the table. He sits with his hands clasped in his lap. He looks like he's about to pray. For all I know, maybe he is.

"I have...had a friend from childhood. We were like brothers. We grew up together and attended the same college. I trusted him completely." Chadwick looks down at his hands as if the thoughts he must gather are pooled in his palms. "After I did the cloning, I had misgivings and confided in him. His excitement took some of the edge off. Remember, this was long before Dolly the Sheep. No mammal had ever been cloned."

"Was he the only person you told?" Jake asks.

"Yes. He kept the secret at first. For a long time, in fact." Chadwick shakes his head. "Only a few people know, but they're exactly the wrong people."

"Wrong, how?" Jake asks.

"They're developing strategic military applications they claim are a matter of national security."

"What are they planning? A master race of cloned soldiers?" Jake asks, squinting in confusion. "How does Madison fit in with that plan?"

"She doesn't. They were working on memory-transfer experiments. When they heard I had successfully cloned a human being, they realized they'd found the perfect testing grounds for their techniques."

"How so?" Jake says.

"Think about it. Two genetically identical people living separate lives with very different experiences and therefore memories. It was a dream come true for them. They could swap Madison and Emily's memories and then swap the actual people into each other's lives to see how successful the memory transfer was."

I've been reduced to a laboratory rat. These people didn't care about my intelligence, my hopes, desires, or my capacity for love--

"Wouldn't their families know the difference?" Jake says.

"If they acted a bit differently, no one would be suspicious. At worst, they'd chalk it up to a bad day or mood. Certainly, no one would suspect that their supposed loved one was really a clone with implanted memories who had been swapped with her twin."

"I can vouch for that," I say. "Until I realized I was someone else and started speaking that thought aloud, no one suspected anything."

"This is insane," Jake says. "Are you telling me there's another you walking around and that you've been living each other's lives?"

"Yes." I fill Jake in on my story—from the first feelings that I wasn't quite myself to meeting Emily face-to-face at my parents' home. I explain that we switched back so I could figure out what had happened to us and how his note on my first day back to work spooked me enough to enlist Gargiulo's help. Jake pays attention but I can tell he's trying to keep up with this stranger-than-fiction story.

"What kind of military application would this have?" he asks Chadwick.

"They didn't disclose that information to me, and I'm not sorry about that. I wish I didn't know any of it."

"So how is she in danger?"

"From what I gathered, this was a highly classified project. I was told just enough to convince me to cooperate. The government wouldn't want the public to know they're testing memory swap techniques on citizens. I was warned many times to keep quiet about our meetings. They weren't polite requests."

"So, I have no chance of returning to my old self," I say. "I'd be in danger if they knew I was aware of who I am and what they've done."

"Unfortunately, I think they already suspect you're aware of the cloning."

"What do you mean?"

"When they started visiting me to talk about the cloning project, I was pretty closed-mouthed. I didn't want to disclose yours and Emily's identities. They came back many times, coercing me more and more. You became suspicious because my health was starting to fail from the stress. Every time they left, I would be on the verge of collapse.

"One night, you were working late in the lab. Everyone else had gone home. You went to get a cup of coffee and saw them coming to pay me an after-hours visit. Unbeknownst to me, you turned on the intercom between my office and the lab. That's how you learned about the cloning experiment. But you mistakenly thought it was still going on. You were extremely upset, and you questioned me when they left. You asked if I was still cloning and whether your work was used in my experiments. You were relieved it had happened only once. But I knew you were in danger. They had already talked to me about switching your memories and your lives. It was such a sick idea. I couldn't let it happen. So, I told you that you were the clone and revealed what they wanted to do. You—"

"I trashed the lab."

"You remember?"

"Parts of it. I wasn't sure if it was real or a dream. When I found out you were alive, I thought it must be a dream because in my memories you died a bloody death. I was convinced I'd killed you."

Chadwick lets out a humorless laugh. "Well, you certainly wanted to kill me, but that didn't go beyond the thought stage. You cut yourself on some glass and I wrapped your hand."

I think back to my reaction that day at the gym when I was wrapping my hands to box. It all makes sense now. The initial peace I felt in that meditative act was disrupted by buried anger, trapped just below the surface, at what Chadwick had confessed.

"Someone in another lab heard the commotion and alerted security." Chadwick pauses. "Hmmmm."

"What?"

"I wonder now if they had one of their people working onsite in security. That would explain what happened next."

Jake leans forward. "What was that?"

"My heart gave out and I was rushed to the hospital. I don't know the time frame, but you came to visit me. It was dark outside. It may have been the middle of the night. I remember your saying something about sneaking in because they'd only let family up. I tried to tell you the rest of it, to warn you of the danger, but we were interrupted."

"By who?"

"I don't know. They were dressed in black and had ski masks pulled over their faces. They were coming for me, but your presence surprised them. They started shooting. I was hit in the carotid."

"Oh my God. I remember. The blood spurting. Slipping in it. Trying to get to you to put pressure on it."

"Yes, I imagine you thought it was futile and ran. And judging by the current state of affairs, they caught you and switched you with Emily."

"In every way." I shiver. "That part I don't remember." But as I say the words, my reaction to the MRI I had comes to mind. The sense of déjà vu. The panic. Was the memory of whatever they did to us triggered by the MRI?

We sit in stunned silence. Jake rises to refill our glasses. I take a quick gulp and savor the river of flames as it makes its way to my gut. I don't want those people anywhere near me again, even if it is to switch me back. Then a question pops into my head.

"Surely there's a hospital record of this and evidence you're still alive. How did you end up hiding out here?"

"I was abducted from the hospital."

At my confused look, Chadwick adds, "By a friend. Jake."

Jake meets Chadwick's gaze, then turns away and stares out the window. Though I don't know him well, I can sense the anger seeping out of him. For some reason, this buoys my spirit. It's as if I can't manufacture enough anger to meet the demand of this fucked up situation and Jake is my back-up production facility.

Chadwick clears his throat. "You seem to have recovered a lot of your memory. What about Emily?"

"No. But she's made peace with that. She's willing to have her memories begin with the present and she accepts Amanda and Brad as her future."

"If that's true, I'd say she has more of herself than you think."

His statement surprises me. "Do you know her, I mean other than..."

"The cloning? Yes. She did some marketing-related work for the labs."

"You kept us both close, didn't you?"

"I felt responsible." He pauses. "Will you be able to move on with your life with your memories beginning at present time?"

"No. I don't remember my work."

"I can help you, Madison. It's the least I can do."

I can't help seeing the irony that the man responsible for my loss of livelihood is the one offering to coach me back.

"But first we have to make sure you stay safe," Chadwick says.

"I'll keep her safe," Jake says.

I can't think about irony now. I have to stay alive. Knowledge is power. I pull a notebook and pen from my bag and have Chadwick repeat the story one last time while I create a timeline and ask questions. I am nothing if not thorough. Jake's expression as he watches me switches rapidly between admiration and exasperation. But I can't help myself. I am a scientist, after all. Even if I can't remember that part of my life, I've been trained to work with data. Once the data is on the page, I'll let my instincts take over. For now it's all black and white.

By the end of Chadwick's story, I know the name of his former friend: Nathan Brixton. I have his last known address, phone number, email address, and his phone number at work. But I suspect Chadwick has disclosed more of his secrets to Brixton than Brixton has to Chadwick. I'm sure Brixton's claims that he had a government job were the understatements of a lifetime. Jake will come in handy figuring out the truth about him.

I push my hair back from my face and glance up at the clock. It's dinnertime. I'm strung out and slightly ill from drinking whiskey on an empty stomach. I need food and a shower. As if reading my mind, Chadwick interrupts my thoughts.

"Shall I order dinner?"

"No," I respond with a bit too much passion. I've spent enough time in his company.

"We need to get back." I stand. "Thank you for the information."

As soon as the words pass my lips, I want to take them back. *Thank you?* This man owes *me*. But I don't say that. Chadwick's expression tells me he knows he's unworthy of my thanks. He fiddles with the collar button of his shirt and twists his neck from side to side as if working out a neck cramp. It's then I see the scar on his neck from the gunshot wound. He catches me staring at him and covers his neck with his fingers.

Jake stands and reminds Chadwick we'll stay in touch via throw-away phones.

Once we exit the security gate, he goes into hyper-vigilant mode. The average person watching him wouldn't notice, but

I'm beginning to know his ways.

"I need to eat, and soon."

"We'll grab a snack on the way and then I'll order you a room service feast when we get to the hotel."

My grumbling tummy wants to argue, but I know he's right. The less time we are in public, the better. "Okay," I say.

"That was easy," Jake says.

"We have no idea whether Chadwick's location has been discovered and we can't afford to stay in the vicinity for too long. I get it."

"What are you in the mood to eat?"

"I'll look at the menu and change my mind, no doubt. But at the moment, I'm thinking a moo-ing steak and a baked potato with a pound of butter on it."

Jake smiles and crinkle lines return to the outer edges of his eyes. "A girl after my own heart."

"And if I never see a bottle of whiskey again, it will be too soon."

"Yeah, it doesn't feel too good on an empty stomach, does it?"

He doesn't wait for an answer because the horn of an approaching train sounds.

"Let's go." He grabs my hand and we race toward an uncertain future.

# Twenty-nine

The yogurt and handful of almonds I ate en route from Chadwick's have staved off the hunger. All I want right now is a hot shower, but Jake reminds me that Gargiulo's guys—they would be the lesser of the evils—found us at the hotel. We sneak back to retrieve his laptop. Then we check in at a new hotel, paying in cash, just in case they found us by tracing Jake's credit card.

"Why are you so concerned about Gargiulo?" I say. "I know he's a mafia guy, but I do believe he's looking out for me."

"So do I. But someday, he'll need a favor. It would be better if he didn't know anything to use against you."

"But he's the one returning the favor."

"Yeah, yeah, the circle of life, mafia style."

He hands me the room service menu. "I'm jumping into the shower. If there's anything close to the steak dinner you mentioned, order it for me."

A quick peek makes my choice easy: the ribeyes. I'll go with a side of creamed spinach, but I suspect Jake is more of a mashed potatoes kind of guy. As I place the order, I make a last-minute decision and tell them not to bring the food for two hours.

Jake emerges from the bathroom minutes later with a towel wrapped around his waist. It's evident he was no doughnut-eating cop in his day.

He catches me looking at him and his friendly smile suggests he's oblivious to the direction my thoughts have taken.

"We need to pick up some clothes," he says.

"Oh, yeah. I forgot about that. I guess I'll dry my things with the blow dryer."

"Excuse my stuff hanging over the shower bar."

I lock myself in the bathroom. Jake's boxer briefs and shirt hang dripping into the tub. I turn the water as hot as it will go. As I lather up, I wish I had a razor to shave my legs. And a tooth brush. And some deodorant. Nothing like living an episode of Survivor in a hotel.

I wrap my hair in a towel and the rest of me in a white, fluffy bathrobe. Then I brush my teeth with soap and my finger.

When I open the bathroom door, Jake is leaning against the headboard, still bare-chested, but in his jeans. He finishes checking something on his phone and looks up.

"Hey, what time is that food coming? I'm starv—"

I silence him with a kiss and straddle his waist. His skin is warm and smells like soap. Through my robe, his strong hands span my hips. He reaches up and guides my face back to his. I have only a second to take in the flash of light-brown M&M eyes before his mouth is on mine. Maybe someday we'll have time for an extended, lingering encounter, but for now it's a series of lightning-quick flashes—fingers trailing on skin, pulling on zippers, tugging on clothes—until we are skin against skin. Electricity pulses through my body and parts of me that felt dead hours ago spring back to life. It's not long before we're staring at the ceiling, gasping for breath.

"Now I'm really hungry," he says.

As if on cue, there's a knock on the door.

"Perfect timing." He pulls on his jeans as I grab for the robe.

Jake tips the room service guy and sends him away. I plop down at the table and uncover the plates, switching them around so Jake has the mashed potatoes and I have the creamed spinach. From a woven basket, I choose a warm roll with caraway seeds and sea salt and spread whipped butter on it. At the first taste, my eyes roll up into my head. Jake stands behind his chair, clearly amused.

"I've been replaced by a dinner roll."

I throw his napkin at him. He catches it with a chuckle and sits down. For the next few minutes, there is no conversation as we savor our medium-rare ribeyes.

"I had you pegged as a vegan. Or a vegetarian, at the least," Jake says.

"I eat a lot of vegetables, but I enjoy a taste of Old MacDonald's farm."

"I eat mostly fish and chicken."

"I figured you for a meat and potatoes guy."

"When I was a kid, my dad had a heart attack and my mom started cooking healthier. My older brother gained a lot of weight after he got married and ended up having a heart attack, too. That's when I got serious."

"Smart. How many brothers and sisters do you have?"

"Two brothers. Frank is older. Tommy's the baby."

I snicker. "So you're the tormented middle child."

Jake laughs. "Nope. I was the most together one. I knew who I was and what I wanted and went after it. I never cared what anyone thought."

"I can sense that."

He raises his eyebrows. "You being sarcastic?"

"Not at all. You definitely seem to have it together. I'd trust my life with you."

"Well, that's good since I'm all you have at the moment."

There's a short pause during which, via mental telepathy, we agree not to venture into that conversation over dinner.

"So, what about you?" he asks.

"What about me?"

"What kind of kid were you?"

For a second, I stop chewing and stare into space. I have some memories, but I'm not sure if they're mine or Emily's. "This is a guess. Probably a nerd, but with a firm grasp of pop culture."

"I'm figuring you're about ten years younger than I am. What kind of music did you listen to?"

"British pop and rock, I think. Radiohead, The Verve, Oasis."

"Huh, that I wouldn't have pictured."

"What about you?" I ask.

"Take a guess."

"Hmmmm. Born in the 70s. Glory days in the late 80s. Either club music or hair bands."

"I was a rock and roll guy. Heavy metal, maybe a hair band or two, if I'm honest." He winks at me.

"Did you ever want to be a musician?"

He chuckles. "As much as any kid, I guess. But Frank followed my dad into the plumbing business and Tommy became a prosecutor. The band broke up before it started."

"A prosecutor, huh? You arrest them and he puts them in jail."

"Something like that."

"When did you know you wanted to be a cop?"

"I never wanted to be a cop. I wanted to be a detective."

"A private investigator?"

"Yeah, but no one was going to hire someone without experience, so after college, I broke my mother's heart and became a cop."

"Where did you go to school?"

"Fordham, BA in Sociology. What about you?"

"Columbia. Undergrad and Grad. Not that it matters. I don't remember any of it."

"Maybe not, but those credentials open doors."

I shrug. "I hope so because I don't know how to be a scientist anymore."

Jake doesn't reassure me. I like that about him. Unlike many people, I prefer cold, hard truth to reassuring platitudes.

And today's truth is "who the hell knows what's going to be?"

We return to a few seconds of regrouping silence to get back on the light track.

"Were you ever married?" I ask. Okay, maybe that wasn't light.

"Once."

For some reason, this surprises me.

"Divorced?"

"Yeah. Didn't make two years. We were young, strong-willed, and as flexible as steel rods."

"Where is she now?"

"Married with four kids. I still see her. We were Frankie's son's godparents. She comes to all the family parties."

"Is that odd?"

"Nah. It's almost as if we were never married. It was so long ago and we were very different people."

"How are you different now?"

"Older, wiser, more understanding. And I know there's no such thing as perfection."

Something about that last bit makes me think about my own life, now far from perfect. Was it ever really? From what I've pieced together, I've spent nearly a decade of long hours in a lab. The few hours I had off I worked out at the gym. There weren't many friends or much socializing. I imagine I kept mostly to myself.

"What are you thinking?"

"Just analyzing what I know about my former life and realizing how far from perfect it was."

"What kept you in it?"

"I think I thought it was perfect. Now, with this hybridized mind, I view it from another perspective. Emily is a social person. I don't think I was."

"As horrible as this situation is, you've found some good in it."

My head jerks in his direction, and I almost lash out that there's nothing good in this, but then I realize his meaning. "It is what it is. I'm not going to kill myself over it."

When our plates are empty, we sit back in our chairs.

"That was good," I say.

Jake puts the tray outside in the hall.

"I need to do some work," he says.

"Do you mind if I watch TV?"

"Not at all."

He settles back down at the table and starts tapping away on his cell phone. I watch the news to see what's happening in a world that doesn't revolve around me. Every once in a while, my gaze returns to Jake. He's intent on whatever he's doing. I suspect it has something to do with my situation, but I don't want to ask. I need tonight off.

Jake types and stares into space. Then he types some more and stares again. This goes on for about twenty minutes. As I watch him, I realize it's comfortable sharing this room with him. I don't feel strange about it. It's as if I've known him a long time. Well, except for the sex part. That was new and exciting. Something inside me knows it won't happen again. It was my "I'm going into battle and may not live to tell about it, and by the way, I'm so freaked out" sex romp. He doesn't have as much riding on the outcome of my case, but I know he understands just what it means to my life. And I also sense he knows what our sexcapade was all about. I don't think he'll be initiating any future contact either. Maybe, when this is all finished...

"Anything good on?" Jake asks.

"Not really. I think I'll turn in."

"Good idea." He yawns and covers his mouth with his fist. I yawn in response and he smiles.

"Long day."

He stands and stretches his arms above his head, making the definition of his muscles that much more pronounced.

I slip out of my robe and slide under the covers. Jake shuts off the lights. In the darkness, I wonder which bed he will choose. Seconds later, he slides in next to me.

"Come here." He maneuvers his arm under me and pulls me in to his chest.

I lie there, staring into the blackness.

"If there were a way to reverse this, would you take the chance and undergo the procedure?" I ask.

"I don't know."

"If they could successfully return my old memories, do you suppose it's possible that what's happened since then might no longer be accessible to me?"

"I don't know."

"I might not remember Emily or the baby. Or you."

"No, I suppose not."

"Would that matter?"

"Only you can answer that, Madison."

I lift my head from his chest and look in the direction I think his face is. "What I meant was, would it matter to you if I didn't remember you?"

The silence seems even longer in the darkness, but then his whisper cuts through.

"Yes."

He wraps his fingers in my hair and pulls my head back down to his chest.

"Get some sleep," he says and brushes his lips across my temple.

# Thirty

The train speeds through the subway tunnels. The nearer Jake and I get to Nathan Brixton's stop, the closer I am to the truth of why Emily and I were used as guinea pigs by the government. My stomach feels sick, but beneath the nervousness, rage simmers.

Earlier this morning, Jake decided the best way to get past the doorman and into Brixton's apartment is to give the name of Brixton's oldest friend. Considering Chadwick has gone underground, we hope his "friend" is intrigued enough to open the door to him.

"What do we do if Brixton doesn't let us in?" I ask.

"I'll lie in wait for the bastard and drag him into an alley the next time he leaves his apartment."

That tells me all I need to know about Jake's mood.

We arrive at the Upper East Side apartment building and the doorman announces Henry Chadwick's arrival to Brixton. There is a pregnant pause. Finally, the doorman says, "Very well, Mr. Brixton." He gestures to the elevator bank and tells us to proceed to the tenth floor. In the elevator, Jake puts on a hat and taps the brim down over his face. When we arrive, I stand out of line of the peephole as he rings the bell and lowers his head so his face can't be seen. As soon as the door opens,

Jake storms in, to Brixton's surprise.

"What the hell is going on?" he shouts, as Jake slams the door.

"We're here to have a nice chat," Jake says. "Just how nice depends on you." Jake gestures to the living room. "After you." Brixton leads us in, casting nervous looks over his shoulder.

His appearance is at odds with the image I conjured up. I pictured someone sinister and dangerous. But this guy has the face of a ferret. Slight in stature, he stands just under five foot seven, but you can tell he's the kind of guy who claims he's five foot nine or ten.

He lowers himself stiffly into a chair. "What's this all about?"

"Do you recognize this lady?" Jake nods in my direction.

Brixton studies my face for a moment. "No, can't say I do."

"I'll give you a hint. You told her secret to whichever government agency you work for."

Brixton's expression moves from confusion to understanding to, unexpectedly, remorse.

"I didn't know. I still don't know."

"You don't know what?" Jake asks.

"What they were doing."

"Let me fill you in. They took two women, each content and successful, and swapped their memories and then placed them in each other's lives."

"Oh, God." Brixton massages his forehead, as if trying to coax some hair to grow, then looks up at me. "But you're well. You seem well."

"Well?"

Brixton flinches at my tone.

"So, what's going on, Nathan?" Jake asks.

"I really don't know much, as I already told—"

"I'll determine how much you know. Let's start at the beginning. What's the purpose of the project and who's behind it?"

Brixton fidgets in his chair and crosses one leg over the

other. "Understand I don't have security clearance for this project, so I don't know as much as you think."

"Every little bit helps. Start talking."

There's no mistaking Jake's growing impatience.

"Rumors circulated that a high-clearance division in my agency was working on strategies against terrorism. The nickname was Project Grey."

"Strategies?" Jake asks. "What kind of strategies?"

"I don't know. I had a sense they were psychological in nature."

"That's all very vague. With so little information, how did you come to recommend two candidates as test subjects?"

"It wasn't as you say. It was a fluke. Someone joked about how they needed a colony of clones to test their work."

"And you knew of a case of successful human cloning."

"Yes. But I didn't know anyone would be harmed."

"And you didn't know they wouldn't," Jake says.

Brixton looks down at the floor.

"Moreover," Jake continues, "you sold out your best friend by revealing a secret he had told only to you."

"I said it in an offhanded way. I didn't know they would take me seriously."

"Obviously, they did."

"Yes. A few weeks later, someone visited my office. He asked questions about the cloning comment. It was obvious he took it all very seriously."

"Name?" Jake says.

"I don't know. I never saw him before and I haven't seen him since."

"Did he threaten you?"

He waits a beat too long before responding.

Jake's chuckle is mirthless. "Oh, that's great. They rewarded you, didn't they?"

Brixton's gaze flitting from side to side confirms it.

"How did it feel to be big man on campus, Nathan?"

For the first time, he makes eye contact with Jake. "It felt good."

In those three defensive words, uttered in a split second, I see the child Nathan Brixton was. Never popular. Never chosen. Never noticed. He felt entitled to the brief recognition he enjoyed. His gaze shifts to me.

"I'm sorry."

He is a pathetic man. He has robbed me not only of my life, but of my rage. But I'm not ready to forgive and forget just yet.

"I didn't disclose the information right away," he says. "Not until they told me about the military men who were sacrificing their lives to volunteer for the experiment."

My heartbeat quickens. "What do you mean sacrificing their lives? Did the experiment kill them?"

"I don't know for sure. I heard they..." He clears his throat. "They weren't the same after the experiment."

"What does that mean?" I ask.

"I don't know. They just said they weren't themselves."

I look up at Jake for the first time during this conversation and his eyes bore into mine. His concern for my welfare is obvious.

"I told them about Chadwick's project, but I think they were hoping for a large colony of clones to test their research," Brixton says.

Colony. If he uses that word one more time, I may strike him. It makes me sound like I'm a dot of *E. coli* on a petri dish.

"In fact, I heard they—"

Brixton suddenly stops speaking.

"What?" Jake asks.

Beads of sweat have broken out on Brixton's brow. He pulls a crisp handkerchief from his pocket and dabs at his forehead.

"What's the problem, Nathan?"

"If I finish that sentence, you'll think even less of me."

"Not possible," Jake says. "Spit it out."

He swallows and his Adam's apple bobs in his skinny neck. "I heard they found another test group."

"Okay," Jake says. "And that disclosure lowers you in my

estimation how?"

Brixton hesitates before continuing. "I don't know who the group is, but they were selected because no one would be the wiser if the experiments failed."

"How do you live with yourself?" I ask.

"There are people much worse than me."

I throw up my hands. I'm wasting my breath. "Who do you think the group might be?"

He shakes his head. "I have no idea. Much of what I know is through the rumor mill. It's vague at best."

Jake blows out his breath and rakes his fingers through his hair. "We're done for now," he says to me. "Got any vacations planned, Brixton?"

"No, why do you ask?"

"Because I need you here in case I have more questions. Got it?"

"Yes."

"Good."

As I step out into the hallway, Jake turns back toward Nathan. "I don't know how Henry ever gave you the time of day. You couldn't shine his shoes. Even after my opinion of him took a nose dive in the last twenty-four hours."

# Thirty-one

Jake and I sit at a restaurant on MacDougal Street in Soho, eating small plates of falafel, hummus, and roasted beets with goat cheese croutons. I guess you'd call this hiding in plain sight. Through the window, the hustle and bustle of the City appears as a collage of black and white and color photographs. The locals hurry by in their monotone neutrals, camouflaged against the drab buildings and streets. The tourists mosey along in bright outerwear, heads bobbing this way and that to absorb the sights. I need a night to be anonymous in the crowd, safe, eating Mid-Eastern comfort food. I scoop up some hummus on a wedge of warm pita bread.

"How are you holding up?" Jake asks.

"I'm okay, all things considered."

Jake nods. "Good."

"Let's brainstorm a bit," I say. "Who could you perform psychological experiments on and if they failed, no one would notice?"

"The insane." Jake responds so quickly, it's obvious he's been pondering the same question.

"So, they kidnap patients from an asylum and that goes unnoticed? What about their families? Don't they question where they've gone?"

"Maybe the tests aren't that long. If a family member visits, they're told the patient is with a doctor."

I consider this, but I'm not convinced.

"What about the criminally insane?" Jake says. "Incarcerated. Maybe the family has given up on them. No one cares."

"That's better, but something still doesn't make sense. These people may be insane in unpredictable and varied ways. That taints the pool. How do you know your experiment is working when you're not sure what normal is for each person?"

Jake swallows a sip of beer. "Good point." He stares into space a moment. "Children in the foster care system. Orphanages."

"Oh, God. I can't even think of that."

"I know. It's gruesome."

"But if this is an experiment, you need more than just a few, isolated people. Brixton kept using the term 'colony.' That points to the need for large groups of people. Large groups of missing kids would raise a red flag, don't you think?"

"What if it were designed as an activity they did with the kids, or a field trip?"

"There would be chaperones. They wouldn't send kids off alone."

I take a bite of falafel and sigh, momentarily distracted by ordinary chickpeas turned into this fried ball of heaven. Suddenly, it hits me.

"Undocumented immigrants!"

Jake's eyes widen. He nods slowly. I can almost see the gears turning in his head.

"That's good. Untraceable. Friends or relatives who might care can't come forward because they're also undocumented or fearful they'll get thrown in jail." Victory is written on his face, but it slowly seeps away when he sees mine. "What's wrong?"

"Where do we start? It's impossible." I say.

"It seems like a needle in a haystack, but it's the best lead we've got." He smiles. "Eat up. We can't afford to get burned out."

A half hour later, bellies full, we walk north on MacDougal. The wind has whipped up and with each breath of air, my nasal passages feel like they've gone into deep freeze. I huddle in my jacket and put my face down to avoid the wind.

We cross West Houston. A homeless man sits against the foundation of a brick building, the smell of pizza wafting through the door. He's absolutely still, wearing a thin, wool coat and a wool hat. Jake hands him a twenty dollar bill.

"Stay warm."

"Thank you, sir. God bless."

My eyes tear up, unrelated to the whipping wind. I'm pretty sure I've gone through my former New York existence immune to such sights. Suddenly, I'm moved by this man. Maybe it's because I'm feeling alone and isolated. Maybe it's Emily's goodness seeping through. I'm not sure, but a part of me has unfolded, broadening my vision, taking me from my head, where I've spent most of my life, to my heart. Is this what they call an epiphany?

We cross Sixth Avenue. I step up on the curb and stop.

"What's wrong?" Jake asks.

"The homeless." The words ride a quick, shallow breath.

Jake's face registers surprise. "Shit." He grabs my hand and we race back across Sixth Avenue, just as the light changes. Horns honk and cars stop short. Damn New York drama queens.

When the homeless guy sees us fast approaching, his eyes widen a bit, maybe thinking Jake has come back to get some change on his donation.

"Sorry to bother you," Jake says. We just realized you might be able to help us."

The man nods slowly. "What can I do for you?"

"Have you heard about any homeless people going missing? People you usually see who maybe you haven't seen in a while?"

The man stares past us for what seems like an eternity, but Jake patiently waits for him to speak.

"Seems I've heard something like that. Gotta be honest though. I stay by myself. I don't hear a lot of talk like you do in the encampments."

Jake nods. "What did you hear?"

The man stares out into the distance again.

"It was at the soup kitchen downtown. I overheard the guy who runs it say a patron was upset about something like that. I didn't hear it first hand, but if you go down there, you can ask him. He's a decent guy. Puts out a nice spread."

When Jake hears the name of the place, recognition flashes across his face. I assume from his police days.

"Thank you, sir. You've just given us our first solid lead," Jake says and extends his hand.

The man stares at it for a second, his hesitation revealing how long it's been since someone wanted to shake his hand. He takes Jake's hand in his and pumps it once up and down.

"Have a good night, now," he says.

A good night? It's freezing cold. How the heck will this guy survive on the street?

"You, too, and thank you for your trouble," Jake says and hands him another rolled bill.

We retrace our steps and cross Sixth Avenue again. My emotions get the best of me. I struggle to hide it, but a sniffle gives me away.

Jake puts his arm around my shoulder and pulls me closer as we walk back to the hotel.

# Thirty-two

Though the offices are officially closed for the New Year's holiday, Jeremy commutes in to meet Reynold. Turner's phone call worried him, and he needs to see for himself the state he's in.

The project is taking its toll on everyone. Stephanie has been silent since Friday night. They've had their differences before and retreated to their sides of the ring for cooling off periods, but this is different. What he's feeling from her isn't quiet anger. It's more like indifference, as if she's made a final decision about their relationship and has moved on emotionally.

On Saturday, she took the kids to an afternoon movie. She informed him of her plans. "I'm taking the kids to the movies." Didn't invite him. "We'll be back in a few hours." Then turned and walked out of the kitchen.

He sat home all afternoon, his feet on the cocktail table, his cell phone in rare silent mode. He stared at the wall, not bothering to turn on the TV. He was going to lose his wife over this project. And his kids. Maybe even his soul. Yet, the panic that arose from these thoughts was not enough to make him back down. Rather, it strengthened his resolve. What he was doing was for the good of the American people. Wasn't it?

Jeremy hears the security door click open and shut. Reynold appears in the doorway and lowers himself into a chair, nodding once in greeting.

Jeremy can't help feeling this uncharacteristic wordlessness is a subconscious form of energy conservation. Reynold was never a man of many words, but used enough in the name of politeness. Jeremy doesn't waste any time broaching his topic.

"I'm concerned about you."

Reynold doesn't respond. There's not even a raised eyebrow of surprise as a response. He seems completely numb.

"How are things going with Turner?" Jeremy winces as soon as he says the words. He's not supposed to know they're still together against his orders. But Reynold, in his altered state, doesn't realize the misstep.

"Well enough."

"You don't seem like yourself. Is the project getting to you?"

"It weighs on me."

"How so?"

"I don't see it ending well."

"Why do you say that?"

"They're no closer to reversing the process to save the military guys."

"Give them time."

"Best case scenario, they figure out how to do it. The SEALS go back to their families."

"That's the goal, Reynold."

"What happens to the civilian subjects? We can't very well reverse their memories and put them back out into the world. Not if there's a chance they remember what's been done to them. Against their will."

Jeremy nods solemnly as his stomach clenches at Reynold's last three words.

"You've put me in charge of operations, but I have no authority over your interrogator. Does anyone have authority over him? He's a fucking loose cannon, assassinating innocent people when he decides they're not useful."

Jeremy tenses at the word assassinating. He feels the rage seeping out of Reynold. Maybe that's for the best, he thinks. Let him get it out.

"Has that happened again since you showed me the video?"

"I don't know. I stopped watching those videos. If I can't change it, I don't want to know."

Jeremy taps his lip with the end of a pen. "Maybe we can return the subjects to their lives after the project ends. Even if they talked, most people wouldn't believe them anyway. They'd chalk it up to mental illness."

"They're not all mentally ill."

"I know, but that's the perception of many people."

"I think it's risky."

"You're arguing against yourself, Reynold."

"That's because it's a no-win situation. We're fucked. Heads are going to roll on this one, Jeremy. Mine for sure, maybe even yours."

Jeremy chews his cheek and tastes the metallic tang of blood. "Times are tough. Life as we know it is being jeopardized by a crazy few. There's going to be some collateral damage in the war on terror. There has to be."

"Performing mind experiments on innocent people without their permission has nothing to do with collateral damage, Jeremy. It's just easier to tell yourself that."

Jeremy feels a combination of anger and defensiveness rising up in himself but mentally tamps it down. This is not the time to pull rank with Reynold in this state.

"And what about Trina?" Reynold asks. "What the hell is she working on that's classified? Is it worse than what I'm doing? Because I gotta tell you, I've become a bit obsessed wondering about the blood that's on her hands while she walks around cool as a cucumber."

A fleck of spit flies from Reynold's lips into the air between them.

"It's not like that. I told everyone their piece was classified to protect the security of yours."

Reynold nods and Jeremy notes a hint of relief in his

demeanor. He considers bringing Turner into the equation to support Reynold. He regrets not putting her in charge of the project in the first place. She would have done the job without complaint.

"Should we bring Turner in on this?"

Reynold's head jerks up and he stares at Jeremy, his eyes blazing. "Is that your idea of damage control?"

Jeremy knows he must tread lightly here. He's lost control of Reynold. Perceived insult might put him over the edge.

"Not in the way you're assuming. I agree with you that this is a big fuck-up, but if we don't fix it, all of our heads will roll. Best case scenario if that happens, they cover it up and we get demoted or fired and find jobs out in the world. Worst case scenario, we become the scapegoats and our names are publicized. Our families are shamed and threatened."

Jeremy sees he's getting through.

"Bringing Turner in would be an all-hands-on-deck strategy."

Reynold considers this quietly.

"No. Let's leave it as is for now. I'm not sure she would hold up any better if she knew what I'm doing."

Jeremy doubts that, but if it bolsters Reynold's confidence, he'll go along with it.

"Did you always know your purpose in life growing up?" Jeremy asks him.

"Pretty much. To serve and protect."

Jeremy chuckles. "Maybe you should've been a cop."

"I considered it, but it wasn't big enough for me. I wanted to do something on a grander scale."

Jeremy maintains his poker face even though this response works in his favor.

"You're doing that, Reynold. You're not helping a mugging victim or reuniting a lost child with his mother in a park. You're protecting over 300 million people from an enemy so vile, we'd be better off if they blew us up than if they took control of our country. Unfortunately, some people will sacrifice their lives in the fight."

Reynold stares into space.

"Do you think everyone has a purpose in life?" Jeremy asks.

Reynold considers the question a moment.

"Yes. Though some people's poor choices make it difficult to see sometimes."

Jeremy nods. "What do you suppose the purpose of those homeless people are?"

"I don't know."

"Maybe it's to sacrifice themselves for the welfare of their country. Civilian soldiers. You know?"

"But they haven't been given the choice."

"Neither have drafted soldiers. Sometimes we find ourselves in dire situations and we just have to suck it up and do the best we can. This is one of those times, Reynold. We can only hope that in hindsight we see the good we've done."

They sit quietly, reflecting on Jeremy's sermon. Finally, Reynold rises. Jeremy walks around his desk and pats his arm. "Reach out if you need to talk. I know it's tough. We're in the trenches together."

After Reynold leaves, Jeremy leans back in his chair and lets out a long, slow breath. He stares at the ceiling and does a self-reality check. *We're kidnapping, torturing, and killing innocent civilians. Am I okay with that? No. We're doing it in the name of national security. Am I okay with that?* He thinks his answer to that should be yes. Part of him wants it to be yes. After all, it's been his philosophy, his mission, something he's dedicated his life to.

If he's being honest with himself, he's not okay with it. But he'll keep going—take it to the bitter end. It's the only way now. His reputation, his life, and the well-being of his family depend on his digging them out of the hole they're in. In the end, his survival and that of his family are of higher importance than a group of unstable people living on the street. If he's being honest.

# Thirty-three

Jake and I blend into the pre-blizzard flurry of activity as we trudge to the soup kitchen downtown. Pedestrians hurry past us, either to the grocery store to buy the requisite bread and milk or home to hunker down. The weather channel predicts at least eight inches of snow. A good coating is already underfoot and it's only 1 p.m. The guy we spoke to on the phone said they'll extend lunch hours and serve a hot meal, but dinner is cancelled due to the blizzard.

A few blocks before the soup kitchen, my Emily phone rings and it brings a smile to my face, but not for long.

"Madison, the baby is sick."

I stop short on the street. "What happened?" Jake walks a few steps more and then pivots quickly when he hears my tone.

"I don't know. She was sluggish and pale. She wouldn't eat. I thought she had a bluish cast to her lips. We rushed her to the hospital and she needed a blood transfusion."

"Oh my God."

"Brad was going to donate blood because I nearly passed out at the thought."

I remember the childhood memory of how my—no Emily's—fear of blood started. I remember Susan's reaction to my performing the cricothyrotomy on Gargiulo, knowing of my phobia of blood. It all makes sense now. It was Emily's memories, not the memories of a scientist who would be very unlikely to be afraid of blood.

"But he wasn't a match, so I had to do it."

"Oh, Emily, are you okay?"

"Yeah, yeah, I'm okay. And Amanda is doing better. She's still in the hospital. I'm here with her now. They're releasing her later today."

I hear the panic in her voice. Her speech is fast and frantic.

"Did they say what's wrong with her?"

"They don't know. They'll continue to monitor her. I have to bring her back next week for some more tests."

"I'll figure out a way to get out there."

"No! It's too dangerous. I just wanted to let you know...and to hear your voice. I feel closer to you than with the people I've supposedly known my entire life," she says.

The sadness in her voice squeezes my heart.

"I know, Emily. I feel the same way. Jake and I are about to check out a lead. I'm determined to figure this out. We'll find a way to fix all of this."

"If anyone can, you will. Let me know how it goes."

"Okay. And give that baby a hug for me. I'll be in touch soon."

I hang up and meet Jake's expectant gaze.

"What's happening?"

I relate the story as we walk the final blocks to the soup kitchen.

When we arrive, we stomp the snow from our shoes and I unwind the cheap scarf I bought from a street vendor from my neck. A line of people, mostly men, waits for food. Six smiling people chat with the people in line while they dish up generous portions. One of the men sees us, sets down his serving spoon, and hurries over.

"You made it," he says with a smile, wiping his hands on his apron and then extending one in greeting. "I didn't know if the weather would stop you. I'm Ray Daniels."

We introduce ourselves.

"You have a nice place here," I say.

"Yes, we do. We've been here five years and most of our patrons are regulars."

He motions for us to follow him behind the food tables. "We get a lot of donations and our claim to fame is fresh food. No canned vegetables here," he says, pointing to the trays. "Today we have stewed zucchini and steamed broccoli with an optional lemon-butter sauce for dipping." He continues down the row. "Saffron rice. Loin of pork. And for those who don't eat meat, baked tilapia."

"It looks and smells wonderful," I say.

At the end of the line is a table full of desserts.

"Chocolate brownies and shortbread cookies," Ray says proudly. "And this is Mary, our chef."

A chubby woman turns toward us with a deep-dimpled smile. "Pleased to meet you. Can I make you a dish?"

"No, thank you," I say. "We're here on business."

At that, Ray leads us across the room to a table away from the crowd. "So what can I do for you?"

"I'm a former NYPD Detective and now a private investigator. We were wondering if you've noticed anything odd in your dealings with the homeless," Jake says.

"Such as?"

"Have regulars stopped showing up? Or have you heard stories about people disappearing?"

Ray leans forward. "Disappearing? What exactly is happening?"

"We're not sure. We're following our guts at the moment, but the trail has led to you."

Just then, the door opens and a man walks in, loudly babbling at a frenetic pace. Ray's eyes widen and he jumps up from his chair.

"Wait here a moment." He rushes over to the man. "James. So glad you made it in. Mary, would you make James a plate? I have some friends I want him to meet." With that, he leads James by the elbow over to us.

"This is my friend James. It just occurred to me he's been telling us a story similar to the one you're asking about. James, these people are interested in hearing about your friends who went for a ride."

James's face breaks into the brightest smile I've ever seen. Ray pulls out a chair for him, and James falls heavily into it, though he is not a large man.

"Did you have some friends who went for a ride, too?" he asks Jake in a childlike tone.

"It's possible. Tell me about your friends."

"They were living down by the piers. They built the best fires. I think that's why they were chosen. I build fires, too, to keep warm, you know? But my fires ain't like their fires. Theirs are bright and tall." He raises his arm to demonstrate the height of the flames. "Sometimes we cook hot dogs on sticks in the fire. And once, one of them bought a bag of marshmallows to toast for some kids who was staying with us."

"So, when did your friends leave?" Jake asks.

"They been leaving. Every week. When they get picked to go."

Jake glances at me with raised eyebrows.

"Who do they go with?"

"The ducks. The ducks take them. I really want to go with the ducks. I gotta make my fire bigger. If I get a better fire, maybe then they gonna take me."

My heart drops when I realize I'm listening to the ranting of someone who is not psychologically sound. I thought we were onto something. Jake looks defeated as well.

"Which pier do the ducks come to?" Jake asks.

"Down by the old seaport. Every week. Maybe tonight. The snow won't bother the ducks. They know how to float."

Mary places a heaping plate of food in front of James. "Bon appétit," she says.

Jake stands and I follow his lead. "Thank you very much, James, for telling us your story," he says.

"My pleasure, sir. My pleasure. Mmmm mmmm, Mary, this is some good food," he says, his focus locked onto his plate, chewing with gusto.

Ray walks us toward the door. "Obviously, James has some psychological issues. He's been obsessed with this story. Tells it every chance he gets."

"How long has this been going on?" I ask.

Ray thinks for a moment. "I'd say about a month. Maybe a month and a half."

"And before that, nothing?"

"Nothing like that. No. He does do a fair bit of talking but it's usually the same stuff."

"And you haven't noticed anyone missing?"

"Not amongst our regulars. Hmmm, actually, except for Pete, but some of the others mentioned he decided to settle with another community."

Jake and I sigh at the same time. "Thank you for your time."

"Sorry I couldn't be more help."

"It's okay. It was a long shot. If you hear anything, give me a call," Jake says, handing him a card.

"Will do. Happy New Year."

Only then do I realize it's New Year's Eve. A New Year's Eve I will never forget.

# Thirty-four

After our meeting at the soup kitchen, Jake and I grabbed a bite to eat and headed back to the hotel for a power nap in preparation for our stakeout. While we slept, the snow piled up and continues to fall. Neither of us has the proper clothes for a night outside in this weather, but the people we're going to surveil don't either. It really makes you think...and stop whining, which, in my defense, I've done only quietly to myself.

Within a block of the piers, we smell the smoke from the fires and see the glow.

"Part of me wishes we could cozy up next to the master fire builders and roast some marshmallows," I say, shivering.

Jake smiles. "I'll take you camping when this is all over."

We stop for a moment as Jake scans the area. "You've just given me an idea. It's a large area to monitor, so we should focus on the people near the fires, near the perimeter."

We find a sheltered spot in front of a deli that is open only during working hours. Too bad. A cup of hot tea would be nice. Jake drags bundled cardboard from a garbage pile. He sweeps away the snow and places it on the sidewalk, insulating us from the cold pavement. We huddle side-by-side and wait.

Jake leans toward me, "So an elephant walks into a bar..."

I chuckle, appreciative of his attempt at lightness, but can't stay in the moment. "What do you think we'll find here?"

"I don't know. Maybe nothing. The weather might not help us. Then again, maybe it will. Hard to tell since we don't know what's happening."

"My mind is stuck in an endless loop of a flock of ducks swooping down and carrying away homeless people."

"I'm pretty sure that won't happen."

"Oh, I don't know..." I say, "Sometimes the craziest things are based in reality. Folk remedies, urban legends..."

Jake shrugs. As his shoulders rise and fall, I lean in and rest my head against him. He, in turn, rests his head on mine. We sit, watching the snow fall, entranced by the tiny, dense snowflakes. Visibility decreases by the minute. The weather channel's predictions were too conservative.

My mind drifts to the conversation earlier today with Emily. I wonder how the baby is doing. Why would she need a blood transfusion? My heart feels heavy thinking about how worried and scared Emily must have been when she was giving blood. Maybe tomorrow I will don my disguise and visit her.

I squirm to get comfortable, the cardboard no longer providing much insulation from the cold sidewalk. "What I wouldn't do for a cup of steaming tea."

A barely perceptible grin graces Jake's lips. At first, I think he is mocking me, but then he unzips his knapsack and pulls out a thermos. "Hot tea." He reaches back into his knapsack and pulls out several small packages. "And cookies."

I rip open a package of Lorna Doones while he pours tea into the plastic thermos cup.

"I feel like I should say one lump or two, but there's no sugar...or milk, for that matter."

"Fine with me. I don't take either." I nibble my cookie and sip my tea. We sit cross-legged facing each other, easy and comfortable in the silence.

As if reading my mind, Jake says, "I feel like I've known you forever rather than just a couple of days. "

"I was thinking the same thing."

"I wish we'd met under better circumstances."

"If not for these circumstances, our paths wouldn't have crossed. I don't think I got out much in my former life."

"You're probably right. I lead a pretty solitary existence myself, immersed in whatever case I'm working." He sips his tea. "I'd like to change that." Our eyes meet. The words are innocent enough, but I know what he really means.

I lean forward and kiss his lips, just once. No passionate lip lock. No unbridled lust. Just my impromptu version of a handshake after a deal is struck. A promise we will give this a chance when the nightmare has ended. If the nightmare ends.

In the distance, a set of headlights appears. Jake turns to look. A vehicle approaches the homeless community. I squint to see through the dense snowfall. An excited shout rises like smoke from the fire, "The ducks, the ducks."

"Oh my God. It's James." I am about to jump up, but Jake reaches over and holds me in place.

The vehicle pulls up in front of the main row of fires.

"Holy shit," Jake mutters.

"What is that?" I ask, confused by the odd-looking vehicle.

"It's a duck."

"What?"

"A duck. D-U-K-W. An amphibious vehicle. It can drive right into the water and float. They were used by the military in World War II."

Confusion and terror build inside of me.

"You were right about there being a bit of truth in even the craziest story. James knew what he was talking about," Jake says.

Two men climb out of the vehicle and approach the people crowded near the fire. It feels like an eternity as we watch them talk quietly. A group of people begins boarding the bus. It looks like mostly men, but then a child steps out from behind a bundled figure. My stomach lurches, my protective instincts kicking in. I struggle to stand and, once again, Jake draws me back down.

"Not yet." He repacks his knapsack and slings it onto his

back. As the vehicle drives off, he pulls me to my feet and we head toward the fires. "We're friends of James," he says to a younger man. He told us about the duck. Do you know where those people are being taken?"

"Don't know the exact location, but it's a shelter. They'll get a warm bed and a hot meal."

"Have you ever been there?" Jake asks.

"Nah, I like being outdoors on my own. It must be pretty comfortable though. No one ever comes back here to sleep."

I feel adrenaline pump through my body. *No one ever comes back!* "I saw a woman and child leave on the bus."

"Yes, ma'am. Edie and her son Jimmy. They've been here a few weeks. A relative was supposed to come get them, but he never showed up. Jimmy'll be better off at the shelter."

I scream a silent "No" as I scan the crowd. "Can we speak to James?"

"You just missed him. He got on the bus."

My breath whooshes out of me. Jake thanks him for the information and we race after the vehicle, if race is the proper word for trudging through several inches of snow.

"Are you okay?" he asks.

I nod, but can't hide my panting.

At the first cross street, we round the corner.

"Let's stay along the river," Jake says. "The only reason to use a DUKW is because you plan to travel on land and water."

I point to the street. "There's not much traffic out because of the weather. Those are probably their tracks."

Jake squeezes my hand. We follow the trail as far as we can before it is covered in snow.

What was once a tourist attraction is now dark and desolate. Businesses have heeded the mayor's warnings and closed early.

"Maybe they're not covered. Maybe this is where they end," Jake says.

We walk onto the pier and stare out at the dark river. Jake reaches into his bag of tricks and pulls out hi-tech goggles.

"Night vision," he says. He scans the river. "I've got them."

I follow his gaze but can't see a thing.

"Son of a gun. Governors Island. They're headed to Governors Island."

# Thirty-five

The day after witnessing James and his homeless friends taken away by amphibious vehicle, Jake acquires a small motor boat through some old contact. By the dim light of a crescent moon, we make our way to Governors Island.

"As a native New Yorker, I'm ashamed to say I have no idea what Governors Island is," I say, the frigid wind nipping at my cheeks as we fly down the East river.

"The Continental Army set up defenses there against the British in 1776 during the American Revolution. Later, it became an army post. There's an old fort there and officer homes. They've been converting it to public park grounds the past few years."

Jake pulls the boat up to a pier and secures it. We keep to the shadows as we make our way past a huge sign that says Soissons Landing. There's not a soul in sight. An eeriness surrounds us.

We trudge through the snow, looking for signs of life. We pass pale yellow, historic homes, no doubt officer housing. However, it's like a ghost town. In the distance, we see lights and make our way to a row of brick, Georgian Revival barracks. Two DUKW vehicles are parked across from the structure and there's a guy taking a cigarette break.

"We're in the right place," Jake whispers.

As if on cue, a loud, shriek makes the peach fuzz on my arms stand on end.

"What the heck was that?"

Jake's face is grim. "The sound of a human being in a lot of pain."

My legs tremble and I grab his arm for a second, afraid I'll fall.

"Are you okay?"

"Yeah."

Jake fiddles with the buttons on his phone. "I'm shutting off the flash on the camera. We can't give ourselves away."

I take the phone from him. "I'll photograph and record. You keep that gun handy."

We round the building, looking for a place to peer in. Several of the windows have small cracks in them but there is nothing to see. We keep on until we hear that horrible sound again from behind a row of windows. It takes my breath away. My fingers trail over the windows looking for any breach in the thick, black paint that covers them. I finally find one. It's tiny, but large enough to put the eye of the camera. I position the camera on video setting and we watch the screen.

A man sits shackled to a chair, his face so bruised and swollen, I'm not sure I'd recognize it as a human head if I saw it out of context. A guy with a crew cut stands in front of him and whacks the man with a short pipe.

"Jake, we have to do something."

"Keep recording."

I turn to look at him.

"If we get ourselves killed, we can't help anyone," he says.

I know he's right, but to stand by and watch this horror is the hardest thing I've ever done. It's difficult to hear the questions the guy with the pipe asks unless he shouts over the screams. Even then, it's hard to understand what is happening.

I continue taking short bursts of video as evidence. Finally, the shackled man is taken away and the guy with the pipe sips from a can of Coke and jokes with another guy who has entered the room. Who are these people? Do they casually cast off the evil of the day when they go home to their families at night? As my mind questions their motivations, another victim is wheeled in. I gasp when I realize it is James.

"Oh, no," Jake whispers.

James's brilliant smile has disappeared. He swivels his head left and right, not sure of where he is. He shakes the chains on his wrists.

"What are you doing?" he screams. "Let me out!"

My heart clenches in my chest. "Maybe we should call the police."

"Madison." Jake grabs my arm and shakes me. "We're not dealing with petty thieves, here. These are dangerous people. They'll just shut down tight, kill all their victims, and go underground."

James makes such a racket, we can hear the torturer's shouted questions. He asks James about people with Arabic-sounding names from Middle Eastern countries.

James sobs. "I don't know! I don't know what you mean."

The guy swings the pipe, hitting James in the mouth. He screams and spits out a spray of blood. The guy accuses him of planning some attack. It's clear James doesn't have the faculties to mastermind a terrorist plot. What are they thinking?

"Nooooo! Take me back to the fire," James cries. "I want to see my friends."

"Did you do the transfer on this guy?" the interrogator shouts to someone behind him. "I don't think it worked."

And then, just like that, he pulls out a gun and shoots James through the head.

I fall back in the snow, stunned by the cold-hearted efficiency of this man who no longer needs James. Puffs of steamy breath explode from my mouth into the cold, night air.

Jake helps me up and pulls me into his arms. Neither of us speaks. They drag James's bleeding body across the floor like a bag of garbage. Tears roll down my frozen cheeks.

"We've got enough," Jake says. "Let's go."

We make our way along the length of the building, keeping

to the shadows. Jake looks around the corner to be sure the smoker is no longer outside. Then he motions for me to follow. The stretch of open field seems wider than before. Our dark forms will contrast with the iridescent snow making us perfect shooting targets.

The crunch of snow underfoot draws my focus away from my racing heart and begins to hypnotize me. I find myself counting off each step in my head and trying to synchronize the white puffs of my breath with Jake's. This wave of obsessive-compulsiveness soothes.

"Hey!"

Step forty-nine. We twirl around. A guy strides toward us. Jake grabs my hand and we run.

"Hey, come back here," the guy shouts, and then "We've got company."

Someone else yells, "What the fuck?"

I glance back again and see two guys chasing us.

"Don't look. Just run," Jake says.

My lungs burn from frozen, dry air and my legs ache. But I forget all that at the sound of the first gun shot.

"Fuck," Jake says. We take cover behind the yellow house we passed on the way in.

I press my back against the siding, panting, exhausted, and then double over as I try to catch my breath.

"You okay?" Jake pulls out his gun and peeks around the corner.

I nod.

"We can't hide. They'll follow our tracks in the snow," he says.

"Don't we have to cross their path to get to the boat?" I ask.

"We'll circle this house. As soon as they clear it, we can cross behind them. You ready?"

"Yeah."

We creep around the house and wait at the front corner until they follow our tracks around the other side. Once they are out of view, we take off toward the pier. We're almost to safety when we see the beam of headlights racing toward us. Gunshots ring out. I can't tell if they're coming from the guys on foot or in the jeep. We cross the landing and run down the incline to the pier. Jake grabs the rope and unties it.

"Get into the boat and lie down."

I don't need to be told twice. I have never been more scared in my life.

Jake jumps in and pulls away as a guy runs to the edge of the pier, shooting at us. Jake lifts his gun and fires one shot. The guy yelps and falls to the ground. A second guy runs up and crouches over him.

Jake navigates the boat up the East River. We race against the freezing wind, thankful we managed to escape getting shot, but there's no escaping the horror in our wake.

***

It's after midnight, but there will be no sleeping tonight. Jake leans close to the laptop, viewing the video footage he uploaded from the camera.

"How did it turn out?"

"Good enough. It can probably be enhanced," he says, not looking up.

I stand behind him and he restarts the video. The sound quality is not that good. It's almost impossible to hear what the homeless men are saying, but their screams raise huge goose bumps on my skin. When the interrogator shouts over them, we hear his questions. He asks the first man about his relationship with the person with the Arabic-sounding name. He inquires about his whereabouts during certain time periods. And then, the big question. Does he have any knowledge of plans for terrorist attacks against Americans?

The homeless man is as bewildered as James was. He shakes his head furiously from side to side. I watch as he is led out and the interrogator waits and jokes with his buddy. Then James is led in.

I can't bear to watch it again, but I know I have to.

I hear Jake's whispered "Oh, no" when he realized it was James in the chair.

My eyes fill with tears at James's confusion and panic. Some of the audio is lost because of my pleading with Jake to do something.

And then I hear the interrogator's words again, "Did you do the transfer on this guy? I don't think it worked."

The gunshot is loud. It startles me just as it did the first time. I jump and let out a high-pitched bark even though I knew it was coming.

Jake wraps his arm around my waist, stroking my back, but my brain has made a connection and I back away, my heart pounding in my chest.

"What's wrong?"

"Brixton said it was some kind of project against terrorism. We assumed they were doing something to alleged terrorists. We were only half right."

"How so?"

"Why would they think random homeless people had any connection to terrorism? It doesn't make sense, right?"

"Not at all," Jake says.

"But then, when that guy isn't getting the answers he wants, he asks if the transfer was done on James. The transfer. Memory transfer. They've transferred the memories from the terrorists to these homeless men and they're trying to torture the information out of them."

Jake lets out a low whistle. "That's inspired, Madison. They take an uncooperative prisoner's memories and implant them into a person who doesn't have the inclination to die for their faith and then torture them into confiding what they know."

"It doesn't seem to be working," I say, shuddering again at what they did to James.

"Not in getting them to reveal the secrets, but from what Brixton said, the memory transfer may have worked a bit too well. Those military guys couldn't be returned to their former selves."

"So, we've got U.S. military guys walking around with the

minds of terrorists." My mind plays with that thought and jumps to another. Emily is a sweet, kind woman, but what if she weren't. Who would I be right now? If the memories of someone like Hitler had been transferred into my brain, what then?

Jake meets my gaze. Something is on his mind.

"What are you thinking?"

"I'm just wondering what role you and Emily play in all of this."

The fear bubbles up, but then logic prevails. "We both have families that would miss us if we didn't return. I don't think we're intended for the same fate. What Brixton said is probably true. When they found out we existed, they said why not. Let's see if the memory swap is so seamless, their own families don't realize they've been switched."

Jake nods slowly, wanting to believe my words.

"You don't seem convinced."

"For now, I think you're probably right. What worries me are the experiments they'll think up in the future. Your existence is just too seductive to crazy minds like that.

# Thirty-six

Jeremy pours himself a cup of burnt-smelling coffee in the office kitchenette, his cell phone held to his ear.

"Do you know what day it is, Jeremy?" Stephanie asks.

Jeremy can tell by her tone this is a trick question, but there's no time to solve it.

"Wednesday," he says.

"That's right. Wednesday. So we got off the train and you kissed me goodbye and walked off to work."

"Okay," he says as he walks toward his office.

"Wednesday, Jeremy. What do we do on Wednesdays?"

And then it hits him—their ritual of having breakfast together at their favorite café. "Damn. I completely forgot. And judging by the smell of the coffee I just poured myself, I'm being punished for it."

"Caffeinated karma," she says without humor.

The line goes silent. For a moment, he thinks the call has been dropped.

"I want us to go for counseling."

Before Jeremy can respond, the security door opens and a disheveled Reynold storms in with a frantic air Jeremy has never witnessed.

"I gotta go." He disconnects the call, wincing as he finally processes what her last words were. He'll explain later. As much as he can.

Reynold rounds the corner into Jeremy's office and pops back out, scanning the rest of the area. When he sees Jeremy, he exhales and his body seems to shrink two inches.

"Go in," Jeremy says and follows him.

"We've got a problem," Reynold says, his voice breathy as if he's panting. "Two people were on the island last night."

"I don't understand."

"Trespassers on Governors Island."

Jeremy's eyes widen. "How'd they get on?"

"Motorboat. They were snooping around outside the compound. We're fucked."

Reynold runs his fingers through his hair and blows out his breath. His right leg jiggles up and down like he's having a seizure. "Someone found out what we're doing over there. I know it."

"Hold on a minute. Is it possible it was just kids having fun? A place to hang out and drink?"

"It wasn't kids. It was a man and a woman."

"Okay, so maybe a place to screw around. Lots of houses at their disposal."

"No. A bunch of guys went after them. There was a shootout."

"A shootout? You mean our guys shooting at them?"

"They shot back. Got Vasquez in the side."

"Shit."

"Somebody found out, Jeremy. They're coming after us." Reynold jumps out of his chair and starts pacing. "We're finished. Our careers are over. We're probably going to jail."

"Reynold, calm down!" Jeremy says, although he is far from calm himself. "There could be a hundred explanations. Maybe drug dealers looking for a place to store some inventory."

Reynold grabs Jeremy's laptop and logs in. He accesses a site and turns the laptop so they can both view the screen.

"This is from the security footage."

Jeremy watches as the couple comes into view. They are

bundled up in coats, hats, and scarves. They stop and exchange some words, then walk along the perimeter of the building, poking at the boarded-up windows.

"What are they doing?" Jeremy asks.

"They're looking for an opening to see in."

Jeremy continues watching. They eventually stop. The woman has something in her hand, but then they lean in to the building and the top halves of their bodies are hidden in the indentation of the window. For a while, nothing happens. Jeremy, impatient to know the ending, is about to ask Reynold for a spoiler when the woman's body flies back and lands in the snow.

"What the hell? What just happened?"

Reynold accesses another file. "This just happened."

Jeremy watches footage from a different camera. This time it's the inside of the building. A man lies on the floor as Jeremy's operatives kick him and then shoot him in cold blood.

"Jesus Christ. You think they saw that?"

"No doubt."

Reynold switches back to the original footage. A few moments later, the couple stalk away and move out of frame.

"What happened next?"

"They were spotted on their way back to Soissons Landing. Two of our guys followed on foot and called for assistance. Vasquez and another guy made it to the pier in a jeep. Vasquez got off a few shots, but they returned fire and hit him."

"How is he?" Jeremy asks.

"Just a flesh wound. He's okay."

"Go back to where they approach the building. Can we get a still of their faces and have the lab blow it up?"

Reynold sits back down and fiddles with the controls, zooming in on the faces.

"This is as close as I can get it."

Jeremy leans in. "That's not bad. Email me that shot and I'll send it to the lab."

Reynold sends the image and then closes out of the program and logs off.

"Let's take this one step at a time and not panic. If we panic, we're going to make mistakes."

Reynold nods in agreement, smooths his trousers, and stands.

"Keep me in the loop," he says to Jeremy. "If we've been compromised, we should probably destroy the footage."

After Reynold leaves the office, Jeremy takes a sip of his coffee, grimaces, and throws it in the trash. He logs back into his computer and stares at the photo a moment before sending it to the printer. As he studies the printout, Turner enters his office, startling him. He lays the photo on his desk.

"Sorry, Boss. It's Reynold. I'm really worried."

"He was just here."

"Reynold was here?"

"Yeah, seconds ago."

"Was he upset?"

Jeremy shrugs. "A bit."

"A bit? Well, then he's hiding it from you. He's more than a bit upset. He got a call last night and went into the bedroom to take it. He never came back. I found him rocking on the edge of the bed with his head in his hands." Turner looks down at her own hands. "He was crying," she says softly.

"We talked, Turner," Jeremy says. "He's better."

Turner's eyes widen a bit and a glimmer of hope shines in them. She really loves him, Jeremy thinks. That could be good or bad.

"Give him some space. The job has gotten stressful and he's not at liberty to discuss it."

As soon as the words are out of his mouth, he realizes his error. Turner's narrowed eyes confirm she's picked up on it. He told her last time her end of the project was the classified one. She won't appreciate being lied to.

"I won't ask him about it if it's going to put more stress on him."

She glances down at the desk and then does a double take at the photo.

"Something wrong?" Jeremy asks as he slides the photo

toward his side of the desk.

"No. I just realized that's Emily."

"Who?"

"Emily Cooke. In the photo."

Overwhelming fear washes over him. He studies the printout. Is Turner right? Between the fuzziness of the photo and the winter outerwear, he can barely tell it's a woman, but Turner's been hanging out with her for a while.

"You sure about that, Turner?"

He hands her the photo.

"Yeah, that's her. What's going on?"

"Do you know the guy she's with?"

Turner looks at it again. "No. Never saw him before."

Jeremy gnaws the inside of his cheek. There's so much Turner doesn't know, even about her own end of the project. She thinks her subject has undergone a voluntary procedure involving memory and her job is to monitor Emily's behavior and ensure she is well. Should he bring Turner all the way in? Tell her the truth about the experiments? Would it serve him in any way? Not yet, he decides.

"I need some time to think things through. I'll call you next week," he says.

Turner nods. "Okay."

"Keep an eye on Reynold. If he gets worse, let me know."

"I will."

After she leaves, Jeremy stares into space a long while, then reaches for his cell phone to do damage control at home.

# Thirty-seven

I've donned my blonde wig and sunglasses for my visit with Emily. The whole way there, my heart is heavy with the horrors I've witnessed and the terror of not knowing how Emily and I fit into this puzzle.

When the door swings open and I see her smiling face, I grab her in an uncharacteristic embrace. As I pull away, I whisper, "We have to be careful what we say in the house."

She nods. "I know the drill."

I pull off my coat and throw it over a chair. "Where's the little bundle of joy?"

"She's napping. She should be up soon for lunch." Emily leads me into the kitchen. "Sit. I'll make tea."

As she putters with the kettle and the cups, I glance around the kitchen, remembering my life here, which was only about a week ago. It seems like a lifetime has passed. I feel older, tired, beaten down. Without warning, my eyes well up and tears stream down my cheeks. I swipe at them and sniff. Emily whips around. She leans down and gathers me up in her arms. "What's wrong?"

"It's been a long week."

Emily nods. "Yes, it has."

"Tell me about Amanda."

"There's not much more to tell. So far, she's recovering. More herself. But I'm terrified. We don't know what caused this. I check on her all night to make sure she's breathing."

Without the bright smile on her face, I notice the dark stains under her eyes and my heart wrenches. There's no way I can add the horror of Governors Island to the burden she already carries.

"How are you doing after donating the blood?"

She swats her hand in the air. "I've made my peace with that fear. I won't say I'm totally cured. I may have to donate more blood. It is what it is. I'd do anything for that little girl."

At that moment, the words "so would I" pop into my mind and my eyes well up again.

"Look at the two of us. Hot messes."

I laugh through my tears.

Emily giggles and pours us cups of steaming Earl Grey and sets a plate of assorted cookies and biscotti on the table.

"Speaking of hot," she says, biting into a sesame seed biscotti, "how's the new man in your life?"

"Stop."

"From the vibes I've been picking up, I'm thinking it's more 'don't stop.'"

I almost spit tea out of my mouth. "What are you, clairvoyant?"

She grins. "Don't need to be."

"Okay, okay, I'll throw you a bone. A small bone." I take a deep breath. "I care about him. I think it's mutual." I pause. "No, I know it's mutual. But it's a complicated time."

We make eye contact and Emily squeezes my arm.

"Once our lives are more settled," I say, choosing my words carefully in case someone is listening, "we'll see where it goes."

"Fair enough," Emily says. "I can't wait to meet him."

"Enough about me. How's Brad?"

"He's doing better now that Amanda is improving. I think he was devastated his rare AB blood wouldn't allow him to be her superhero."

Something flashes in my mind. It's that same feeling that triggered the slow return of my memory months ago. I try to retrieve it, but I can't.

"What's wrong?"

I shake my head. "I forgot what I was about to say." I give her a certain stare and she knows I'm referring to our condition.

And then I blurt out the question, though I already know the answer to it. "What blood type are you?"

"O positive, just like Amanda."

From the recesses of my mind, from the halls of Columbia University's Genetics Department, an image of a Punnet square pops into my mind. The simple Punnet square that allows you to take the blood types of two people and predict which blood types their children will have. And here's the problem. From what Emily has just told me, there is no way Brad is Amanda's father.

Emily sees the expression on my face and her eyes widen. "What's the matter?"

I am saved by Amanda's cry.

We both break out into smiles and hurry to her room. I get there first and reach down to pick her up.

"Hi, baby girl," I coo. She rewards me with a magnificent smile and grabs a piece of my blond wig. A wave of emotion washes over me. I wonder if she recognizes me. When I look over at Emily, her eyes are filled with tears and I'm reminded again of how connected we are. But then a darkness creeps in. A thought I can't retrieve taunts my mind. I pull Amanda onto my shoulder and she, surprisingly, nestles into my neck. I pat her on the back as I follow Emily back to the kitchen.

She prepares lunch for Amanda as I continue to coo in baby talk and extract my hair from her chubby, little fists.

"Have you been going to the gym?" I ask.

Emily turns around and makes a face at me. "Yes. My favorite thing in the world."

I laugh. "What have you been doing?"

"Treadmill, some weight machines. The free weights are

just too difficult. Trina was worried I was getting lazy."

"How is Trina?"

"She's good. She keeps pushing me. I'm so delighted. Can't you tell?"

I burst out in laughter. "I really adore you."

She looks at me with a pleased expression. "Right back at ya."

We take turns feeding the baby. Before long, it's time to go. We hug each other so tightly, it hurts. I kiss Amanda's full cheek.

"Take good care," Emily says.

"I will. You, too. And be sure to keep in touch about Amanda."

As I walk to the train station, I notice the shops and the bustle on the main street and I feel a pang. Just a few weeks ago, this was a place I wanted to escape. Now there's a comfort to it that draws me in and makes me want to stay. Whether that would continue to be the case in happier times, I'm not sure. But for now, with everything upside down, it feels secure and safe and warm.

I run to make the train and fly through the doors just as they close. I fall into a seat as the train pulls out and replay my visit with Emily. My mind immediately returns to the story about the transfusion and my realization that Brad can't be Amanda's father. I have Emily's memories of the in vitro she went through. I know Brad donated sperm. Is it possible the wrong sperm was used to fertilize the eggs?

The dark shadow crosses my mind again. I think about the crazy situation I've found myself in. For there to be yet another weird situation in the middle of the existing one could be a coincidence, yet the odds of so many strange things happening to the same people seem high.

What's the easiest explanation then? The one where coincidence doesn't play a role. It flashes in my mind like a neon sign. Bile rises up in my throat.

As the train doors open at Merrick, I run outside and vomit the contents of my stomach onto the platform.

No, Amanda is not Brad's daughter. She is not any man's daughter. Amanda is a clone.

# Thirty-eight

I want to be me again. I want to remember my life. I need to remember my life. With my stomach still queasy, I walk up Merrick Avenue toward Dr. Snelling's office. I must find out whether there's any hope. Returning to my former self is the only chance I have to figure this out and keep Emily and Amanda safe.

I should call Emily and tell her the epiphany I had just minutes after leaving her house, but how can I do that to her? How can I tell her Amanda is most likely her clone? I need to contact Chadwick and find out how many others that bastard created. Tears roll down my face and the urge to smash my fist through a plate glass window of one of the shops I pass is strong. Even if I figure out what role we play in this sinister experiment, even if I safely extract ourselves from it, if the world ever found out what we are, there would be no peace, no security. We'd be circus freaks pursued by a frenzied media—demonized by the religious right, coddled by the left, pursued by scientists with both noble and ignoble intentions. My body shakes as I sob. There's only one person I can share this with.

Jake picks up on the first ring.
"You okay?"

"No," I say, my voice trembling.

"What happened?"

"I think Amanda is a clone."

Silence. I think we've been cut off and then, "Jesus."

"I haven't told Emily yet. I want to be sure. I'll call Chadwick later, but first I'm on my way to Dr. Snelling."

"For what?"

"I need to talk to him."

"I don't know, Madison. I don't think that's a great idea in the state you're in."

"I need to know if there's some way to get the old me back. I need the strength and the logic of who I was to solve this."

"You are strong and the most logical person I've ever met. Please just come back to the City. We'll figure this out together."

"I'll be back soon, but I have to see Snelling first."

Jake lets out his breath. "Be careful."

When I arrive at Snelling's office, the waiting room is empty and the receptionist is putting on her coat. I tell her I don't have an appointment, but she doesn't seem to mind. I almost slip up and tell her my name is Madison instead of Emily but catch myself.

Seconds later, Snelling exits his office. "Emily, so good to see you again."

We shake hands and he ushers me into the office, reassuring me when I make apologies for showing up without an appointment.

I settle into the couch. Yes, that's right, the couch. I don't have the strength to vie for equal stature. I need help.

"Are there any circumstances under which you could violate therapist/patient privilege?" I ask.

Snelling's face registers surprise but then goes neutral again. "A few circumstances. My discretion would play a role. In general, if I knew you were a danger to yourself or someone else, I could report that. Also, if you were involved in a court case and your emotional state was introduced, then the court would have the right to order your records."

I nod, thinking the only life that may be in danger is my own...and Emily's and Amanda's. The powers that be, whoever they are, wouldn't let my situation be known in a court of law, no matter what.

"I'm going to tell you a story. You're going to think I'm a raving lunatic. I'm not. But even if you think I am, pretend I'm sane and give me straight answers. Can you do that?"

"Of course."

I take a deep breath. "Some covert research department in the government has figured out a way to transfer memories from one person to another."

Snelling's eyebrows leap up, but I continue.

"Their goal is to transfer a terrorist's memories to a less resistant person to extract information about future terrorist plots."

Snelling is dead calm. "Go on."

"Apparently, they tried this experiment on some military guys with disastrous results. They couldn't return them to their former selves. I'm guessing someone's head rolled for that snafu. They decided to use civilians—civilians who..." I make quotation marks in the air. "...'don't matter' and won't be missed to continue their experiments in the hope of getting it right. I'm one of their victims. There are others I know of, as well."

"Hmmmmm." He fiddles with his watch in the silence.

I stop and wait for his reaction.

"How do you know this memory transfer experiment has happened? Do you have memories of this being done to you?"

"No. But I know I am not who everyone thinks I am. My name is really Madison Thorpe. I've been given the memories of someone named Emily Cooke. And we've been switched into each other's lives."

"What do you mean by switched?"

"They've moved me to Emily's home and they've moved her to my home."

Snelling squints. "I'm not sure I understand. How would that be possible? Wouldn't your families notice you look nothing like the person you're supposed to be?"

I look down at my hands. "There's another piece of the story I can't tell you that makes that a non-issue."

"I see."

"You just have to accept my word on that. But I need to know...in your research experience, is there a way to access my former memories if they've been transferred to someone else. Do they still exist somewhere in my brain? Could they be accessed via hypnosis? Or maybe drugs?"

Snelling holds up his hand. "Slow down. I have no knowledge that memory transfer is possible. We could try hypnosis. It certainly couldn't hurt."

"Last time you said there was a higher mind that controls the lower mind. I feel like my higher mind knows who I am. If you can get to my higher mind, it might be able to get me back to where I need to be."

Snelling nods slowly. "You've obviously thought this through."

"I have nothing else to do but think."

"All right. Let's do a ten-minute session to see how receptive you are to hypnosis. Get into a comfortable position. Feel free to recline on the couch if you like."

As I lean back, I feel my pulse quicken. Now that this is happening, I'm afraid. I've already had my mind messed with in a serious way. I don't know much about hypnosis except the occasional stage act I've seen. Will I lose control over my thoughts? Will I be unaware of what is happening around me? Will hypnosis exacerbate the memory issues I have?

"I want you to raise your eyes to the dot of light on the ceiling," Snelling says.

I follow his direction and force myself to focus on the light. There's no time left for fear. Lives are at stake. His voice is soft. His sentences are like undulating waves. He emphasizes certain words as he explains what will happen during the session.

"Five, four, three, two, one..."

***

Trina drives home from Jeremy's office with unshed tears clouding her vision, her throat aching from her tight composure. As she enters her home, her grandfather's brogue echoes in her mind. She reaches for the bottle of Jameson and pours herself a generous portion. *God gave you a nose to smell and a tongue to taste, lass. Don't be slamming back a good whiskey like medicine*, he always said. And so she doesn't.

She takes a sip, rolls it over her tongue in a slow wave, swallows. Then she sits at the kitchen table. Thirty-two years old. Ten years as an agent. She went from the tough love of her family in Hell's Kitchen to the tough love of the agency. She made her job her life, worked long hours, no time off. She didn't socialize with work colleagues, had no outside friendships. At night, she grabbed take-out or microwaved a meal and watched the news. Every other week, she talked with one of her brothers. On the rare occasion when they got together, she enjoyed her nieces and nephews, but then Monday came around again.

She was good at compartmentalizing her life. Until Reynold. They couldn't be more different and yet their bond was immediate. Trina was used to a certain brand of toughness in the guys she grew up with. Despite Reynold's height and build, one might underestimate him with his gentle manners and attention to his wardrobe. Inside, however, he was as tough as they come—the only man she'd ever met who could be her rock. Yet here she sits, powerless to help him as he unravels.

Trina takes another sip of whiskey. Reynold is her match in strength and control. She tries to imagine something so horrible it would break her but comes up blank. Then she remembers something he said to her one night in bed. *The biggest badasses are the most fearful people in the world, and the thing they're most afraid of is admitting to themselves how afraid they are.*

For weeks, that sentence resonated in an uncomfortable way. Slowly, she came to realize she was afraid. Afraid of being afraid. Afraid of never having a family. Afraid of having a family. Afraid of completely opening herself to another person. Afraid of never opening herself to another person. Afraid of being alone forever. She wasn't fearless as she had thought. She had just spackled the fault lines so thick, she couldn't find them anymore. But Reynold saw through it all. With one sentence, he blasted through layers of protective plaster. It was terrifying. It was also liberating.

"I'm afraid," Trina says aloud, the words echoing in the silence of her kitchen. "I. Am. Afraid."

Her cell phone lets out a burst of three chimes. A code flashes across the screen. She curses under her breath, slams back the rest of her whiskey, grabs a bag from her closet, and hurries out the door.

\*\*\*

Snelling's watch beeps. My eyelids drift open. I am relaxed but alert.

"So what do you think?" I ask. "Can hypnosis help me to get back to who I was?"

"You seemed receptive. We should set up some sessions to go further. I need some time to ponder what you've told me and to work out a plan."

"Okay."

"I'll give you a call in a few days to set up our first session."

"Thank you."

"No problem." Snelling stands and extends his hand. He precedes me to the door. When he opens it, I'm surprised but pleased when I see who is standing on the other side.

"Trina!"

"Emily. I didn't expect to see you here."

"It was an unscheduled visit," I say.

"Trina and I were planning to grab some dinner," Snelling says from behind me. "Would you like to join us?"

As I turn to decline his invitation, my peripheral vision catches a flash of movement.

Trina extends a hypodermic needle toward me.

My conscious mind doesn't have time to reason, but danger is imminent and muscle memory kicks in. I deflect her arm and she tries to grab me. I throw a hard hook and her head bounces back. My often criticized hook is not looking so bad now, is it? Like a punching bag clown, she springs back up in attack mode.

Snelling weaves his arms through my elbows from behind to restrain me. I jam my heel back and up and he screams out in pain as I connect with his testicles. I then launch myself at Trina and end up on top of her, pummeling her face. When I'm convinced I can get away, I take off. I dart down a side street before running for the train station, fumbling for my phone to call Emily. She picks up on the first ring.

"Don't say a word out loud," I say, panting. "Trina is in on it. They know I'm on to them, but they think I'm you. Take the baby and leave right now. Get on the railroad to Jamaica. I'll meet you onboard in Merrick. You got that?"

"What! Yes, yes. Oh my God."

"Do it Emily. Now!"

# Thirty-nine

With my adrenaline surging, I need to pace. Instead, I make myself small and sit against a wall on the cold cement of the elevated railroad station so I can't be seen from the street below. Mixed with the adrenaline is the bitter rage of betrayal—first by my mentor Chadwick, then by my country. But the hardest to take is Trina's. I thought she was my friend. I shared my life and my fears with her. My existence is now officially a complete lie. I can't bear to think about it. That's just as well. Better to focus on keeping us safe. I take out my phone to cash in a favor with Vincent Gargiulo.

The West-bound train to New York City pulls into the station. As the doors open, I scan the platform in each direction and see Emily's head pop out from a door a few cars down. I board the train and make my way to her. She sits with Amanda resting against her shoulder, her knee bouncing up and down repeatedly though Amanda is already asleep. When I lay my hand on her leg, she stops twitching but her eyes are wide and questioning.

"Gargiulo's sending a limo to Jamaica Station to pick you up," I say. "I told him my daughter and I are in danger. You have to be the Emily who saved his life."

"Okay."

"Tell him it's just safer for Jake to continue without you. You need to make sure the baby is safe. As a macho-gangster man, he'll accept that."

"What are you going to do?"

"I'm not sure yet. I have another twenty minutes on the train to decide."

"Please stay in touch, Madison. I'm really scared."

"I will."

We hug as we pull in to Jamaica station. I kiss Amanda's temple and watch them exit the car. As the train creeps away from the platform, our gazes lock, our mutual fear a powerful magnet. I know Gargiulo will keep Emily and Amanda safe, but the control freak in me wishes I could keep my eye on them.

Just before the train goes under the East River on its way to Penn Station, I decide to visit Chadwick to get the truth about Amanda. I call Jake to let him know. At Penn, I have to take a crosstown and then an uptown train to get to Grand Central Station. I'm grateful for the rush-hour crowds, as crazy as that sounds. Safety in numbers.

As I navigate the throngs of commuters at Grand Central, I can't stop thinking about baby Amanda. Before now, only animals have been cloned, and not entirely successfully. Dolly the Sheep survived only half of a normal sheep's lifespan. She died of a lung disease typical of older sheep and also developed arthritis prematurely. Some scientists hypothesize that when Dolly was born, she was already the age of the sheep from which she was cloned.

If that theory is true, Amanda's age, from a cellular perspective, is dependent on when Chadwick cloned her from Emily. Was it when Emily was a baby--the same time I was cloned? Did he put those cells on ice until Emily was an adult and unable to conceive and then create Amanda? Or did he clone her when Emily's fertility problems surfaced, meaning those cloned cells were already Emily's adult age? What if Amanda's recent illness has something to do with her cloning? My rage builds again when I think of what Chadwick did. At the same time, I wouldn't be here if not for him.

I enter the ticket area for the train to Chadwick's. As I scan the boards to find my connection, someone grabs my arm. I twist and throw a punch about head height. My wrist is grabbed before I make contact.

"Nice hook."

I stare up at the face that has become increasingly beautiful to me.

"You should see what I did to Trina."

Jake wraps me in his arms and pulls me into a bear hug I want to lose myself in.

"You are the most stubborn woman I have ever met. I could strangle you."

"You're doing a pretty good job," I croak from his tight grip.

"Sorry." He pulls back. His face is a stew of emotions: relief at seeing me, concern, and something else. I don't have the courage to speculate.

"I have the tickets. Let's go," he says.

Once we settle on the train, I explain in whispers the new horrors I've uncovered and my fears for Amanda's health. His hand reaches for mine. Comfort overpowers the flutters I know I'd feel if our situation weren't so dangerous.

"We'll get to the bottom of this," he says.

I rest my head on his shoulder and try to quiet my mind.

When we arrive, we scan our surroundings, both of us on high alert.

"Did you call Chadwick to let him know we're coming?" I ask.

"No. I wasn't moved to extend him that courtesy."

At the security gate, we once again identify ourselves as the Smiths.

"You're not on the list of visitors," the guard says after scanning the list.

"No? We spoke a little while ago and he said he was going to call down and let you know," Jake says.

The guard picks up the phone to call Chadwick. I hear it

ringing through the handset.

"He's not answering. But I know he's up there. Probably still tied up with the cable guys. You know what? Go on up."

"Thank you very much," Jake says.

"That's some fine security," I say as we move out of earshot of the guard.

Jake shakes his head. "I'm not surprised. You can't believe the things I've seen."

As we walk toward the building, a motorcycle races through the parking lot toward us. Jake pushes me back to safety.

"Asshole," he mutters.

When we arrive at Chadwick's apartment, the door is slightly ajar. Jake stops, then motions for me to stand back. He pulls out his gun and holds it barrel down as he silently enters the foyer. I sneak up to the open door and watch him enter the living room and then disappear as he crouches on the other side of the couch. Then, he's up and racing down the hallway to the bathroom and the bedrooms. I hear him kicking open doors and I know something is very wrong.

I make my way into the living room. Chadwick lies on the floor with a bullet wound to the chest. His blood has dripped onto the beige rug. I kneel over him to check his vitals. No, no, no! He's dead. The danger is closer than I thought and without Chadwick, there will be no answers. He can't die yet. I start chest compressions on him just as Jake returns. "Call 911," I say.

"He's dead, Madison."

I continue CPR, desperate to revive him, until I feel Jake's hand on my shoulder.

"He's gone," he says softly. "We need some time in here before we call the police." He helps me to my feet.

I try to push off the surprising sense of sadness that has washed over me. Though I am angry with Chadwick, he was my mentor, the one who believed in me, gave me a chance, and trained me. The fact I can't remember most of that obviously doesn't matter to the part of me registering this sadness.

"When Chadwick sent me after you, he told me he had some sensitive information hidden away," Jake says. He said he should destroy it, but he couldn't bring himself to do it. His ego was obviously still being fed by his little experiment."

"No. I don't think so," I say. "It may have started out that way, but I think after he realized what he had put in motion, he was remorseful. He may have decided he needed that information intact. Maybe as insurance, or maybe as future reference."

"Future reference for what?"

"In case something went wrong as it has with Amanda."

"You think her illness is related?"

"It could be."

"We need to find those records then. Look any place you think a paper file, DVD, or thumb drive could be hidden. And try not to touch anything with your bare hands. They're going to dust this place and we don't want your fingerprints showing up in odd places."

My first stop is under his kitchen sink, where I find a pair of rubber gloves and pull them on. I practically crawl into the cabinet searching for anything that might be taped up under the sink. There's nothing. The cleaning products seem to be legitimate aerosol cans, but I check them just in case.

"I'll search the other rooms," Jake says.

I open the refrigerator next, which is relatively bare. I check the mayonnaise jar for a false bottom. Nothing.

In the cabinet to the left of the stove, I find a dozen jars of spices and herbs. On the counter is a package of Amish-style oatmeal cookies. I proceed to the pantry and pull out shelf by shelf, examining the items on each one. Then, I run my hands underneath to feel for any hidden items. Unopened, five-pound sacks of flour and sugar are on the bottom shelf. I skip over those but pull the shelf out all the way, thinking he may have dropped something in the dead space in the base of the pantry. Once again, nothing.

Overhead, I notice a light is blown out. I climb on a chair, unscrew it, and look inside the socket to see if anything is hidden. I don't bother with the working lights, thinking the heat from the bulbs would not make it a good place to hide electronic files on a flash drive.

When I've searched the entire kitchen, Jake returns with a grim expression on his face.

"I don't see anything. His decorating leans towards the stark side, so it's not like there are lots of places to search."

"There's nothing in here either. Did you find his computer?"

"Nope. Whoever killed him must have taken it."

"Jesus, I hope there was nothing on there about Amanda. Brixton didn't seem to know about her. Chadwick must have kept that to himself."

Jake leans against the stove. "We need to make a move. I'm thinking we should call the police. It'll look suspicious if he's found after we leave."

I nod but my attention focuses on those Amish-style oatmeal cookies. Jake follows my gaze.

"Don't tell me you're hungry."

"No." I slide out the bottom pantry shelf again and retrieve a sack of flour. "Remember that movie *Witness* with Kelly McGillis as the Amish woman?"

"Yeah."

"She hid Harrison Ford's bullets in the flour so her son wouldn't find them." I inspect the seal on the flour, but it's hard to tell if it's been tampered with. I slide my finger under the seal and open the mouth of the sack. This is going to be messy. I place the sack in the middle of the sink.

"That's the movie where she takes a sponge bath at the kitchen sink, right?"

I flash Jake a look that must appear scathing, judging by the flush that creeps up his face, and then plunge my hand into the flour.

When that turns up nothing, I carefully close the sack, replace it on the shelf, and pull out the bag of granulated sugar.

As soon as I reach in, I feel a plastic bag.

"Is there something there?" Jake asks.

I carefully pull out a zip lock bag with a flash drive in it.

"Put it back." Jake reaches under the sink and pulls out a plastic shopping bag with the name of a local grocery store on it. He places the sugar and then the bag of flour inside and ties a knot in the bag.

"I'll put this in my knapsack. Make it look like we stopped at a store, just in case the police search our things."

"Good thinking."

We wash up, making sure there is no residue of flour or sugar in the sink. Then, Jake goes out into the hallway, closes the door, and smashes it in with his foot.

"He had a heart condition, right?" Jake says.

"Yes."

"When he didn't answer, we sat in the hall and waited a while, but then, remembering the guard told us he was up here, we got worried and broke down the door. We found him with the bullet wound. You did chest compressions while I called it in. Sound good?"

"Yes."

While Jake calls the police, I phone Emily.

She picks up with a strained "hey" and I know she's letting me know Gargiulo's there and she's not at liberty to speak.

"Just pretend I'm Jake calling," I tell her. "Chadwick's dead." I hear her gasp. "This is bad and getting worse by the minute. We have to be careful."

I hear sirens approaching in the distance.

"I've got to go. The cops are on the way."

"Be safe," she whispers.

When the police arrive, Jake's credentials get us out of there fast. Once they know we're not the next of kin, they're only too happy to let former-cop Jake go, especially after he mentions the cable company was supposedly here before us and the guard at the security gate confirms it.

As we leave, we spot an unmanned cable company van in the parking lot. Jake walks around it and then pulls open the back door.

"Huh."

"What?" I ask.

"I'm betting there's a report of a stolen cable van. Remember that motorcycle that almost hit us?"

He points to a narrow metal ramp inside the back of the van.

"That was the getaway vehicle."

# Forty

The children are especially rambunctious this evening, and Jeremy summons every ounce of patience to get them to bed without losing his temper. But when Kaylee wraps her skinny Muppet arms around his neck and the scent of Johnson's baby shampoo drifts up from her downy hair, he softens. Stopping off in Robbie's room, he kisses his temple and ruffles his hair.

"I love you, Dad."

"I love you, too, buddy."

Back in the kitchen, Stephanie holds out what seems to be a glass of soda, but he spots the bottle of Jack Daniels on the counter. He takes a much needed sip. He's thought about this moment all day and realizes the only option left in his bag of damage-control tricks is fear.

Stephanie leads the way into the den, out of earshot of the kids. The fire he made after dinner still glows in the fireplace. It lends a warmth to the room he doesn't feel. He stares at the orange embers and remembers happier nights. When Robbie was a baby, they'd put him down to sleep and then have a drink or watch a movie. Many times, they'd end up tangled on the floor in front of the fire. In fact, he's pretty sure Kaylee was conceived during one of those encounters.

"Have you thought about what I said on the phone today?"

Stephanie asks.

He continues staring at the fire, remembering the counseling comment he hung up on to deal with Reynold.

"I don't need to think about it. If that's what you want, that's what we'll do."

Stephanie's expression relaxes.

"But not now," he adds and she looks startled.

Jeremy holds up his hand. "Steph, there are serious things happening right now at work. Very serious things."

Concern flashes in her eyes. "What kind of serious?"

"You know I can't tell you that."

"I know, Jeremy, but if we're talking about imminent terrorist attacks, we need to protect our children."

"It's nothing like that. A project at work has run off course. There could be consequences for my unit. If that happens, losing my job might be the least of our troubles."

"What does that mean?"

"I'm not sure yet."

"News coverage? Would you be named?"

Jeremy shrugs. "Possibly."

She studies his face. "You don't seem upset. Why not? You know what that would mean to our standing in this neighborhood and our kids at school."

"There are worse things than bad publicity."

"Are you in danger? Are we all in danger?"

Jeremy thinks about the military guys, with their terrorist memories, hidden away, their families believing they are missing in action. He considers the number of homeless men who have been tortured and murdered. Even if his own people didn't silence him permanently, once the public found out, some crazy would eventually take him out. He'd always have to be on guard, always hovering over the kids to keep them safe.

"Jeremy? You're scaring me."

"No, we're not in danger," he says.

She stares at him a second longer and then exhales. She has no choice but to believe the lie. Again.

His cell phone interrupts the silence.

"Chadwick's taken care of," the voice on the other end says.

"You found him." Jeremy says, carefully choosing his words in front of Stephanie.

"Yes we did. Got his laptop, too. It's with the techs."

"Great. Let me know what turns up."

When Jeremy hangs up, he mentally adds another tick mark to the list of people he's had to have killed. He turns to find Stephanie staring at him.

"Who's 'him'?" she asks.

"I can't tell you that, Steph."

"What happened to 'him'?"

Jeremy doesn't respond. Something in her eyes changes. She stands.

"I'm going to bed."

When Jeremy leans in to kiss her, she turns her face away.

"You can sleep in the guest room tonight."

# Forty-one

Just out of the shower, I sit in the dark hotel room in front of Jake's laptop. Drops of water drip from the ends of my hair. My body is clean, but the residue of death and fear cake my spirit like tar. I won't be free until I know the truth.

There are several files on Chadwick's flash drive. Some are lists, others tables, but all of them contain code words, dates, and even characters in other alphabets. I'm bleary-eyed after scrolling and skimming. Too exhausted to attempt to figure out any of it.

"Anything important on the drive?"

"I don't know. It's encoded."

He frowns. "We'll put our heads together and try to crack it in the morning when we're fresh. It's been a long day."

"Understatement of the year." I stretch my arms toward the ceiling and yawn.

"Are you hungry?" he asks.

"Not at all."

For some reason that makes him grin.

I feel my face flush. "What's so funny?"

"That's a first." He walks up behind me and starts rubbing my shoulders.

I sigh in relief, oblivious to how tight my shoulders were.

"What's a first?"

"You're not hungry."

I slap my hand back at him and am rewarded with his husky chuckle. He dips his head down to kiss my cheek. At the same moment, I lift my face to reply. His lips land on the corner of my mouth instead, setting off a chain reaction. He reaches lower and catches my mouth again. His is hungry and searching. I reach my arms up around his neck and he pulls me from the chair. He backwalks to the edge of the bed, scooping me up into his lap. I curl into him, against his warm skin. His fingers stroke my cheek and slip into my hair.

"You look sexy with wet hair." His lips touch the skin under my jaw and make their way along my neck to just under my ear.

I shiver.

His chuckle is more the feeling of warm breath than a sound. "That's your spot," he whispers. I feel his grin even though I can't see it.

I graze my fingernails down his back. He freezes. "You're not the only one paying attention," I say.

"Touché." He picks me up and tosses me lightly onto the bed.

As he moves over me, he takes a playful nip at my nose. For this brief moment, we have all the time in the world. That he can make me laugh in the midst of horror is nothing short of miraculous.

Tracing his face with my fingers, I memorize every angle. I read the stubble of his jaw like it's Braille. I notice the exact location of the gold flecks in his brown eyes. He allows me this indulgence, waiting patiently until my hands still. My fingertips rest lightly on his cheeks. He smiles with his eyes and I feel myself falling into their depths. I want to hide out in them forever, cherished, perhaps even loved.

"What are you thinking?"

I shake my head.

"Big secret?" he asks.

I stare into the space behind him, my vision blurring as I

consider my words. "I was thinking..." I look back into his eyes. "I feel safe with you."

"Good," he whispers as he slides into me and brings his lips to my temple.

This time it is painstakingly slow. Silent. Our gaze remains locked, searching, until the very end when his eyes close briefly but then stare into mine with an intensity I've never seen. He lies next to me and gathers me into his arms.

"Good night," I whisper into the darkness. I wait for the echo.

"I love you," he says.

For a moment, I'm stunned. My chest thuds. I'm like a glow worm in the dark room.

"I love you, too."

He exhales as if he's been holding his breath. It makes me feel protective of him. I squeeze closer into his embrace. Our synchronized breath lulls me to sleep.

***

My eyes fly open. The green glow of the clock displays 3:33 AM. A memory rises up from my past as a scientist. I'd jolt out of bed with an answer that had stumped me during the day at the lab. Just as in my past, an epiphany has come to me as I slept.

I throw my legs over the edge of the bed and then remember there is reason to be quiet. I glance over at Jake. He lies on his back, his head tilted toward his shoulder. He is a peaceful sleeper, I think, as a smile touches my lips. I reach out to stroke his hair, but stop myself, not sure if he's also a light sleeper. There's still so much I don't know about him.

I push the thought away and pull on a bathrobe. As the laptop comes out of Sleep Mode, the screen brightens, causing tiny blind spots in my vision. I squint at Jake. He hasn't stirred. I access the first file on the flash drive.

This is what woke me. It is a list of codes and dates. I scroll through them. As I thought, there is repetition of one of the codes. I'm not sure why my brain thought that was significant, but I continue my analysis.

The first code on the list is 1F.0. It is followed by a single date—Emily's birthdate. I let out my breath.

Below that entry is an indented listing with the code 1F.1. This time there are two dates. The first is also in August, just a few days after Emily's birthday. But it's the date at the end of the row that has me hyperventilating. It's my birthdate. This must be Chadwick's summary of when he harvested the cells from Emily and when I was born.

What, then, is the rest of this list?

The next main entry is 2M.0. As with the 1F.0 record, there is only one date at the end of the row. That one falls about three months after Emily's birth. The indented entry is listed as 2M.1 and that one, like 1F.1, has two dates.

An eerie feeling creeps over me. I count the number of main listings that have only one date. There are twelve of them. Each has one indented entry that contains two dates with about ten months between them.

Nathan Brixton's words are like a ghost that's come back to haunt me. *Colony of clones.* Chadwick lied. There's more than just one clone. According to this, there are twelve, created from twelve different people.

But something still bothers me. I roll the mouse up and down, staring at the screen, but not seeing it. The thing that drew me here in the dead of night was the memory of one of the codes being repeated.

The last main entry is 1F.1. That's me again! A chill spreads through me when I notice the indented entry beneath mine—1F.1-1. The first date on that entry is a year and a half ago in May. The second one, almost ten months later, is March 29th of last year. March 29th is Amanda's birthday.

"No!"

At my shout, Jake jumps up in bed. "Are you okay?"

I stare at him, the horror completely filling me.

"What's wrong?" Jake reaches for his jeans. He pulls them on, his gaze never leaving mine.

"Amanda isn't a clone of Emily."

"That's good, right?"

"She's a clone of me."

Jake's eyes widen. He sits back on the bed, his jeans still undone. He curses Chadwick under his breath.

"God, Jake. Clones aren't always as healthy as the original subjects. And now we have a clone of a clone. Human, no less. It's never been done before. There's no data to access. I wonder if that's what's wrong with Amanda."

"Are you sure about what's in that document?"

He pads over to the desk and leans over my shoulder. "Walk me through it."

I show him the twelve coded main entries. "These are the original subjects. The date associated with each is the date of birth. So, this first one is Emily."

"Wait, what do you mean by twelve original subjects?"

"Chadwick lied to us. I'm not the only clone and Emily isn't the only original subject."

"What!"

"See these indented entries, one under each main entry? Those are the clones. I'm thinking the first date is when the cells were harvested from the original subjects and the second is the date of birth." I point to the indented entry after Emily's. "That's me and my date of birth."

"Okay, so what's the proof that Amanda was cloned from you?"

I trail my finger down to the last listing. "Notice how the codes for the original subjects are in numerical order. At least from one through eleven. But the twelfth one doesn't follow that pattern. It's a repeat. My code. 1F.1. And this indented entry beneath it? That's Amanda's date of birth.

"Jesus. So Amanda seems to be the only clone of a clone." Jake stares at the screen. "Hmmmm."

"What?"

"Almost every clone was created within days from the original subject, who was a baby, and born nine months or so later. So the clones are just about the same age as the subjects.

Like you and Emily. But not Amanda. According to her harvest date, you were already an adult."

I jump out of the chair and start to pace. "That son of a bitch. He stole my cells while I worked side-by-side with him, never the wiser."

"Hey, take a look at this. The codes either have the letter F or M in them. Female or Male?"

"Makes sense."

I sit back down. My rage has dissipated a bit. I'm an unemotional scientist again, ready to crack the Chadwick code.

I review the first file one last time. "Unless there's a file of real names and contact information somewhere, we'll never know who these other people are."

"If Chadwick kept his records at the lab, we could eventually match up former patients by the dates of birth."

"True."

I open the next file and find a series of tables—twelve to be exact. Each table seems to be detailed information on each clone. I access my table and examine the data. Even though it's no longer a surprise, I feel chilled when I read my "origin" is 1F.0—the code for Emily. The rest of the table lists notable dates. If I had to guess, they are the dates Emily's cells were taken, various status dates during cell division, implantation date into Regina, and follow up appointments to be sure everything was going well. I scroll through dozens of pages of notations in code and symbols.

On the second to last page, there is a section called Abnormalities. It says None with a note next to it. *1F.0: Infertility - Poor Responder. Monitor.*

"What does Poor Responder mean?"

I'd forgotten Jake was reading over my shoulder.

"Chadwick was noting any abnormalities from the cloning. In my case, there weren't any." My fingers tremble as I point to the screen. "His note refers to Emily, who is infertile. Poor Responder means she produces less than the optimal number of eggs per cycle despite fertility medications."

Jake's brain makes the inevitable leap. "So, as her clone, if you have the same condition, you'd have to do in vitro fertilization to become pregnant."

"That's right. But as we know, IVF didn't work for her." In the silence that follows my statement, I let that new knowledge sink in. I will never get pregnant.

I can't bear to let Jake see the tears in my eyes. I scroll to the final page of my record.

"Huh. Look at the last line on the page," Jake says. "That's the date we visited him."

I glance down and see the words "I'm sorry." I shake my head, in awe at how one man can screw up so many lives.

"What are those words after the apology? Is that Russian?"

I squint even though they are the same size as the other words on the screen. "Technically, no. Those are Cyrillic letters, but the words are not Russian."

"You know Russian?" Jake asks, the surprise evident in his voice.

"A bit. I studied it in college. These are actually English words coded in Cyrillic letters. It says 'Protect dem.'" I stare at the screen, tapping my lip with my index finger. "Them! There's no 'th' sound in Russian. It's 'Protect them.'"

"Brilliant," Jake says, planting a kiss on my forehead. "Protect them. Protect the clones."

"I can't protect them without any identifying records."

"We have to search his office again and find those records. But first, I think we need to pay Nathan Brixton another visit. We've got to find out who's behind the Governors Island project." He walks toward the bathroom. "I'm taking a quick shower."

I stare at the closed door and let thoughts and feelings wash over me. Now that I am sure, it's time to tell Emily about Amanda and the other clones. I take a deep breath and let it out slowly, then reach for my phone. She answers on the first ring.

"How are you?" I ask.

"Fine. Amanda and I are in a suite off of Gargiulo's office, so I have some privacy to talk now."

I pause to figure out how to break the news.

"Madison? Are you still there?"

"Yeah. Just thinking."

"What's wrong?"

"I wish I could tell you this in person, Em." I exhale and go for it. "Amanda is a clone."

"What?" It comes out like a jagged whisper.

"When you told me Brad's blood type, I knew she couldn't be his biological daughter. I thought maybe samples got mixed up during the in vitro process."

"But you found out that's not true?"

"Yes. I have Chadwick's notes. He cloned about a dozen people. They're not named, but I was able to figure out from key dates that Amanda is one of them."

"My God. I can't believe this. This is a nightmare."

"There's more."

"Just tell me. I'm all right."

"Amanda is a clone of me."

I give her a moment to process that.

"You're a clone of me so isn't it kind of the same thing?"

"Not necessarily. I'm wondering if her recent health problems are related. When this is over, I'll make it my life's mission to research this, Emily, but for now, we have to stay alive. If anyone ever finds out about us..."

"I'm really scared, Madison. I know this is probably the safest place I can be right now, but it gives me the creeps. I made the mistake of Googling Gargiulo."

"He's a ruthless thug, but he'll keep you and Amanda safe."

Emily sniffles. "I'm trying to remember that."

My heart breaks for her. "I wish we could all be together, but it's too dangerous. I'll fix this, Em. I promise."

"I know you will."

# Forty-two

Jeremy twists at the waist to the right and then to the left, a victim of the thin, cheap mattress in the guest room. He takes a swig of coffee and sits at his desk. The photo of Emily catches his eye. He stares at it a moment, wondering how the hell she showed up on Governors Island. Could Turner be wrong? He squints at the photo again. Between the graininess and the winter wear, it's hard to tell.

As if conjured up by his thoughts, Turner appears in the doorway. Her bruised and swollen face features a zig-zag line of stitches.

"What the hell happened to you?"

"Emily happened to me."

Jeremy motions for her to sit.

"When I got home from your office yesterday, I got an alert from Snelling. Emily was in his office and needed to be subdued chemically. I grabbed my kit and raced over expecting to find a madwoman. But she seemed perfectly composed." Turner shrugs. "Maybe I hesitated a second too long, I don't know. She saw the needle. It got physical. As you can see, I lost."

"Where is she?"

"I don't know. Not at her home, cause I checked."

"When did this happen?"

"Yesterday. Late afternoon."

"Why the hell am I just hearing about it, Turner?"

She looks him straight in the eye. "Because I had some thinking to do."

Her icy calm tone takes Jeremy by surprise.

"What's going on here?" she asks. "Who is Emily and what does she have to do with Reynold's project? I've thought it through over and over again. I can't figure it out."

"It's not for you to know, Turner. Trust me. It's for your own protection."

Turner snorts. "I thought you'd say something like that, but I don't feel protected. And watching Reynold getting closer to putting a bullet in his own head hasn't inspired confidence either."

"We're in damage control mode. The less everyone knows, the better."

Jeremy pushes a button on his phone and bypasses the pleasantries with the person on the other end. "Is she at work today?"

"No. Figured she had a relapse from last week, but she's not at the apartment either."

"We've got a problem. Stake out the apartment and bring her in."

When he hangs up, he turns to Turner. "Go back to Emily's house and wait for her to show up. Bring her in."

Turner glares at him a moment without responding, then stands and storms out of the office.

# Forty-three

So here we are again, in the lobby of Nathan Brixton's apartment building, waiting for the guy at the desk to announce us. I'm not sure what to expect during this visit. Jake and I have already agreed the man is not to be trusted. This means no talk of the additional clones. Telling him what is happening to innocent homeless men seems like a harmless trade for information we need. However, we decided even this was too much information for the self-serving Nathan Brixton, world class sell-out.

The doorman gives his approval and tells us Brixton's floor, even though we already know it. On the way up in the elevator, Jake winks, but his rapidly pumping cheek muscle belies his attempt at seeming relaxed.

Brixton waits in his doorway. His eyes are wider than usual, giving him the appearance of a tarsier, a nocturnal primate I once saw on a wildlife show with eyes as big as its brain. He greets us with a nervous hello and leads us into the apartment. Jake declines his invitation to sit and gets right down to business.

"I've seen some things this week that turned my stomach and made me angry, Nathan. I need answers. So this is how it's going down. I ask you a question. You give me the answer. No second chances. You don't respond, I hurt you. Any questions before we begin?"

Now I know why Jake thought we didn't need to trade information to get answers. The conquerors of terror have become the terrorists.

Brixton's face is ashen and clammy. His Adam's apple bobs up and down in his scrawny neck.

"First question. What is the name of the person in charge of the department working on this counterterrorism project?"

"I don't have the clearance to know the answer to tha—"

Jake makes a wrong-answer buzzing sound. He grabs Brixton's hand in a lightning-quick motion and bends his finger back as far as it will go.

Brixton lets out a high-pitched squeal that makes me wince and starts to hyperventilate.

"Tell me the name."

"The doorman knows what you look like. If something happens to me, you'll be the first person they come looking for."

"There won't be any evidence. I'll chop you up in little pieces, put you in a box, and Fed Ex you across the country. The name, Brixton."

"You don't know what these people will do to me."

"The only thing you have to worry about right now is what I'm going to do to you if you don't start talking."

Jake increases the pressure on his finger and Brixton lets out another scream.

"The name, Nathan, or you'll never use this finger again."

"Steele. Jeremy Steele."

"Good answer. Where does Mr. Steele work?"

"At the Chrysler Building."

"I imagine security is tight."

"You've got to have the right fingerprints. And I've heard rumors about what happened to people who strolled into the reception area without good cause."

Jake grunts. "I bet. Any idea where Steele lives?"

"No. I don't know him personally. Don't even know what

he looks like. I don't work in that building." Brixton pauses, thinks for a minute. "I would imagine his personal information would be unlisted considering his security clearance and the nature of his work."

"Probably right about that."

"Is he married? Does he have kids?" I ask.

Brixton's eyes narrow. "I don't remember any specific details about his family life, but for some reason I have the sense he is a family man."

"Fair enough," Jake says.

"How old is he?" I ask.

"I don't know."

"Any hunches?"

"Fortyish?"

"Why'd you pick that number?" I ask.

Brixton sighs wearily. "It used to be that more seasoned people oversaw the classified projects, but the trend now is the young, rising star. He would've spent some time building his career and getting noticed, so mid-career seems about right. If he were older, I probably would have crossed paths with him at some point."

I nod. It sounds logical.

"Well, Nathan. This concludes our question-and-answer session. It's been a pleasure as usual. As before, please don't take any vacations."

Brixton massages his finger as we walk to the door.

Jake turns. "Just a reminder. This conversation is between us. No sharing."

"I understand."

"Oh, and by the way," Jake says, "Chadwick's dead. They found him."

Brixton's eyes widen to perfect circles and shine with unshed tears.

# Forty-four

Vincent Gargiulo sits in his office, dunking toasted Italian bread into his coffee. Always an early riser, he's been up since 6 AM. With his first cup of coffee, he listened to the radio news channels, flipping stations now and then for a different take. Now, he lingers over his second cup of coffee, while reading the newspaper Vito delivers every morning.

If he's honest, reading isn't an accurate description. What he actually does is turn the pages slowly, while looking at the photos. Vincent Gargiulo has deduced he is dyslexic, but he's the only one who knows.

Back in his school days, they didn't have that diagnosis yet, so he was considered lazy and unruly—labeled a poor student. But that was only in a school system that insisted the way to learn was by using your eyes to read words. Vincent failed out of school, illiterate by their standards, but he continued to learn and hide his disability by listening.

He loves culture. Classical music. Opera History. Classic literature, which he listens to on audio book. He knows now he is not a stupid man. In fact, he's pretty damn smart.

A baby's cry distracts him from his page turning and a smile forms on his lips. That little Amanda is a breath of fresh air in his world of tough guys. Someone taps lightly on the door that leads to a small apartment behind his office.

"Come in," he says.

Emily, with her tentative smile and wide eyes, peeks around the door.

"Good morning. I'm sorry to bother you so early, but I need to get diaper cream for Amanda. I didn't think to put that on the list."

"No problem. I can send one of the guys."

Emily steps into the office and clears her throat. "Do you think I could go along?"

Vincent lets out a hardy chuckle that culminates in a wheezy cough. "Cabin fever?"

Her face turns pink. "A bit."

"I understand. Sometimes I feel a bit claustrophobic with all these guys around." He points a sausage-like finger toward the door. "Go get that beautiful baby of yours and join me in a cup of coffee and then I'll have Vito take you to Key Food."

Emily nods and retreats into the apartment.

Gargiulo stares after her. Though he can't read words on a page, he's a scholar when it comes to reading people. His reading of Emily tells him something isn't quite right, though he doesn't have a clue what it is. She seems off balance and nervous. Granted, she has good reason with someone out to get her, but he can't help feeling her nervousness is due to his presence. He wonders how the brass-balled woman who saved his life and then came to him a week ago to ask for his protection, bantering with him in the process, could have turned so tentative and unsure of herself.

He presses the button on the intercom.

"Vito, bring Mrs. Cooke a cup of coffee and some breakfast, huh."

A few minutes later, Emily returns with the baby.

"Heh heh heh, there she is. Miss America." He reaches out and takes the baby from Emily. He sits her on the edge of his desk and leans in close to talk to her, unable to stop himself from falling into a bit of baby talk.

Vito knocks and carries in a tray of coffee, toasted Italian bread and butter, assorted biscotti, and a half of a cantaloupe melon filled with ricotta cheese.

"That looks great," she says, selecting a *giugiuleni* sesame seed cookie from the plate and dunking it in her coffee.

"So, how are you holding up?" Gargiulo asks.

"I'm doing okay. Amanda keeps my thoughts in a happy place."

Gargiulo smiles at Amanda. "Yes, you do, don't you, Miss America?"

Amanda giggles and reaches for Gargiulo's nose.

"So, does your husband know where you are?" he asks Emily, without looking up.

"No. He thinks I'm helping out a sick aunt."

"He's not your problem, right?"

"No! Not at all. He's a good man."

Gargiulo starts a game of peek-a-boo with Amanda and she kicks her legs in glee.

"You know, you seem like a different person than the one who saved my life."

Silence meets his comment. He glances at Emily and notices she has stopped chewing her biscotti. When she realizes he's staring at her, she swallows.

"It's been a stressful time. The baby was rushed to the hospital and needed a blood transfusion. When my husband wasn't a match, I had to give blood. I'm terrified of anything to do with blood, and—"

She stops suddenly. "What's wrong?"

"You said you're terrified of anything to do with blood. How can that be after what you did to save my life?"

Emily's eyes grow wide in the silence. "I guess my super hero drive kicked in at the right time." She gives a false chuckle. "Lucky for you."

Gargiulo assesses her through eyes that don't miss a trick. "Yes, lucky for me, indeed."

***

An hour later, with her things hastily packed into the diaper bag and Amanda in her arms, Emily leaves the apartment to meet Vito.

Gargiulo still sits at his desk. "Do you want me to babysit her while you're at the store?"

Emily flashes her brightest smile. "No, that's okay. She loves going to the grocery store."

With that, she follows Vito out to the car. She forces herself to make cheerful small talk, trying to act as if everything is normal, like she isn't going to make a run for it as soon as she's out of Vito's sight. Gargiulo is getting too suspicious and she's let too much slip.

Inside the grocery store, she doesn't waste any time. Diaper cream will have to wait. She scans the store looking for an alternative exit. Not finding one, she walks back to the refrigerated section and enters the back area for employees only. There has to be a loading dock somewhere in the back for food deliveries.

"Can I help you?"

Emily twirls around. A middle-aged man in a white apron stares at her.

"I'm being stalked by an ex and he's out front. He's very violent and I need to get out of here with the baby."

The man is instantly concerned. "Shouldn't we call the police?"

Emily shakes her head. "He is the police. Believe me, I'm going to end up dead if you don't help me."

That's all it takes. The man leads her through the back warehouse to the dock.

"Is there a train near here?"

The man points. "About six blocks up that street. Are you going to be okay?"

"Yes, thank you for your help." She walks briskly out of the store, looking back to be sure Vito isn't following her and dials Madison's number.

\*\*\*

"Yo, Boss, there she is."

Gargiulo turns in the direction Paulie is pointing and chuckles.

"That poor bastard Vito is going to be sitting outside for a long time before he wises up."

Paulie laughs.

"Follow her, but at a distance."

Paulie drives a block behind her.

"She's headed for the train," Gargiulo says. "Pull over. I want you on that train. See where she goes. But stay invisible."

"Okay, Boss."

"I'll take the car back and tell Vito he's been ditched," Gargiulo says. "When you get on the train, call Vito and let him know where you're headed. I'll have him meet you with the car."

Paulie gets out of the car and Gargiulo walks around to get in the driver's seat.

"Let me know what's happening," Gargiulo says and pulls away from the curb.

# Forty-five

Jake and I make our way to the lab to search Chadwick's office for records related to his cloning hobby. To say I'm nervous would be an understatement. The safety of Amanda, as well as all those anonymous people, depends on our finding those records. If they get into the wrong hands...I can't help shuddering at the thought.

Jake puts his arm around my shoulders and gives me a squeeze as we walk down the avenue. "You cold?"

"Not really. Just thinking of what's at stake. We have to find those records."

"We will. But if we don't, take comfort in the fact they're hidden so well."

"I guess. But not finding them is not an option."

"I know." His voice has a humorous tone.

"What's so funny?"

"Your control-freak ways."

"I'm not a control freak."

When I look back at Jake, his eyebrows are raised and he sports a grin. "In a good way."

I smack his arm and he pulls me close.

"I adore you, Madison, control freak or not."

Long-dormant butterflies in my solar plexus flap their

wings.

"Even though I'm the human equivalent of a counterfeit designer bag?"

"What? You're insane." He kisses my nose. "And too smart to believe that. You're not just your DNA. Your environment, your experiences, all of that shaped you to be the woman you are. The one I adore, as I might have mentioned a few seconds ago."

"Yes, yes, nature versus nurture. I know. But at my foundation, all of my potential springs from someone else's genes."

"That's ridiculous. Potential is infinite. And from what you say, you and Emily are nothing like each other. And by the way, I've mentioned twice now that I adore you. Don't know if you heard me the first time...or the second time...or now—"

I throw my arms around his neck and hug him tight, overcome by emotions too numerous to analyze.

"Hey, hey." He pulls back and looks down at the tears running down my face.

"I don't know what I'd do without you. You've kept me sane through all of this."

"You're the sanest person I know. You don't need any help with that. And you *are* unique." He touches my chicken pox scar. "I bet Emily doesn't have a chicken pox scar on her right temple."

"What is it with my chicken pox scar?" I ask. "You're obsessed."

"Nah, it's just that you're this super-competent person and that scar reminds me you were once a vulnerable, little girl, scratching itchy blotches." He leans in and kisses me.

I caress his cheek and press my forehead to his. Behind him, puffs of steam rise from the manhole covers on the avenue. Beneath the grates in the sidewalk, the subway rumbles. The streets are desolate, the residents of New York City sleeping in on this frigid, Saturday morning.

"Come on. Let's go find those records." He kisses my nose and grabs my hand. "I contacted a friend with some connections about Steele. With any luck, he'll find out where the bastard lives."

"Then we just have to figure out what to do with that information."

"One thing at a time."

When we enter HC Labs, I nod at the security guard and head toward the elevator bank. The building is eerily quiet.

I lead Jake to Chadwick's office. "You start here. He also has a small lab down the hall I'll search."

I try a few keys until I find the one that fits the door of the lab. The coating of dust on the counters indicates just how long this place has been unused. I scan the room, then start with the cabinets and drawers.

\*\*\*

Emily approaches the apartment building, her heart pounding. Though mid-afternoon, the sun has slipped behind a cloud and the day has gone dark. Amanda sleeps soundly on her shoulder and Emily's arm aches from holding her. She's moments away from getting inside and lying down, but eluding Gargiulo has not left her calmer. She can't shake the sense someone is watching her. She scans the street before making her way into the building.

\*\*\*

Paulie follows a half block behind Emily. He sees her look around one last time before slipping into the building. As soon as she's inside, an Asian guy in a suit steps out of a car and quickly follows her in. "A fucking Fed, he mutters." He knows this doesn't necessarily make him one of the good guys.

He texts the address to Vito. By the time Paulie enters the lobby, both have disappeared. He looks at the elevator display and sees the elevator is still climbing. He texts a range of higher floors to Vito and runs up the fire stairs, taking them two at a time. His gut tells him something isn't right.

He peers out at each floor to see if they have exited the elevator. On the sixth floor, he spots Emily walking down the corridor, her back toward him. Behind her, the elevator door is still open, held in place by the guy in the suit. He watches as the guy peeks around the door and follows Emily. She hears him behind her and turns, a startled expression on her face.

"Hi, Madison," the guy says.

Emily doesn't respond.

"I need you to come with me."

Emily grips the baby closer to her chest. "I'm not going anywhere."

He reaches out to grab her elbow and she swings her arm at him, her keys strategically between her fingers like claws.

"Son of a bitch." The guy strokes his jaw where the keys cut him.

"Is there a problem here?" Paulie calls out.

Both the guy and Emily look his way.

"No problem. Just helping my wife in with the baby," the guy says, digging his fingers into her upper arm and placing the palm of his hand on Amanda's back as she sleeps. Big mistake.

Emily transitions from woman to lioness in a split second. She elbows the guy and stomps on his instep, extracting herself from his grip.

Paulie whips out his gun and strides up the hallway. "Step away from her."

At the sight of the gun, Emily gasps and ducks against the wall.

"You're interfering in government business," the guy calls out.

"Nothing good, I'm sure. Step the hell away from her and the baby."

The Asian guy fires a shot. Amanda howls. Emily screams and presses them tighter against the wall. Paulie returns fire, grazing the guy's shoulder. He grunts and fires his pistol again, but he's off-balance from the hit. Paulie watches as Emily's body jerks, her arms open, and Amanda falls to the ground, Emily right behind her. The guy has his gun raised at Paulie and another shot rings out, but this one comes from behind Paulie. He spins around with his gun and sees Gargiulo huffing and puffing, his face a deep red.

Gargiulo lowers his arm with the gun and strides by Paulie as if he's not there. He picks up Amanda and then feels for a pulse in Emily's neck.

"Oh no. Oh no." His head dips as he makes the sign of the cross. He rubs Amanda's back.

"Help me," the guy in the suit whispers.

Gargiulo looks down at him. Then, he raises his gun and puts a shot right between his eyes.

"Boss, we gotta get outta here," Vito says.

Gargiulo nods. "Grab her bag." He walks over to the dead agent and examines the ID tag hanging around his neck and grunts. "Says he's Dr. Andrew Peng of HC Labs. But if he ain't a Fed, nobody's a Fed."

"Should we just leave her here?" Paulie says.

Gargiulo stares down at Emily one last time. "Can't do anything else for her but take care of her little girl. He kisses Amanda's forehead. Let's go."

# Forty-six

I sigh for about the third time in a few minutes as I survey the mess around me. I've searched every inch of the lab, even slicing into the sheetrock of the wall where there seemed to be a groove, but it turned out to be just a poor taping and spackling job.

My stomach growls and I realize I'm thirsty as well. Digging through my bag for a mint to hold me over, I see the flashing message light on my phone. Before I can access it, Jake appears in the doorway, a hammer in one hand and a piece of paper in the other.

"Hey, how's it going in here?"

"No luck. How about you?"

"I still have a few places to check, but good news on the Jeremy front. My contact sent his address." He waves the paper in the air. "He lives in White Plains with his wife and two kids."

I grab the paper out of his hand and stare down at it, not believing our good luck.

"The kickboards," Jake says.

"Huh?"

He points with the hammer to the bottom of the lab counters. Before I can respond, he walks around the lab counters and uses the other side of the hammer to dislodge the bottoms of the counters. Then he gives the same treatment to the moldings around the room.

"I've got to finish up inside."

He captures me in the crook of his elbow and kisses my temple, then stares at me a second longer than anyone else would. I'm amazed at what can be communicated in just one second.

"I'll check these out and meet you back in the office," I say.

I watch him leave, then stuff Jeremy's address in my pocket and start pulling the rubble out of the way to check in all the crevices. Halfway through, I remember my blinking phone and stop to listen to my voicemail.

Nothing could have prepared me for Emily's breathless message.

"I think Gargiulo's on to us. He knows I didn't save his life. I screwed up and told him I'm afraid of blood. I slipped away and I'm taking a train to the apartment. Call me."

Oh no, oh no, oh no. What is she thinking? She can't go to the apartment. The message from Emily was hours ago. I call her back, my chest pounding. Her phone rings and rings.

\*\*\*

Vincent Gargiulo stares at Amanda sleeping on his office couch, barricaded with pillows to prevent her from rolling off the edge. He barely knew Emily and yet her death has left him frantic with pain. Questions race through his mind. Why did she run away? Whose apartment did she end up at? Who was the guy he killed in the hallway? Why was he following her? Paulie agreed with Gargiulo about the guy being a Fed. He certainly dressed the part. But none of it makes sense. Why was a federal agent tailing her?

He rubs his eyes and takes a sip of scotch. His usual red wine isn't strong enough for the occasion.

A phone rings and he pats his pockets before realizing it's not his phone. He looks around the room. It's coming from

Emily's diaper bag.

He rummages through the bag. Maybe it's her husband. How the hell does he tell the guy his beautiful wife is dead?

"Hello."

Silence meets his greeting, followed by a woman's voice.

"May I speak to Emily, please?"

"Who's calling?"

"A friend."

The voice sounds oddly familiar.

"Do you have contact information for her husband by any chance?" Gargiulo asks.

"Her husband? Why?"

Gargiulo pauses. "I'm so sorry to have to tell you this. Emily is dead. She was killed this afternoon."

Gargiulo hears panting on the other end. "Oh my God. What about Amanda?"

"I've got her. She's safe."

"Are you at the club?"

"Yeah."

"I'm coming. Don't do anything or say anything to anyone until I get there."

It's only after the line goes dead that he realizes the caller knows about the club and, obviously, him.

***

Emily is dead. I dry-heave over the lab sink. My stomach is empty but that doesn't stop it from trying to purge. The muscles in my solar plexus ache from the exertion. Emily is dead. How can that be? A feverish heat radiates from my skin, but my insides are ice cold. I shiver uncontrollably. Emily is dead.

I grab my bag and race out the door to find Jake. Halfway there, I stop short in the hallway, my brain flooded with thoughts. With Emily gone, Amanda is motherless. I'm the only one who knows what she is and can protect her. But the only way to do that without revealing the cloning secret is to be Emily.

I've been Amanda's mother before. I can be it again, better this time. Without my memory, I've got no past and no future as a scientist. I wipe the tears from my cheeks. I head to Chadwick's office and stop again. For this to work, no one can know I've switched again. Chadwick trusted his best friend and look where it got us. No one can know. Not even Jake. I stifle a sob and exit through the fire stairs, realizing I'm never going to see him again.

An hour later, sitting in a racing cab just minutes from Gargiulo's club, my phone rings.

"Where the hell are you?" Jake asks. "I found Chadwick's records."

"Where were they?"

"In a walled up space under his book shelves. So, where'd you go?"

"I have to handle something," I say.

"Handle something? Where are you?"

In response to my silence, he continues. "Tell me you haven't left without me, please."

"I'm sorry."

"Jesus. How can I protect you if I'm not with you? Tell me where you are and I'll meet you."

I start to cry again. "I can't." The thoughts that were just a foggy idea have formed into a cohesive plan. I hate what I'm about to do to him. My heart screams "What are you doing?" over and over again.

"I love you," I whisper and disconnect the call.

A few minutes later, the driver pulls up at Gargiulo's. After climbing out of the cab, I take a few deep breaths of cold air before entering the club.

Everyone looks up as I walk toward Gargiulo's office.

I knock on the door and enter before he gives the go ahead. His ruddy face drains of all color when he sees me in the doorway.

"Madre di Dio," he whispers. "Twins?"

I don't respond.

"You're the one who saved my life. I can tell."

"That's right."

"Who are you?"

"Where's Amanda?" I ask.

He points to the couch where Amanda sleeps peacefully. Relief and gratitude collide in my chest. I have to stop myself from gathering her up in my arms. I brush a lock of hair from her forehead. She stirs but doesn't awaken.

"Who are you?" Gargiulo asks again.

I walk over to his credenza and pour myself a shot of whatever he's drinking. It burns all the way down and I cough. I take a seat opposite Gargiulo.

"Emily Cooke. Amanda's mother," I lie.

"And who was the person who died today?"

"Her name is Madison Thorpe. Tell me what happened."

As Gargiulo narrates, holes in my plan develop, but by the end everything has fallen into place. He has her diaper bag and her wallet is in it with her Emily identification. So no one who finds her in front of her apartment will doubt she is Madison. The guy Gargiulo shot, an agent playing the role of Dr. Andrew Peng, can't tell anyone what happened, though he may have made a call before he followed her into the building. That's a chance I'll have to take.

"Here's the official story," I say, "and I need you to stick with it or that little girl's life will be in grave danger."

Gargiulo nods and sips his drink.

"You don't know anything. You weren't there. You never met Madison Thorpe before. You only know Emily Cooke, who saved your life. However, if you left evidence behind and the police question you, make up some story. But leave Amanda's name out of it. She was never there. That's very important."

"Is that all you're gonna tell me?"

"It's easier to lie when you don't know the truth."

He nods in agreement. "True enough."

Amanda whimpers in her sleep and I lift her in my arms. My heart that earlier screamed "What are you doing?" seems to know now. I inhale her baby scent and whisper "We're going to be all right, sweetheart."

But will we be all right? I turn to Gargiulo. "I need your help with one more thing."

"Name it."

"I need to borrow some muscle and a car."

# Forty-seven

Exhausted and barely believing it's the same day Jake and I set out to Chadwick's office, the same day I learned Emily was dead, the same day I traveled to Gargiulo's club to get our story straight, I slam the car door and cross the street. Despite the chill in the January air, two bundled-up children play outside. I pause on the sidewalk and watch as the boy makes a layup.

"Hi."

The boy stops dribbling the basketball and stares at me. He's old enough to know he shouldn't be talking to strangers.

"Hi," the little girl calls out.

"Does Jeremy Steele live here?" I ask.

"Yes, that's my Daddy."

"It is? Today's my lucky day."

"Do you work with him?" the girl asks.

"Not really. But we have some things to discuss. So what's your name?"

"I'm Kaylee."

"What a pretty name."

The boy walks over, basketball in hand. "I'm Robbie."

"Hi, Robbie. Nice to meet you." Robbie awkwardly sticks out his hand and I shake it.

How ironic that a man without qualms about torturing innocent people has taught his children good manners.

I crouch down to pick up a rag doll from the lawn. Kaylee immediately sits cross-legged on the grass.

"Me and my Mommy sewed that."

"You did a great job. I love her yarn hair and button eyes."

Kaylee nods. "Inside of her there's a piece of paper with a dream on it."

"A dream?"

"Yes, Mommy said everyone has a dream inside."

"And what's your doll's dream?"

"She wants a puppy. That's my dream, too."

I can't help chuckling.

"My dream is to be a basketball player for the Knicks."

I look up at the boy. "Judging by that last shot you took, that dream may come true."

He smiles broadly.

Just then, the front door opens and a man steps out. He looks to be about forty, attractive, thin but athletic—not quite the sinister, cigarette-smoking man from the X-Files I expected. He walks over.

"Can I help you?"

"Jeremy, right?"

"That's right. And you are?" Then his eyes widen as he recognizes me.

"I was just getting acquainted with your lovely family," I say, standing up. "My name is Emily. Emily Cooke."

"Come on, guys. In the house now. It's getting colder," he says.

"Awwwwww," Kaylee whines.

"It was nice to meet you, Kaylee. And you, too, Robbie."

This time they both shake my hand and I even get to shake the hand of the doll. I watch them walk inside, a smile on my face.

"Delightful children. Well-mannered, personable—they have a bright future ahead of them."

"What do you want?"

His eyes bore into mine, but then his gaze shifts to a spot over my shoulder. With an awesome sense of timing, Gargiulo's guys, who have no idea what my mission is here today, have stepped out of the car to stretch their legs. I almost laugh out loud at how menacing they look.

"My friends were nice enough to drive me over here. They work for Vincent Gargiulo. You know who that is, right?"

"Of course."

Jeremy's gaze darts between them and me.

"Madison Thorpe was murdered earlier today by one of your agents, who's also dead."

Jeremy's eyes get wider. Obviously, he hasn't heard the news yet.

"That's where it ends. If anything happens to me or my daughter or anyone I care about, information about your little projects will be broadcast to the world. You'll be infamous. Your children will find out who their father really is. Strangers who fancy themselves avenging angels will make the rest of their lives a living hell. Just like you've done to mine."

I glance over my shoulder at Gargiulo's guys and then back at him.

"I have no desire to be a headline in the news, so I'll stay quiet...for now. But your torturing of homeless men stops now."

Jeremy swallows. "I don't know what you're talking about."

"No? Would you like to see the footage I took the other night? A very gentle man was shot in the head after attempts to get terrorist memories out of him were unsuccessful."

At that statement, Jeremy's rate of breathing increases. My hypothesis about what they've been doing on Governors Island is obviously correct.

"I'm not the bad guy," he says.

I can't help laughing at that.

"I've seen some horrible things the last twenty years." Jeremy rakes his fingers through his hair and stares into space. "This new breed of terrorist will not comply, will not succumb. We're under attack by people who are not afraid to die. They don't care if their families, their children, are hurt either."

"That's one point in your favor then. I believe you do wish to keep your children safe. I think you'll agree my request is more than fair. Homeless torture stops now, and you forget I and anyone I know exists. Or your kids are going to grow up really fast."

Jeremy looks like he might vomit. He nods.

"I'm glad that's settled."

I turn and walk toward the car. Once inside, I lean against the seat back, my body shaking uncontrollably.

"Everything okay?" Paulie asks.

"Yes. Just one more stop."

\*\*\*

The sun has long set on this January evening, leaving the brownstone dark and forlorn. I climb the stairs of the front stoop, pulling my coat tightly around me to keep out the cold wind. My stomach roils as I ring the doorbell.

When Regina answers, she breaks into a smile of surprise. "Madison."

I shake my head. "No, it's Emily."

She's quiet for a few seconds, squinting at me, her head cocked to one side. "Come in. Can I take your coat?"

"No, I'm a bit chilled."

I sit at the kitchen table and she puts a kettle of water on the stove. Finally, she sits across from me. "Is everything okay?"

I look down at the table, unable to meet her gaze as I tell her the ultimate lie. "Madison has been killed."

A long silence follows and I finally lift my face. Her eyes are wide, glassy, and burning with an intensity I have never seen.

"What happened?"

How I long to tell her the truth. That it's Emily who is dead. That I need to take her place to protect Amanda. But I know I can never see my parents again if I'm going to pull off this charade. It's safer for everyone involved, if my parents think I am dead.

"She was shot in front of her apartment."

Regina leans forward and stares at me for a long time. Just when I think she's gone into shock, she speaks.

"Will you be safe?"

"I hope so. Madison and Jake found out the name and location of the guy in charge of this mess. I was there today. By the time I left, he understood what was at stake if he doesn't leave us in peace."

Regina shakes her head in confusion. "You and...Madison. How was it possible?"

I stare into her eyes. "Think of the simplest explanation, even if it doesn't seem possible...yet."

Regina nods and I know she and Richard probably lay in bed many a night pondering how Emily and I could have existed. I know the word "clones" had to come up. They are scientists, after all.

"Amanda?"

I won't speak the word "clone" again. I will forget I ever knew the truth, for Amanda's safety. But Regina clearly remembers that photograph of the baby and how she looked exactly like me.

I nod.

"Oh my God." Regina brings her fist to her mouth, ignoring the whistling kettle. "She'll never be safe."

I rise and shut off the gas.

The sob she's been holding back erupts. There's no containing the torrent of anguish that pours forth. I turn and put my hands on her shoulders and she reaches up and grabs my wrists.

"She's going to be all right. I promise you. No one knows about her and we need to keep it that way."

Regina nods as the tears spill down her face.

"I'm going to protect her."

"I know you will," she says fiercely.

Just then Richard comes in the front door, a bag in hand. "Watson!" He calls out my childhood nickname. I instinctually start to respond before catching myself. But Regina's eyes widen at my blunder. Richard registers the mood in the room and Regina's red eyes.

"What's happened?"

"Madison," Regina whispers. "She's dead."

Richard sits down heavily at the table. My heart breaks for their pain. I have never seen my parents, the stoic scientists, this emotional.

When Regina gets to the part about how Amanda is a clone and how I'm going to take care of her, she slips up and refers to me as Madison instead of Emily.

Richard sits up straighter. He looks at me intently, as if his brilliant mind is working through some problem. He nods slowly.

"I need to pick up Amanda and take her home."

They stand. I pick up a pen from the table and write Jake's number on a napkin.

"Can you let Jake know about Madison? Tell him—" My voice breaks and I take a breath. "Tell him she loved him. Very much."

Regina stares at me, her eyes filling again, and engulfs me in a tight embrace. We stand wrapped in each other until, finally, she kisses my cheek. "Give that little girl of yours a big hug for me."

When Richard hugs me, I let out a sob. Before he releases me, he murmurs something at my ear. I'm not sure, but I think it's "I'm proud of you, as ever."

Outside, I descend the stairs and look back at my parents, huddled in the doorway, one last time. I smile through my tears at these people who raised me, and know me, and are willing to sacrifice it all for the safety of a little girl they've never met. Beyond any doubt, it's clear as they gaze at me, eyes shining with tears and pride, that they know exactly who they wave goodbye to.

In the car, I wipe the tears from my face. "Take me to Amanda. And then home."

\*\*\*

As Vito pulls to the curb, I gather up Amanda in my arms. My sleeping angel.

Paulie looks back at me. "You gonna be okay?"

I nod.

"You ever need us, you know, give a call."

"Thank you. No disrespect intended, but I hope I never see you again."

Paulie chuckles. "I can understand that."

"So can I," Vito mutters under his breath, garnering a smack from Paulie.

They wait until the front door opens before they pull away.

"Emily!" Brad opens the door wide. "Why didn't you tell me you were coming back tonight?" He is so innocent of all that has happened and so happy to see us, his family. It's all so normal and safe.

"I'm home," I say, and then for many reasons, some I can't articulate, I start to cry.

Brad envelops us in a warm embrace.

"It's okay," he says.

"I know."

He takes Amanda from me, wraps his arm around my shoulders, and we walk up the stairs.

# Forty-eight

Bright sunshine and mild temperatures mock the painful emptiness I feel. A piece of me is missing. Today is Madison's funeral.

I skipped the wake and service, afraid that even with my disguise someone would notice the resemblance. Instead, I followed to the cemetery and stand under a tree at a distance from the burial, pretending to mourn someone named James Hitchcock Moore III. The blonde wig and sunglasses are added protection should the distance not be sufficient.

People step up to drop a rose onto the casket. I wait patiently for them to leave so that I can pay my last respects.

As they exchange their last hugs and climb into their cars, a man walks in my direction. My heart starts to pound. I look back down at the gravestone. My body jolts when I realize he is just a few feet away. He stops short and stares at me.

"You look just like her," he says. "I'm Jake."

"I guess the wig's not that great a disguise. That's why I didn't chance the funeral."

Jake's face is so pained, I want to gather him up.

"It's not the wig. I...I just know that face."

My eyes fill with tears. "She loved you, you know."

Jake clears his throat and looks away. My tears spill over in an unrelenting stream. I raise my sunglasses on my head to swipe them away.

When he looks back at me, his expression is first shocked and then pained again.

"Madison gave me Jeremy's contact information before she died," I say. "I paid him a visit. Gargiulo provided some muscle for effect."

He forces a smile. "Madison would have been proud."

"Amanda has to be protected at all costs. What she is—if anyone knew, her life would be in great danger."

My gaze locks on his as I speak these words, willing him to read between the lines, to recognize it's me, to know I love him but that I have a greater purpose now. But I know none of this will be.

Finally, our conversation exhausted, I realize it's best to get going. I have to fight with all of my strength to pull myself away. We say our goodbyes and stare at each other awkwardly one last time. Just as I turn to leave, he reaches up and cups my cheek in his hand. He stares into my eyes a long moment. Very slowly, he brushes his thumb across my chicken pox scar. I gasp and hold my breath. He leans in and kisses my cheek.

"Be well...Emily." He turns and walks away.

# Forty-nine

It's been almost a year since that day of forgotten Crock-Pots and Cheerios on the floor. A year since the inkling I was not who someone wanted me to be. So much has changed and yet many things are the same.

Amanda, now a year and a half, flies wildly with her arms in the air, a crazy daredevil of a child, as Brad pushes her higher and higher on a swing. Her enthusiasm is infectious. As I watch them, I wonder if I was the same at her age.

We fell into a comforting rhythm, she and I. Each time she reaches for me, I melt, and almost always think of Emily, hoping she is smiling down on us. In my heart, I know she is and that she has had a hand in this understanding that has grown between us.

Brad's hearty chuckle sounds and I wonder what Amanda has done now to delight him. Actually, enchant is a better word, for he is surely under her spell. I smile and the warmth of the sun caresses my cheeks as a rare breeze ruffles my hair. Life is good. Though I wouldn't have chosen this life, I am content. Some people search their entire lives for meaning, to uncover the purpose for their existence. No such exertion was required on my part. My purpose was thrust into my arms one cold, dismal day, and each day since has grown brighter.

It hasn't all been easy. I sense I wasn't one to dwell on the past in my former life as a scientist. Today I don't dare look back. I fear being swallowed up by what could have been. In the same vein, the future seems a dangerous place to spend too much time. Instead, I cling to the present like a security blanket, moving from day to day, appreciating the small joys that each brings. While I didn't get what I thought I wanted, life has given me what I need to fulfill my purpose and I've come to realize there are infinite, alternative realities in any one life.

Don't think for a moment that all this domestic normalcy has numbed me to the dangers that lie around us. After the funeral, I received a box in the mail, filled with the files Jake found at Chadwick's office. Many an evening, after Amanda fell asleep and Brad retired to his spot on the sofa to watch a ball game, I sat with those records and compared them to Chadwick's encoded documents. All of the clones have now been accounted for. They all have names. With any luck, I'm the only one who will ever know them, and their identities will remain tucked in a weatherproof box, buried three feet under my deck.

Amanda's squeals interrupt my thoughts. Brad lifts her high in the air and grins up at her. He's a good dad, a good man. As soon as he puts her down, she dashes toward the grass just outside the swing area. Giggling uncontrollably, she runs wild in zigzags and circles, making me laugh and bringing Emily to mind again.

When I think back on those few weeks last winter, it's always the people who spring to mind. The brilliant scientist who helped so many couples conceive and then let his ego get the best of him. His best friend who betrayed him. Bad guy Vincent Gargiulo who turned out to be a lot of good guy, too. Jeremy Steele, loving husband and father and torturer of innocents. Jake.

The duality does not escape me—the ultimate duality the intermingled cells and minds of Emily and Madison. I still don't remember completely who I was and, in light of recent events, I won't try to imagine who I'll be in the future. All I know is what is here, right now, in this moment.

My name is Emily Cooke. I am a wife, a mother, and protector of an innocent.

As my gaze follows Amanda, a movement in the distance catches my eye. A man walks toward a bench across the park, on the other side of the grass. My body reacts before my brain catches on. This is not the first time he has come. It comforts me to know he watches over us. Sometimes, my mind drifts and I wonder if he misses me as much as I miss him. But then a fierce sensation in my core makes me hope he doesn't.

"How about getting some ice cream?" Brad calls out.

Amanda giggles again as he puts her on his shoulders. I stand and meet them on the grass, gobbling the exposed skin on Amanda's leg as she fingers my hair.

As we walk away, I look back one last time. The man stands up, glances our way, and then walks in the opposite direction.

*Be well, my love. Be well.*

# Author's Note

This novel has been in the works for a long time. I started it in November 2009 during NaNoWriMo (National Novel Writing Month) as a way of keeping up my writing chops while I marketed *The Benefactor*, my first novel. Over the years, I rewrote it several times, creating new characters and subplots. With each addition, I felt the story went deeper and became more interesting. I hope you feel the same.

After so many years, some of my story's settings have changed in real life. I remember researching uninhabited islands in the New York area. I visited Governors Island when it was undergoing major construction and renovations and was open only on weekends during the summer. There was something about it in that state, along with the very limited access to the public, that made me know immediately it would be the bleak and dangerous winter setting for a horrifying scene in my book. If you visit Governors Island today—and you should—you wouldn't perceive what I saw back then.

When I finished writing the novel, several authors and savvy readers read it, as did my wonderful writing group. Their suggestions were helpful in making it even tighter. But just as I was preparing to put the finishing touches on the manuscript, life stepped in and my focus went elsewhere.

When I finally returned to *Mind Games* just a few months ago, all hell had broken loose in the world. My husband and I were holed up in our New York City apartment, in a neighborhood called the "epicenter of the epicenter" of the pandemic. The world as we knew it had changed drastically. No more hopping on the subway to head down to the Village or uptown to Central Park. No more grabbing a drink in a funky bar or a crowded, 100-year-old café. No more adventurous dining or listening to bands in packed venues. Without a car to take even a short drive for a change of scenery, we were left with a masked walk to the local grocery store every ten days as entertainment. But we're surviving and have a keener awareness of the little things that make life so beautiful.

To be honest, I considered not publishing this book. My settings had changed in real life. The way people live has changed. I felt I should make major revisions to reflect all these changes. But the pandemic taught me an important lesson. Life is short and uncertain. It's time to let go of crippling perfectionism and analysis paralysis. This novel is ready to be birthed into the world. My story in no way reflects the world in which we now live. But I hope it carries you away for several hours and entertains you and makes you think.

It's time for me to move on to new projects and keep creating, whatever that means in my future. I wish you new adventures, too. Peace, health, and love to you.

Margaret Reyes Dempsey
Jackson Heights, 2020

# Acknowledgments

Many people provided support during the creation of this novel.

My darling husband, Richard, participated in numerous brainstorming sessions over the years, helped with edits, provided counseling during bouts of despair, and created the cover art and design, my author website, and social media banners. I love you.

My writing group: Geri, Pat, Linda, Terri, and Julie. I can't thank you enough for the edits and advice you provided over the years.

The Dollbabies, my group of writer friends, provided inspiration, encouragement, and love. Covid kept us from our beach house retreat this year. Hope to see you all in 2021.

Malissa Smith & Lisa Creech Bledsoe, bloggers and boxers who inspired me to give my protagonist a passion for boxing, edited my boxing scenes. Any errors about boxing technique are mine alone.

Family and friends read early and final drafts of my manuscript and offered suggestions, opinions, and enthusiasm. Thank you for your generosity.

M. Shefflewitz, affable AF, kept me laughing.

Jon, who went from child to man during the writing of this

book, accompanied me in my fact-checking missions and was always a source of joy and wonder. I love you, Sweet Boy.

# About the Author

Margaret Reyes Dempsey was born and raised in Ozone Park, New York. She lives in Jackson Heights, New York with her husband, cat, and a few imaginary characters that make an appearance now and then. You can find out more about her books on her website www.MargaretReyesDempsey.com or by following her on Facebook at facebook.com/mreyesdempsey.

Thank you for reading *Mind Games*. If you enjoyed the book, please tell your friends, consider posting an online review, and help spread the word on social media.

Made in the USA
Middletown, DE
14 December 2020